D0070286

Sleepless Nights

Sleepless Nights

The Drew Smith Series

Norwood Holland

Windmill Books Ltd.

∞

Washington, DC

Sleepless Nights.
Copyright © 2011 by Norwood Holland

All rights reserved.

Limited First Edition printed in the United States
Signature Book Printing, www.sbpbooks.com

ISBN 978-0-983-16560-6
LCCN 2010941286

This is a work of fiction. All of the characters, organizations and events portrayed in this novel are either products of the author's imagination or are used fictitiously.

Publisher's Cataloging-in-Publication
(Provided by Quality Books, Inc.)

Holland, Norwood.
    Sleepless Nights / Norwood Holland. -- Limited 1st
ed.
    p. cm.
    LCCN 2010941286
    ISBN-13: 978-0-9831656-0-6
    ISBN-10: 0-9831656-0-2

    1. Street life--Fiction. 2. Urban fiction, American.
3. Detective and mystery stories, American.   I. Title.

PS3608.O48345S54 2011   813'.6
               QBI11-600010

Dedicated to

Kay Frances Mebane Holland
(1933 – 1995)

My mother first introduced me to books
and thus began this journey
into the wonderful world of literature

Acknowledgments

The road to publishing this first novel has been filled with detours, potholes, and uncertain turns. I stayed the course through the countless obstacles and never would have reached this point without the encouragement and support of family and friends.

Forever patient in guiding me through the process of writing and rewriting, thanks to my writing coach and editor Peter Gelfin with the Editorial Department, and Basil Buchanan for his editorial support and partnering with me in this publishing venture.

I am greatly indebted to my major financial supporters Lauren Hicks Barten, Mr. & Mrs. Lloyd and Sally Buchanan and daughter Amelia, my aunt Judith Saunders Burton, sister Norma Holland, Glenda Fitzpatrick, Lorne Gates, Joy Hill, Cheryl Kidd, Robyn Sims, Jean Smith, Haroldene Moten Pratt, Leslie Rogers, George Richards, Theresa Williams Stoudamaire, Acquanetta Wheeler, and Adrian Williams. I would be remiss not to mention the rallying support from that classy group of contributing supporters, the Fisk University alumni Class of 1973.

Thanks to the Kickstarter Project *Sleepless Nights* launches the Drew Smith Series with three more volumes to follow.

Chapter 1

T HE NATION'S CAPITAL sweated under a searing sun and hazy skies. The sauna-like air bathed the city in humidity, and as the day was hot, so was the spot. The Feds kept cruising through. Under the big Dutch elm on the corner of Eighth and Kennedy, the three chilled in spite of the breezeless heat. Perched on the wall exchanging the word on the street, hood gossip including the latest lock-ups, convictions, and releases, they waited and watched for prospects.

For Gee, idle time with Tyrone and Jinx didn't used to be so boring. The two planned to unload the last of the crack cocaine, re-up for tomorrow, and call it a day. Gee was just hanging. The sun was beginning its descent, growing less intense, while the ever-present heat continued rising from the asphalt streets, concrete sidewalks, and red brick houses.

"Gee, man, where dat nice ride of yours?" Tyrone focused on his feet, admiring the new Air Jordan Jumpman sneakers.

"Home. Parked."

Tyrone looked up, a toothpick poked in the corner of his mouth. "Why ain't you driving?"

"Gas is expensive, besides walking is good exercise."

"If I had a car I wouldn't be walking on a day like this. Would you Jinx? I'd be chilling, rolling in the conditioned air. Know what I mean?" Tyrone grinned revealing his stained uneven teeth. "Forget dat, I be exercising e'ry day all my life. Enough of dat shit. Ain't dat right Jinx?"

Jinx ignored Tyrone's prattle. Gee could tell he was anxious to get off the corner, watching the intersection, hoping for customers on foot or mobile.

"What time is it?" Jinx looked to Gee. His thoughts focused elsewhere.

"Four-fifteen." Both he and Jinx knew Tyrone didn't own a watch and never would own a car.

Soon they would have to leave. The Kennedy Street crew was due to show up with more heat, brandishing automatic weapons. Eighth and Kennedy was one of the few spots where independent hustlers operated, priming business until the evening rush and lucrative late-hour trade. The corner then became the crew's exclusive domain, any encroachment with a competing sale would be a challenge, and a drive-by spray of hot lead was the response. Coexisting with the fearless crew on its turf was one of the perils of working the open-air drug market. For now, a détente existed between the crew and the indie hustlers, and yet another danger was lurking around the corner.

The houses on this block of the Petworth neighborhood sat on a hill with steps leading down to the sidewalk bordered by a four-foot stone wall. At the van's approach, Tyrone eased up off the wall and strutted to the curb, pulling up his baggy jeans. Sunlight glinted off the perspiration beads sprinkling his forehead. Not particularly good-looking, his best feature was a striking complexion, smooth like dark chocolate. Though his glow was appealing, it failed to compensate for or distract from his irregular teeth. His hideous mouth had a talent for telling tall tales and not much else.

The two extra-large t-shirts and double underwear of briefs and athletic shorts camouflaged his agile but slight frame and gave the illusion of bulk. Tyrone dressed more for style than comfort. Seated on the wall, Gee and Jinx watched the white Chevy van slow its roll.

"Bet I get two dubs for these dimes," Tyrone said, concocting a scheme to beat a couple of crack-heads by doubling the street value. "Look like suckas to this bidnissman."

Jinx eyed the approaching van. "Handle your bidniss and watch yourself."

The opposite of Tyrone's, Jinx's complexion was pitted and dusty. He was ruggedly handsome but for the menacing scowl. Rarely did he smile, and the unkempt Bantu locks lent him a treacherous air.

Gee looked to the corner while Jinx kept an eye on the two in the unfamiliar van. Should it be necessary, each plotted his best escape route. In front of them, the van came to a stop. The driver rolled down his window.

"Was up?" Tyrone stepped closer to the driver, sizing up the two solidly built guys.

"Twenty." The driver said placing his order.

Gee could tell Tyrone was reconsidering his suckas. The message ran telepathically to all three. *Jump out.* Driver and passenger appeared too straight and older than the average crackhead. Though age was no criteria, just the law of averages, one could never be certain of people's private habits and few factors alone were determinative, these two men just didn't look right.

"Hold up." Tyrone stepped back and pretended to kick the street litter for a hidden stash, which was actually safely tucked away in the pocket sack of his briefs. Most cops didn't like to tickle a suspect's balls, but then again some took a perverse pleasure in it.

Gee spotted a patrol car turning the corner and leapt off the wall. "Jump out! Jump out!"

Instincts kicked in and the chase began scattering like roaches under sudden light. The two undercover cops jumped out of the van, feet pounding the pavement as they gave chase, one after Tyrone and the other on Gee's heels. The squad car's siren began to wail. Jinx escaped into a nearby alley. Red, blue, and white lights flashing behind him, it sped down the alley, bouncing over potholes and uneven pavement, to cross the street and dive into the next block, homing in on Jinx racing to stay ahead.

Through the opposite alley, Gee sprinted, laughing along the way, around the corner then into another alley toward Georgia Avenue. His stamina would easily outlast the older cop, already panting halfway through the alley. Ten feet behind, the cop ignited a burst of energy increasing his stride closing the gap and almost within reach. Gee tipped a trashcan in his wake, startling a jumbo rat into scampering across the cop's feet. Horror-struck, the cop stumbled over the trashcan, regained his footing and grabbed his revolver, and aimed at the rat. In seconds, both the rodent and Gee had disappeared.

Gee wasn't a drug dealer, nor did use them, in fact, he didn't have the slightest interest in that illegal activity. He wouldn't even smoke reefer. He would soon start his final year at George Mason University to complete a bachelor's degree in computer sciences. Selling drugs was the business of Jinx and Tyrone, his childhood friends. Gee didn't have to run. He did it for the thrill of the chase, playing decoy, distracting the cops, helping Jinx and Tyrone in their escape. To him, it was just a game.

On Georgia Avenue Gee slowed to a casual walk, recovering his breath a craving for a cold grape soda developed. He'd catch up with Jinx and Tyrone tomorrow. Or would he? Maybe hanging with those two wasn't such a good idea. Back in the day dodging the cops was fun when he was a kid, but now it seemed dangerous, stupid. Gee realized he'd outgrown that scene, Tyrone and Jinx as well.

It was time to get ready for work, shower maybe catch a catnap. Two squad cars pulled up to the stoplight and eyed him. From a peripheral glance Gee noticed the vehicle but continued to stroll. His street training had taught him how to blend avoiding suspicion feigning unawareness. The light changed and the cruiser passed. He released a breath of relief turning into the Korean market at the corner of Georgia and Ingraham.

The icy air conditioning brought up chill bumps that made the hair on his arms rise, but it felt good. He went straight for the coolers in the rear, and after selecting the cold drink, he turned toward the cashier, but abruptly stopped. Something in his chest tightened and forced him to suck in his breath.

She stood browsing the shelf in a pink halter-top and Daisy Duke cutoffs. Back when she was a cheerleader at Coolidge High, pretty and popular, she always had that effect on him. Marie Davis was out of his league, and now she was finer than ever. Unaware of her admirer, the shapely mocha-colored girl focused on the canned goods. He had to say something.

"Marie?" Her name softly slipped off his lips.

She turned in his direction but didn't seem to recognize him. Three years had passed, and at the age when boys turn into men.

"Yes?" Her curious expression changed to recollection and she smiled.

Known around the hood as Gee, the Spanish kid, Gustavo Agusto Garcia had been quiet and shy with a studious bent, a bit of a nerd a class ahead of her. Her look of intense interest told him that she, too, had noticed how much he had physically changed. Against her memory, the transformation must have been sudden and surprising. She was not the first to notice his metamorphosis. Coming into manhood, putting on the freshman ten and then some, playing on the soccer team, and spending a lot of time in the weight room at George Mason, he had reached a point in his life where he attracted rather than repelled the honeys. His confidence had grown as well.

"Gee." She greeted him with a hug.

While puzzled by the assumed familiarity, he welcomed her soft fragrant embrace. He couldn't believe he had it going on like that.

"Wow, you sure look good." She stepped back, her bright gray-green eyes appraising him with amazement and delight. "Still at George Mason?"

"Final year, coming up. How about you? Heard you were at Spelman College."

"Two down, two to go. Good to see you. How's your summer?"

"Just working."

"Where?" She returned to searching the shelves of canned tomatoes.

"Waiting tables at the Farragut."

"Are you kidding? I heard it's a great club. I've never been there."

"What are you doing tonight?" He recaptured her eyes and her interest.

"Why?"

"I could get you a seat at the bar for the last show. Maybe when I get off we could hang out." The old Gee would never have been so bold to ask Marie Davis out.

She smiled. "I'd like that."

"Meet me at the door around ten. It has to be ten, that's when I take my break."

"I'll be there. That all you're getting, a soda?"

"Yeah, thirsty. What's up with the tomatoes?"

"My mom's making pasta."

The matronly Korean cashier grinned at the handsome couple placing their items on the counter. Growing up in the same neighborhood and attending the same schools, Gee and Marie were acquainted with each other's faces, family and friends, but had never really known one another. Now it seemed like a mutual attraction and Gee wondered what his chances were. He walked her home, two blocks out of his way. The police had chased off his afternoon boredom and brought the revelation that he had outgrown a childhood relationship. Now here was the possibility of inventing a new one.

∝∾

Friday, August 4, 10 p.m.

Standing at the entrance to the Farragut Tavern in his bistro uniform, starched white collar, black slacks with matching bowtie, and black full length apron, Gee met her taxi with a big grin. The valets were jumping to greet the crowd gathering for the night's final performance. As Marie emerged, conversation lulled among a lingering group of young men. Gee closed the cab door and positioned himself between her and the gawking admirers to escort her in.

Guided through the lobby past the hatcheck room, Marie gazed about at the stylish crowd. Under the portrait of Admiral David Glasgow Farragut, harried bartenders filled the constant flow of orders. The Tavern continued its nautical theme with anchors adorning the walls and mural-sized canvasses dramatizing the Navy's first admiral leading his fleet to the capture of New Orleans in 1862 and Mobile Bay in 1864. The rustic bar and décor evoked an authentic Civil War milieu.

Gee followed closely, steering her toward the bar, his eyes glued to the backless halter dress with its silky material clinging to her curves.

"Who's performing tonight?" she asked.

"Boney James, you heard of him? He's played on the radio a lot, especially WHUR."

"Don't know the name but I'll probably recognize the sound."

Gee scanned the bar. "I see the perfect spot for you. I'll put you next to Tio and Mr. Drew, they'll look after you. The show starts in about thirty minutes, I got to get to my station. I hope you don't mind sitting at the bar."

"Not at all, I'm glad just to be here with you."

Gee took her hand and maneuvered through the crowd around the bar. "I was worried. A woman alone at the bar can bring the dawgs out--if you know what I mean."

She laughed. "Gee, you're funny."

"I'm serious. I know those guys; they'll be hitting on you left and right, fine as you look." The corner of his mouth turned up, dimpling in. "I know the bruthas."

"That's cute the way you do that."

"What?"

"That thing you do with your mouth. It's cute."

Gee pretended to look puzzled and did it again.

"See, that's it," she said.

It was a tic, a reflexive action, and a habit so subtle only those making the closest observation would notice. It expressed many things, sometimes his puzzlement, indifference, or even annoyance, the way another might shrug.

Gee halted at a vacant stool next to Drew Smith and his sidekick Julio Mejia and apprehensively greeted them. "Tio, Mr. Drew, this is my friend, Marie. This is Mr. Drew and Mr. Julio. He's my uncle—well sort of."

Marie's eyes widened and she smiled. "Wow! This is really something. You're Drew Smith, the famous lawyer."

"Only famous in your neighborhood. Call me Drew. I can't break Gee of the Mr. Drew, he's been calling me that since he was knee high."

"You're always in the papers. They call you D.C.'s Johnny Cochran."

"Like I said, only in your neighborhood."

"Tio," Gee addressed Julio, using the Spanish title for uncle. "Would you look after her for me while I finish up my work, please? Keep the dawgs away?"

Julio snickered. "We'll play bodyguard."

Drew laughed and clapped Gee on the shoulder. "Don't worry, Gee, she's in good hands. We'll keep the dawgs, wolves, MacDaddy's, and any other lecherous creatures at bay until you say when. We're waiting for a table. Perhaps Marie will join us for dinner." Drew looked to Marie who looked to Gee for approval. A beaming grin gave her the answer.

Surprised and speechless with gratitude she nodded her acceptance.

"We'd be pleased to have you. Right, Julio?"

"Wow, this is so nice, thank you.

"Gee, we'll make sure she don't give out those digits," Julio said. The distinguished looking Latino with wavy hair glanced over at the bar and Drew's gaze followed. The young men from the sidewalk had moved inside, and from a distance, Marie still held their attention. "Here comes your boss," Julio said.

"Gotta go." Gee stepped away, but stopped to look back before disappearing behind the swinging kitchen doors.

His boss Theo was a dark man with an athletic build and an assured air. "Drew, Julio your table is ready."

The manager and maitre d' carried himself in a way that left little doubt he could handle any rough situation. He escorted the three to the best seats in the house. While Julio was getting better acquainted with Marie Theo whispered an inquiry in Drew's ear. Drew smiling shook his head in a negative gesture then nodded toward the swinging doors where Gee was emerging from the kitchen balancing a large tray. Theo's eyes connected the pretty young girl and Gee. He then understood, and the men exchanged approving nods.

At a stage-front center table, Marie was treated to dinner, and after the show, Drew and Julio released her back into Gee's care. The young couple planned to finished the evening at a popular hip-hop hangout.

Chapter 2

Friday, August 4, midnight

DREW NUDGED JULIO as they crossed the Farragut parking lot. "Come on, one more drink with me?"

"Nah, man, Chevy's waiting up for me. Got a full schedule tomorrow. Son number two's competing on 'It's Academic.' Start taping at nine. Chevy'll kill me if I'm not there cheering him on. Then at eleven it's the soccer league playoff. Sons three and four, they're starting."

"That leaves one and five."

"Number one son, doing his own thing chasing skirts, only thing on his mind, no time for his family, but number five got nothing but time. Just hanging with his old man."

"How's Li'l Medhat?"

"He's become a spoiled brat, but he's my spoiled brat."

A moment of silence passed between the two as they crossed the parking lot.

"Nina's boy is turning out to be quite a fine young man. She must be proud."

"Gee's a good kid."

"There's something about him."

Julio looked Drew directly in his eyes for a moment then glanced away. Drew knew what provoked that reaction in his old friend, a subject that had long lay silent between them as it would continue Drew let it pass. "Come on, just one drink?"

"Where?"

"The Palais. I want you to meet this dancer."

"A dancer at a titty bar? Nah, man."

"She's hot."

"Nah man, I can't see that now. That's foreplay for me. I need to go home."

"You'll be ready when you get there, all warmed up, Chevy will love you for it."

"She'll love me anyway. You forget I'm Eveready. That's how we got five boys. So you dating a stripper now?" Julio shook his head with disapproval.

"Exotic dancer. Puerto Rican girl, name is Angel."

"Ay, estas loco? When you going to stop roaming around like some alley cat hunting pussy?"

"Wait till you see her."

Drew had heard the speech countless times about how he needed a wife. It would calm him down, avoid the dangers of kicking it with the hos. With five boys and a wife Julio loved more than anything, he couldn't understand how anyone would want anything else. In his heaven on the altar of love, there was no other life; Julio would preach the virtues of marriage and family. Drew turned a deaf ear even though he envied Julio.

Julio shook his head again. "No thanks, bro. I'm heading home."

Undeterred, Drew headed downtown alone.

∞

Friday, August 4, 11 p.m.

Jinx had not been as lucky as Gee and Tyrone in their getaways. Running east through the alleys for three blocks toward Kansas Avenue, he couldn't shake the cops in the squad car. He had discarded the drugs, but four blocks away, trapped in a dead-end alley, he gave up. The cops unable to recover any drugs gave him the rough treatment anyway and took his two hundred dollars pocket money then sent him on his way. A day's earnings gone and no way to re-up. Angry and humiliated, he vowed to get even.

Later that night sipping forty-ounce malt liquors on the porch, Jinx and Tyrone tried to catch a breeze. Jinx was still seething, feeling beaten down and bitter. It seemed a way of life. Few knew him by his given name, Jeffrey Legere. He got the nickname Jinx by being a playground bully and always the center of trouble. Never outgrowing the name or the chip on his shoulder, he was still known around the hood as Jinx. He considered himself a hardcore thug, a true street soldier. Not much of a follower, no crew would have him, but Jinx was determined to be a gangsta to be reckoned with.

"I'm tired of working the corner peddling rocks." Jinx idly twisted his braids. "I need to get paid some big money. With a big enough roll I could blow this town, go somewhere else. Maybe go live with my sistah in Richmond. D.C. ain't no place for a black man like me."

"There be a whole lotta black men like you here," Tyrone said.

"I don't mean just black, I'm talking about something else."

Tyrone turned up the forty and chugged a long swig, then wiped his mouth with the back of a hand. "If I had a job like Gee, I'd be set, man."

"Fuck a job, and fuck that Spanish boy."

"Hey man, Gee got it sweet, college man and all. Why you doggin' Gee? He got you that job at the Farragut last summer. We been boys since the playground, he be looking out for you."

"Fuck the Farragut."

"Wish I had a job there. Don't care if it's bustin' suds. It's a check, free eats, and you get to see all those famous musicians. No jive, I wish I had a job like that. Why you let them fire you, man?"

"Cause I'm a different kinda black man. Ain't no goddamn dishwasher. That's for them no-speak-English Spanish boys. Should go back and stick up the place. I'd show 'em."

Tyrone sat up. "You sound serious, man."

"You got that right."

"If you talking robbery with arms, holding up that kinda place, you talkin' big time now. Lotsa money be flowing through the Farragut."

"You down with it?

"Quit playing." Tyrone took another swig.

"I'm as serious as a heart attack. I know where to get guns."

"For real?"

"Tattoo. I'll talk to him in the morning."

"You got a plan?"

"Ain't got no plan, but give me time. We'll get the guns first."

Jinx spotted his mother coming down the block, returning from the Kenyon Bar and Grill or some other funk-ass joint, tottering on some man's arm, drunk as a skunk. She must have got lucky. The dude was carrying a brown bag and a shirt in one hand and steadying her with the other. Giggling like a coy schoolgirl and batting her eyes, Jean Legere was trying to look sexy. His mama's ridiculous act was just what he needed this fucked-up night.

The man followed Jean up onto the porch but froze at the sight of the two tough guys and their unfriendly glare. Jean Legere was on top of it.

"Don't pay them no mind. That's my son Jeffrey and his friend Tyrone." Despite the assurance, he eyed them with suspicion and a friendly smile.

"Boys, this is my friend, ah…" She cackled. "I'm sorry, what's your name again?"

"Henry, folks call me Henry, *Jean*." He had probably reminded her more than once that evening.

"Well come on in, Henry Jean." She let out another cackle.

"How you fellows doing?" Henry offered a handshake.

"Wassup?" Jinx ignored the hand.

Tyrone looked away without speaking. Henry grimaced and dropped his hand.

Jinx sized the man up as he followed Jean into the house. Early forties, and judging by his farm-boy accent, probably up from some rural Virginia county or one of the Carolinas doing construction work. The building boom in D.C. brought a lot of that type to the city. About six feet and solidly built with broad shoulders in a tank top, sinewy upper arms, a light brown complexion, graying temples, and the beginnings of a paunch.

Jinx could remember way back when his mama was pretty. Now, Jean Legere looked well beyond her thirty-five years, with sagging breasts, a washed-out complexion, a beer gut, and alcoholic red eyes. Jinx shook his head in sympathy, that country Jethro had no idea what she had planned.

⚯

The Palais was Drew's favorite of the District's bars featuring exotic dancers. A connoisseur of sorts, having at some point visited most, he claimed the diversity of the Palais's talent gave it a certain cachet. With three runways it was like a three-ring circus, with black, white, Asian, Middle Eastern, and Latin girls performing in the front, middle, and rear of the saloon with tables grouped at the foot of each runway. Over a speaker system to the dressing room, the talent was cued to assigned stages. Each girl would give a ten-minute set and then work the floor, further picking the patrons' pockets.

Angel was nowhere in sight on any of the stages nor working the floor. The next set was announced over the speaker system. "Lolinda, stage one, two minutes. Sunshine, stage two, two minutes. Angel, stage three, two minutes."

Drew looked for a seat at stage three, where a busty long-legged redhead began her finale, prancing in stiletto heels, nude except for black fishnet stockings and a garter belt, a club favorite not because of her lanky legs but for her carnival-like contortionist display, lying on her back, spreading her legs wide, and flexing. Her fuzzy landing strip revealed a true redhead.

"Ah baby," a pleased patron said, "tighten that honey hole." Amazed at this rare feat, every man leaned in for closer inspection. "Work it girl. Work it." For exercising this talent, she was generously rewarded.

Unable to find a seat near the stage Drew meandered over to the bar and ordered a beer. Two familiar District patrolmen chatted with the bouncer at the door. On their beat, stopping by to enjoy a peep, they were much like most of the other men there, in their twenties and thirties. Drew could count the middle-aged men like him. The moneyed ones were usually there for a particular dancer. While young men parted with their precious singles, blowing hard-earned wages on drink and tips in appreciation of a momentary thrill, the older men with deep pockets wanted more and patiently waited till closing.

Angelica Morales looking over the audience as though it were her's alone descended the staircase like a movie star making her entrance. Drew was the first to notice. Poised and confident, Angel's hair was up in a French braid. Other dancers used their long hair as a seductive prop, tossing it around as a part of the act. Petite and shapely with a caramel complexion, Angel's glamour and unique allure needed no props. To Drew she was a star. He watched each deliberate step, her red toenails peeping through open-toed, high-heeled, marabou-trimmed, red satin slippers.

Gliding off the staircase in a sheer black camisole over a red lace thong and matching bikini top, she smiled at the eager men. Drew couldn't take his eyes off her. Angel could turn him on like no other. That is, no other recent woman. He had only been seeing her a couple of weeks. It was a shame she had that habit. No one would know from her appearance she was a crack addict. He hated the notion that she supported her habit this way. As much as he wanted her, he wanted more to help her. She spotted him at the bar and smiled at him. Then she took the catwalk and began her masterful pole dance as he watched lost in her performance. He watched and waited content until her act ended, she then made her way towards him.

A man stood up from a nearby table and moved into her path. She seemed to recognize him—a tall youthful Latino, slim and dark, with long hair pulled into a ponytail tied with rawhide. What the hell kind of business did the man have with his Angel? Drew only spoke a few words of Spanish but thought he heard her say *hasta luego, luego.* She was putting him off. Her attention returned to Drew as she swept by the man.

"Hey baby, you're late tonight." She took his hand and caressed it. "Where you been?"

"I had another date." He smiled and enveloped her red-nailed fingers, the most affection they were permitted while she was on duty. A kiss or hug might give other patrons ideas, so touching the dancers was strictly forbidden.

"Who is this other woman you're dating?"

"More importantly, who is he?" Drew nodded in the man's direction.

"Who?" She pretended to look around.

"The fellow you were just speaking with."

"You're jealous, how sweet. He's nobody, an old friend from New York. We on for tonight?"

"Most definitely."

Suddenly a drunk was in Angel's face. The short and brawny Latino wedged himself between them. "Hey Mami, you look so good. Was your name?" The man balanced a drink in one hand, wrapped the other around her waist and attempted to pull her close.

Angel forced a smile while pushing him back. Drew yanked the shorter man by his collar. Strong, squat, broad-shouldered, bulging with the muscles of a man who worked hard with his hands, he twisted out of Drew's grip.

"Hey!" Drew pointed to the bartender's mirror. "You see that sign? No touching the dancers."

"Was it to you?" The man stood angry and defiant.

"I think you've had too much to drink."

"Oh yeah? Then why don't jew finish dis." He splashed his drink in Drew's face."

Angel pushed the man away as Drew turned to the bar and gave the man his back. The bartender, who kept a baseball bat under the bar, leaned in to see if Drew was all right. "I'll take care of him, Drew."

"Don't bother." Drew lifted the dishtowel from the bartender's shoulder and wiped his face while watching the man through the mirror behind the bar. Then Drew wrapped the towel tightly around his right hand.

Angel grabbed his arm. "Drew, please, don't."

The man's friend was attempting to pull him away but the squat drunk pushed him off and held his ground. Unsteady on his feet and proud of his action, he was unprepared when Drew turned abruptly and unleashed a right hook that crunched bone and broke teeth. Cold-cocked, the man fell onto his back amid a sea of feet.

His cohort flashed a knife. The crowd backed off, tripping over chairs and one another. The police were making their way through the crowd. The knife-wielding man charged. A deft jab nicked Drew's forearm and tore into his jacket sleeve. Drew twisted his arm, snagged the knife in the fabric, and pulled it from the man's grip. The blade hit the floor and disappeared. Drew snapped an uppercut and followed with a swift kick to the groin. Clutching his crotch, the man fell to his knees next to his friend.

The officers stepped into an already defused situation. All three men were handcuffed and transported to the Third District Precinct.

∞

Tyrone fell asleep on the loveseat. The TV light sporadically illuminated the unadorned walls of the meagerly furnished living room. Without air conditioning, the musty old sofa and loveseat stored the summer's humidity, giving off an odor that assaulted even accustomed noses. Tyrone's snoring competed with the TV volume.

Reclining on the sofa, his bare feet propped on the rickety cocktail table, Jinx watched a gangsta flick, his thoughts divided between the TV and planning the stickup. He had heard enough talk while locked up for distribution, and he had been locked up more than once; he knew how it was done. He could do it. His mind was made up.

Only one problem: they needed a getaway car. They could steal one, or maybe borrow Gee's. Then he had another idea, but Gee didn't have the heart, and Tyrone couldn't drive nothing but his motor mouth. He would give it some thought. Maybe there was a way.

Suddenly Jinx heard his mother cursing upstairs. Mufuckin' Henry must have thought he was spending the night. Ain't no breakfast served here. Let's be steppin' lightly. If Jean couldn't handle him, she would soon be downstairs for help. It wasn't the first time. The fool didn't know that once the bottle was empty, his pleasure done, it was time to pay up and be on his way.

Clump, clump of her bare feet on the worn steps, cursing all the way. "Jeffrey," she yelled, "Jeffrey!" At the living room entrance, her loud gravely voice forced him to look up. She continued her tirade. "That man won't give me my money. Get my money and get him out of here."

The man eased down the steps buttoning his shirt and shaking his head. At the bottom of the staircase, she stepped into his path.

"Watch it woman. I'm leaving. I don't owe you no money. You didn't tell me you was no ho."

"You know what the deal is, and if you didn't, you better act like it." She sneered in his face, hands on swinging hips, head bobbing in sync punctuating every word. She stood red-eyed and foul-mouthed, her knobby knees and bony stick legs exposed beneath her oversized t-shirt under which protruded two sagging sacks. Her hair screamed out every which way like she had stuck her finger in a light socket. How could any man lay down with her? Must be the older you get, the less looks matter.

She shot her son that get-him look. Jinx pulled himself up from the sofa and looked to Tyrone, now fully awake. The scene for a shakedown had been set.

"You owe my mama some money, man?" Jinx glared stone-faced.

"If this is a setup, I ain't game. I don't owe her nothing, she didn't tell me she was a ho."

"You calling my mama a ho?"

"I call 'em like I see 'em."

"And you ain't go'n pay this ho?"

"You got that right. The way she look, I should get paid for fuckin' her."

Tyrone snickered and Jean Legere cut him a sharp look. Tyrone put back on his hard face. Henry turned to walk out the door.

"Hey," Jinx said to the man's back. As Henry turned, Jinx's hard right slammed into the man's cheek. He may not have been ready for the steal to the face, but he was quick to raise his own defense. Dodging Jinx's follow-up left, Henry came back with a forceful left hook to the jaw. Stunned by a single punch, Jinx fell back over the cocktail table and collapsed onto the sofa.

Like a dazed fighter coming back from a knockdown, struggling to beat the count, his mother's ringside taunts echoed in his ears. "Git up boy, git him." But Jinx was having trouble summoning the wherewithal. Time was moving in slow motion. He staggered to his feet and leaned on the wall to steady himself. Then collapsed again.

Tyrone stepped up. Tyrone was a better fighter. He wasn't good at too many things but he was known for a good scuffle, a skill acquired from having a big mouth that many tried to shut. He came to this fight with a wealth of experience and followed Henry outside. Jinx staggered to the door to watch.

"Hey Jethro, where you think you going?" Tyrone dogged the man down on the sidewalk.

"Name's Henry."

"I say it's Jethro, you hillbilly muthafucka."

"Don't you try it."

Jean pulled Jinx back inside, slammed the door, and turned the deadbolt. He knew it was for fear the man would re-enter, and Jinx didn't want that either. When Tyrone didn't return, Jinx knew his friend probably got some of the same and went home to lick his wounds. Jean wasn't finished, her tirade resumed.

"A couple of punks, both of you." She stood over Jinx. "Why didn't you get my money? A waste, that's all you are, a waste, I didn't raise no faggot."

"You didn't raise me. I was raised in foster homes and juvenile detention. And your money—"

"Shut up—"

"If it was your money why didn't you get it yourself? Know why? 'Cause you couldn't turn a decent trick if you tried. Look at you, an old alcoholic ho. I'm sick of you and your shakedowns. It's always about you, never about me and Tamika. Just you."

"Don't talk to me like that, I'm still your mother."

"You ain't no mother." He stepped to her, glaring down into her face, fists balled at his side. She backed away, turned, and quickly retreated up the stairs. Her bedroom door slammed and the lock turned.

Jinx collapsed face down on the sofa and buried his head in the throw pillow. Life had dealt him a bad hand, that's the only way he could see it. Adrift and alone on the river of life, no family to love him, no woman to anchor him, to share his hopes, his dreams and his plans for the future, he had nothing to offer. The few women who had taken an interest usually lost it after sex. He never really clicked with a female. Hell, he never really clicked with anyone.

This wasn't a thug's life. A day's frustration and anger overflowed. He cried, whimpering into the pillow, stifling his sobs. He couldn't go on living this way. He'd rather be dead.

Saturday, August 5, 2 a.m.

Drew Smith walked into the interrogation room, hands cuffed behind his back, escorted by a smiling uniformed officer, young and proud of his prisoner, the city's most revered criminal attorney. Police Chief Richard Washington, a dark-skinned man carrying a few extra pounds, regarded both with contempt.

"Look at you," he said to Drew with palpable disgust. The usually dapper attorney stood without necktie, belt, or shoelaces in his torn Italian designer suit and rumpled shirt. Drew smiled at his old friend from twenty years back when together they solved the Arab playboy murders. "Get those cuffs off him," the Chief snapped.

The young officer's grin disappeared and he sheepishly fished for the key.

"Smith, I only get out of my bed at this hour to piss or for national emergencies."

"I already look like shit, I hope you don't plan to piss on me. Thanks for taking my call." Drew massaged his freed wrist. "Don't worry, I won't sue the department for false arrest."

The Chief glared at the befuddled officer. "What do you want?" The cop quickly stepped out, fumbling with his extra handcuffs. The Chief waited for the door to close. "As far as the Department is concerned, there was no arrest."

"How about false imprisonment?"

"What false imprisonment? Cut the crap Smith, you were involved in a barroom brawl. The police simply detained you for a statement."

"Nice spin, but it's bullshit, they were out to get me. They saw I was attacked. The man threw his drink in my face and his friend came at me with a knife. Your officers were more anxious to arrest me than my attackers. Look at my suit." He waved the slashed sleeve about. "There was no probable cause for my arrest. I'm a victim of the city's rampant crime."

"Save the courtroom theatrics. You weren't arrested. It's your reputation among the rank and file. They don't like you for making them look like Keystone Cops in court. Besides, why's a man of your stature hanging out in a titty bar at one in the morning?"

Drew gave the Chief a puzzled look. "Checking out the tits. What do you think?"

The Chief's gruffness gave way to a smile. "Ask a dumb question, get a smart answer. Smith, you have a talent for turning black into white before a jury's eyes. Don't destroy your public persona. No sooner you were in handcuffs, a scanner jockey for the *Post* had a reporter here. Thanks to your quick call, I gave orders to issue the standard no comment and officially deny your arrest. There's no paperwork. In the interest of your clients, we wouldn't want the public to know what a whoremonger you are. Quiet as it's kept, you're known as a regular at those sleazy dives."

Drew displayed a grateful smile. "Thanks, Chief, I knew I could count on you."

"You need therapy. That ghost riding your back for the past twenty years must be a heavy burden by now. Get some help."

"I don't need any help."

"The hell you don't. What's a successful, wealthy, good-looking, sought-after man like you doing whoring around and making an ass of yourself?"

Drew turned to check himself out in the two-way mirror, using the palm of his hand to smooth the close cut wavy hair, straightening the lapels, then inspecting his ragged sleeve. In his early forties, Drew maintained a youthful and handsome appearance.

"You're an important man in this city—"

"Yeah, a regular pillar of society. Hey, can you give me a ride?"

Silenced, he shook his head and watched Drew preen like a peacock. Drew checked both sides of his profile and yanked up the belt-less slacks that hung low on his waist. "Can I get my tie, belt and shoestrings back?"

"No problem."

"What about my two amigos?"

"The two you fucked up? They're at Howard Hospital. One is having his jaw reset and they're trying to pry the other's testicles out of his asshole. No charge on them as well."

"That's fair." Drew laughed. "Next time they'll think twice."

"What happened to that timid young man just out of law school? You've grown cocky and arrogant. Don't let your celebrity status go to your head. It'll come back to bite your ass."

"How about that ride?"

"Where to?"

"The Palais."

"It's after two. It's closed."

"That's where my car is parked."

"Okay, but then you're going straight home, right?"

Still preening, Drew didn't respond. It was none of the Chief's business.

Chapter 3

Sunday, August 6, 5:00 a.m.

IN THE NIGHT'S last darkness, Drew Smith bolted up from a deep sleep. Sweat beaded his forehead and his hands were shaking. It was the dream again. He eased back, baffled and bothered. Medhat had been dead for more than twenty years and yet from time to time his old buddy would pay him these haunting visits. What was it all about?

He had never felt so alone, bereft, and shaken.

Then a thought and a smile came over him. He was looking forward to spending the afternoon with Julio, Chevy and the kids. Morning came blue-gray across Rock Creek Park's treetops, bringing the promise of sunlight.

∞

Sunday, August 6, 6:00 a.m.

Not far across town, Mrs. Glenda Fitzpatrick suffered a mild asthma attack and couldn't sleep. The octogenarian decided to sit in her rocker near the open window of her second-floor bedroom. Six a.m. according to her clock, and soon she would go downstairs, prepare her tea and toast, and then get ready for Mass. For the moment she decided to just rock and watch the sunrise, pray her rosary, and thank the good Lord for giving her another day. As she puffed on her inhaler, something caught her attention down on the street. The rocking stopped. She put on her glasses, moved the wavering sheers aside, and leaned in to watch.

∞

Sunday, August 6, 6:30 a.m.

Jinx and Tyrone quickly crossed the parking lot to the rear kitchen entrance of the Farragut Tavern. Each checked the other's mask, and with an "Okay," Jinx pulled his Glock 17 from his waistband and released the safety. Tyrone did the same. The door was open and kitchen activity could be heard. Jinx tried the screen door but it was latched.

With the barrel of the gun, he tapped on the frame and stepped back out of view. Tyrone too pressed his back against the wall. The doorway darkened as someone appeared. The latch lifted, a head stuck out and met the barrel of Jinx's gun. Naomi's mouth dropped open.

"Oh, Jesus."

"Back up." Jinx flung the door open and with the gun in her face forced her back into the kitchen.

"Oh Jesus."

Her fear coursed through his veins like a jolt of speed. The big dark-skinned bitch with the feisty attitude, who once gave him orders, was now taking orders from him.

"Everybody down on the floor!" Jinx ordered waving his gun entering the small kitchen.

The intruders had interrupted Josh the chef, Naomi the cook, and Rodney the dishwasher. The three had been busy preparing for the Farragut's famous Sunday brunch. Biscuit mix still covered Naomi's hand as she tried to towel it away. Her biscuits a brunch staple were always in demand. Jinx watched as she lowered her heft down onto the floor. Rodney and Josh did the same, all looking stunned.

"Watch 'em," he told Tyrone, then moved out of the kitchen down the hall to the stairwell leading up to the manager's office.

Jinx's stealthy ascent up the old Victorian mansion's staircase, two steps at a time, made the varnished worn wood creak under his weight. Gun in hand, he faltered at the closed door. Maybe Theo wasn't there after all. It was locked. He knocked and waited, then knocked again.

He could shoot off the lock, but the ricochet might catch him. Instead, with a single solid swift kick, the old wooden door swung open, splintering at the jamb. Once inside the small room, Jinx snatched off his mask and smiled at the piles of cash lying on the desk.

But something wasn't right. The window was open. Theo must have heard the commotion and ducked out the window onto the roof of the breezeway connecting the new dining room. "Damn." Jinx stuck his head out and looked up and down the street—no one. Only Michigan Avenue's sparse early morning traffic could be heard.

He bagged the money, put his mask back on, and returned to the kitchen. Tyrone stood over the three terrified workers.

"Let's go," Jinx said.

Tyrone's eyes suddenly widened.

"Jeffrey Legere?" Naomi said. "Boy, you ought to be shamed of yo'self."

Jinx looked to Tyrone.

"Your mask," Tyrone said, "you got it on wrong."

Jinx felt his face. "Damn."

"Do you really think you can get away with—"

"Shut up, you fat bitch. My bad, and now you die." He looked to Tyrone. "Shoot 'em."

"What?" Tyrone's eyes grew wide with fear. "The guns was just for show. Dat's what you said. Won't be no shootin'."

"She recognized me. They gotta go, all three of them."

Tyrone shook his head.

"Shoot 'em before I shoot you." Jinx pointed his gun at Tyrone's face. "You want to join them?"

Tyrone stepped back, pointed his gun at Naomi's frightening stare, closed his eyes and pulled the trigger. He jumped back at the sound and recoil.

"Oh my God, Sweet Jesus!" she cried out. Tyrone opened his eyes. The bullet had torn into her shoulder.

"You fuck-up, get out my way. Let me show you how it's done." Jinx stood over Naomi as she begged for her life. He pumped two rounds into her skull. Blood and flesh splattered the floor and wall. He moved on to Rodney, who defiantly looked up. "Sorry bro," Jinx said, and methodically shot him in the same manner. Finally, he stood over Josh. "Yeah, it's me muthafucka. I told you, you hadn't seen the last of me. But I've seen the last of you. Say goodnight." He squeezed the trigger.

Tyrone was shaking.

"Let's go." Jinx grabbed his backpack from the floor and stepped to the door. Tyrone had not moved. "Come on, man!"

"You said no shooting. You killed three people."

"We're in this together. Let's go, someone was upstairs, they got away. We gotta get the fuck outta here. Feds be here any minute. Let's go!"

Tyrone finally moved, following Jinx out the door. They ran across the parking lot and down the block. When they turned the corner, the car was gone.

"That no good mutha—"

A horn sounded from behind them. It was Gee coming around the corner from circling the block.

Jinx yanked the driver's door open. "Move over, God damn it." Gee scooted over to the passenger side, looking back at Tyrone. Distant sirens approached from the east. Jinx stomped the accelerator, going west.

"If you're going to speed, don't take North Capitol," Gee said. "Cameras on North Capitol."

Uncertain at first, Jinx gave Gee a bitter one-sided smile. "Thanks."

He crossed North Capitol and took a series of side streets back to Georgia Avenue. The ride was silent. Tyrone looked like he was going to be sick. The car soon came to an abrupt stop in front of Jinx's house. He grabbed the backpack and jumped out. Again Tyrone was slow to move. "Come on, muthafucka." Tyrone lethargically pulled himself up out of the car.

As Gee eased back behind the wheel, he glared up at Jinx. "What happened back there?"

"You don't wanna know. Just remember what I said. Now get out of here."

Gee drove off.

Chapter 4

N EWS OF THE Farragut robbery came that afternoon while Drew was visiting Julio and Chevy. Drew was shocked and angry, but somewhat relieved to know Theo and Gee were all right. The Farragut was his favorite hangout. It would never be the same. Tragedies like that have a way of changing things. Back home, he fell into a deep funk. Being around Julio's happy family always increased his own discontent and loneliness. Because the dreams had kept him awake again the night before, fatigue forced him to take an early evening nap. He jerked awake when the phone rang.

"Drew, it's Theo."

"I heard about the robbery, Theo. How you holding up?"

"The police had me at the station all day. They think I had something to do with it. They want me back tomorrow. Will you go with me?"

"I don't think you need representation."

"Drew, they've pretty much accused me of masterminding it. I did that once, but not this time. I learned my lesson. They're trying to build a case on me. I need your help."

Drew sighed. "I'll try to move some things on my calendar."

"Thanks Drew. Believe me, I didn't do it."

"I believe you, any idea who did it?"

"You know Drew, I thought I heard a familiar voice. Just can't place it."

"Think about it. I'll call you later."

Early in his career, Drew had represented Theo on an armed robbery charge. It was a fast-food restaurant, an inside job, and Theo, the inside man. He was no more than a kid, eighteen with no juvenile record. Drew put up a vigorous defense and got him a light sentence. After serving three years and parole, Theo turned his life around, started a family, and stayed on the straight and narrow. Drew attributed the holdup to youthful indiscretion. Theo knew his mistake and always regretted it. When he came out of the joint, it was Drew who helped him get back on his feet, finding him a waiter's job at the Farragut, where over the years he was promoted to manager.

The police would pressure Theo with threats and intimidation, preying on his fear, and Drew once again wanted to be in his corner. It was more than curiosity and loyalty to Theo drawing Drew into the case. He personally knew all the victims. The place and the people killed were dear to him.

Drew called his secretary, apologized for disturbing her Sunday evening, and explained he needed her to contact the parties first thing tomorrow morning and reschedule a deposition. When he hung up, the phone's staccato tone signaled a message. He entered his password.

"Hi Drew, it's me, Angel. Sitting here thinking about you, hope you're not still mad at me. I'm off tonight. Interested in getting together? I could use the company and dinner. Give me a call when you get this message. Please."

She wanted to come over. After the incident at the Palais Friday night, maybe it wasn't wise to keep company with that kind of woman. Maybe he'd best be cool with Angel. But the mere sound of her voice had physically aroused him. Give her up? Soon, very soon. He dialed her number.

✧

Sunday, August 6, 9:00 p.m.

Jinx and Tyrone agreed to regroup later and divvy up the take when Jean would be out of the house. Around six she usually made her way down to the Kenyon Bar and Grill. Jinx caught the evening news, and the robbery was the big story. Against the Farragut backdrop, the TV reporter said nothing Jinx didn't already know, and that was a good thing.

Tyrone arrived in a more collected state. Jinx counted off the five hundred dollars for the guns, then divvied up the remaining thirty three hundred. Each had a share of one thousand six hundred fifty dollars.

"This all?" Tyrone picked up his share.

"That's it. Most of the take was in credit card receipts? What you think? I'm cheating you?"

"Didn't say that. But now you mention it, what's to stop you from cheating me?"

"I wouldn't do that to you, man. We're in this together."

"Don't seem like it was hardly worth it. This ain't no big money. Not enough for three people to die."

"Shut up about that."

"All it takes is for Gee to snitch."

"Shut up, fool. Gee won't snitch."

"What'll you do, kill him too?"

"You got a problem with that? Why you so concerned with Gee? Forget about Gee—"

"I can't, and I can't forget those people you shot—"

Jinx pulled his gun and pointed it at Tyrone. "You're just a faggot. You couldn't even pull that trigger. Shut up and get out of here. Faggot. Your uncle must have butt fucked you good. Turned you into a complete bitch."

Tyrone stood defiant. Growing up, he'd suffered continuous sexual molestation at the hands of an uncle. Expecting sympathy and understanding, he'd confided in Jinx. But Jinx used it to his advantage, turning it on his friend with ridicule and taunts directed at Tyrone's manhood, the ultimate smack in the face. Tyrone has big issues of guilt and shame, and would violently lash out when his manhood was questioned. Jinx knew how to get a rise out of him, taunting him with their secret, aggravating the man's personal torment, then channeling the rage toward Jinx's chosen target. As Tyrone shoved the money in his pocket, Jinx smiled, keeping him in check at gunpoint.

"We shouldn't be seen together for a while, so stay away from here."

"Sure, Jinx, whatever you say. Just put that gun away. It's me, Tyrone. Remember?"

Jinx lowered the gun when Tyrone walked out of the bedroom, and listened as his Timberland boots hit the step boards and then the front door slammed behind him. Shoving the gun under the mattress, he felt around and pulled out another two thousand dollars. With a fistful of money, thirty-five hundred dollars, he laughed out loud. Tyrone and Gee were history. He'd never be bothered with them again. Now it was time to go settle up with Tattoo.

∞

Sunday, August 6, 10:00 p.m.

"Who is it?" A woman peeped through the lattice door.

"Jinx, I'm looking for Tattoo."

"Hold up." She closed the interior door.

Seconds later again the door reopened. The lattice door unlatched and swung open. Tattoo was about six feet with a slight but muscled build. "What's up? You got my money?"

"I got your money. Like I said I would." Jinx stepped in, keeping an eye on Tattoo. The Hispanic stood shirtless and barefooted wearing low-hanging jeans and, from what Jinx could tell from the exposed hairy belly, nothing else. His wicked smile and dark eyes always made Jinx wary. With a well-toned body, the man had a sensuality felt by both men and women. He flaunted it dangerously.

"Come in, have a seat." Tattoo led Jinx into the neatly furnished one-bedroom apartment. With all the bright colors and fancy décor, it must be the woman's place. She sat on the sofa painting her toenails, never looking up to acknowledge or speak to Jinx. Jinx couldn't stop staring at her. "Angel, give us some privacy."

Frowning at the interruption, the barelegged woman in the black teddy replaced the top on her nail polish. Damn. What would it be like to have a woman like that? Probably high-maintenance. She ambled into the bedroom, showing off that fine ass of hers, and closed the door.

Jinx pulled out a bankroll. "Dat your woman? This her place? Why we meeting here?"

"You got a lot of questions, Jinx. Right now I'm asking the questions. How much is there?"

"All of it. Count it." Jinx dropped the money on the coffee table.

"I will. Later."

Jinx stood to leave.

"What's your hurry? Sit down. Let's talk business." It was not a request, but an order, and Jinx eased back down. "What you do with dose guns?" Tattoo tilted his head curiously.

"What you mean?"

"Who you kill?"

"What kind of question is that?" Jinx grew uneasy. He feared few men, but Tattoo was one. There was a cold indifference in the black eyes, windows to a hollow soul, dull and flat like primer paint that neither glistened nor sparkled. Tattoo sent out a chilly vibe and that Asian tattoo across his back might as well have been a skull and bones.

"Again, you asking too many questions. Yesterday you come to me wanting a couple of guns on credit—just guns, no caine. You been making your money selling caine on the streets. I figure you needed the guns for protection. Maybe somebody hassling you? Or you got a job to do? Which was it?"

"I'm here to pay for the guns. The rest is my bidniss. I'm out of here."

"Not so fast. You not buying no caine. That means you don't need no money, don't need to work the streets." Tattoo smiled. "You heard about the Farragut?"

"What's that?" Stricken with fear, Jinx tried not to show it while wondering what Tattoo knew.

"It's all over the news. You're hot, man. I put you and two guns together. You better lay low. Maybe get out of town. You ever hear of Santo Domingo?"

"Who dat?"

"It's a city, my home in the Dominican Republic. I'm getting up an operation. I could use a man like you, not afraid to use a gun."

Jinx looked him in the eye, but Tattoo looked away when the bedroom door opened and Angel stepped out. It didn't take her long to get dressed to go out, but then it didn't look like she put much on. Jinx checked her out from head to toe as she strutted to the door. The dress was backless and her strappy heels were retro. The highlights of wavy auburn hair set off her caramel complexion. Neither her bare legs nor her red toenails escaped Jinx's attention. He was aroused just looking at her.

"Where you goin'?" Tattoo snapped.

"Out."

"Where?"

"I'll be with Drew if you must know. And don't wait up for me, papi chulo." She threw him a teasing kiss and strutted out the door. In the wake of her sweet fragrance, she left Tattoo looking angry and jealous.

Whoever this Drew was, the man was beating Tattoo's time. And one thing was for sure. She was definitely high-maintenance.

Tattoo turned his attention back to Jinx. "As I was saying, you need to lay low. I'm willing to help."

Chapter 5

Monday August 7, 7:00 a.m.

"WAKE UP." Drew placed the mug of steaming coffee on the nightstand next to the bed. Angel stirred and looked up through sleepy eyes. Drew had already showered and dressed. "I got someplace to be in an hour."

"I don't want to get up." She pulled herself up, exposing her breasts. Nina had always been modest, and even when it was just the two of them, she would always pull the sheets around her top. Why did Nina creep into his thoughts while he was with another woman? Another question for the therapist, which reminded him of the day's to-do list: find a therapist.

"You can go back to bed when you get home."

"It's not the same, I'll be all awake." She sipped from the mug and watched Drew pick a tie from his closet then step to the mirror and mechanically loop the knot. "Let me lay here and sleep. Come back for me on your lunch hour."

He stood over her. "Let me feel your head." His fingers massaged her scalp.

"What are you doing?"

"Checking to see if I banged your head on that headboard."

"Oh, silly." She smacked his hand away. "You don't trust me."

"Hey, you're a crackhead, remember?"

"I smoke cocaine. I'm not a crackhead."

"What's the difference, the amount you smoke?"

"Shut up. What, you think I'd rob you?"

"Back a truck up to the door and empty the place. One thing I've learned over the years, druggies can't be trusted."

"I have principles. I support my own habit."

"With my help."

"You should help me more. Marry me and let me move into your big beautiful house."

"You done lost your mind for sure."

"You wouldn't marry me? I'm not good enough?"

"Oh, I'd marry you in heartbeat, sweetheart, if you didn't have so much baggage. I can't deal with the drugs, the dancing, and the other men. I'm crazy about you, but not that crazy. Just give me my one or two nights a week."

"Help me, Drew."

"Kick the habit, go back to school, and get a regular job. Then we'll talk about the future." The sincere dejection in her eyes pulled him down onto the bed. He took her hand. "We'll see."

"Is that a proposal?" He only winked. "I can do that for you, baby. Help me?" She clutched the coffee mug in her hands as if drawing hope from its warmth.

"Don't do it for me. Do it for yourself. You have to want it. And I don't think you want it that bad. Now get dressed. I got to go."

"Please, Drew?" She looked desperately sad. "Let me sleep in. I'm tired, if I get up now I'll just drag through the day. Please? Please?"

Her pitiful eyes overcame his better judgment. "I'll leave a spare key for the deadbolt on the counter. The alarm code for the keypad is DREW. Stick the key under the doormat when you go."

She gave him a goodbye kiss and slid back down under the covers.

⚬⚬⚬

Monday, August 7, 9:00 a.m.

The media was on an all-out blitz about the crime that shocked the city. Public outrage echoed from the halls of Congress to the District Building, and down through every neighborhood barbershop, beauty salon, and café, wherever city folk gathered. The press vented, quoting citizen sentiment and city council members, while the mayor provided thirty-second sound bites promising the criminals would be brought to trial. The hue and cry for justice put pressure on the mayor and thus the police chief to produce immediate results.

The WPA architectural municipal building, once a WPA project, stood sandwiched between the postmodern Superior Court and the U. S. Department of Labor. Drew arrived at the Indiana Avenue entrance of police headquarters to find Theo nervously waiting on the steps. They shook hands, then Drew pulled him aside for briefing. Theo explained how he'd been counting the receipts, heard shouts from the kitchen, first tried to investigate, then instead decided to flee. He'd run nearly three blocks before finding a payphone to call for help. Satisfied with Theo's explanation, Drew led him into the Municipal Building.

They took the elevator to the third-floor Violent Crimes Unit conference room. Drew recognized the players: Chief Washington, Lieutenant Mike Lowry, and the first response detective, Terry Blankenship. At Drew's entrance, conversation abruptly ceased mid-sentence. The two detectives seemed surprised and annoyed. The Chief flashed a friendly smile as though Drew had come to save the day.

Lt. Lowry, short and stocky with a buzz-cut and a square jaw, was every bit the ex-marine. In his late thirties, he was beginning to soften, and his thin lips seemed perpetually turned down in a frown. Although he gave no obvious outward signs other than a tough, superior air, Drew sensed the man was a racist. But living and working in a predominately minority city, Lowry knew how to suppress his prejudice in a politically correct charade. He and Smith had bumped heads many times before. Defeated on more than one occasion in court, Lowry made no effort to hide his disdain for Smith.

Their history had lurched toward war ten years prior. On his way to the office one morning, Drew came out of the Foggy Bottom Metro station and witnessed the manhandling of a disabled elderly black panhandler. Smith and two other witnesses told the bully to stop. That's when he flashed a small gold badge and said he was a plainclothes cop. What they saw didn't look like a policeman following procedure but a burly thug pushing and shoving a frail old man. As he hustled the panhandler away, a growing crowd followed him, protesting the rough treatment. Lowry subdued the ugly crowd by demanding identification from the three leading protestors. He then ordered uniformed officers to arrest Drew and the two women. The officers were polite, professional, and as taken aback as everyone else. Lowry ordered them to write up summonses for disorderly conduct, and told Smith to plead guilty and take his medicine. He had no idea who—or, more importantly, what—Smith was. Lowry yelled at the gathering crowd with the most menacing tone. "Any of you doubt I'm a police officer now? Any of you? What more do you want? My cuffs?"

The press got ahold of the incident, and when the then Lieutenant Richard Washington was asked about the decision to arrest Smith and the others, he'd said that people who interfere with the police are subject to arrest. Smith filed a complaint with the Civilian Complaint Review Board. It turned out the panhandler was never arrested, and the case against Smith and the others was dismissed for failure to prosecute. When Lowry never showed up at trial, the Review Board dismissed Smith's complaint as moot.

Now the Chief gave Drew a vigorous handshake. His presence signaled that the Farragut case was being given high priority. It may have been Lowry's investigation, but the Chief was exercising his dutiful oversight.

"Who's the good cop and who's the bad?" Drew said, breaking the ice as they sat down.

"There are no bad cops here," the Chief said. "Surprised to see you here, Smith, but if I remember correctly, some years back you represented Jackson on his prior robbery conviction."

"My client was convicted, served his time, paid his debt to society, and has since been a model citizen. A victim, like the others, he had no involvement in the preparation or perpetration of this horrific crime."

Lt. Lowry's eyes narrowed. "Then why are you here?"

"To make sure you don't make him a scapegoat."

The Chief held up a calming hand and turned to Drew. "Since counsel is present, no need to Mirandize."

"Is Theo a suspect?" Drew asked. The Chief shrugged. "I believe he signed a sworn affidavit yesterday. May I see it?"

Blankenship pulled the statement from a file in front of him and handed it over. Drew read while the others waited in silence. Once done, he handed the affidavit back.

"Can we begin now?" the Chief asked.

"Certainly," Drew said. "My client stands by his prior statement."

Lt. Lowry looked to the Chief, awaiting the go-ahead. It came with a nod.

Lowry smirked. "Jackson, you seem more at ease today. Can you tell us something new?"

Theo looked to Drew, who avoided his eyes. It was important that Theo appeared to answer freely.

"Yesterday was a rough day." Theo shifted in his chair. "It's hard to keep it together once you've seen three of your coworkers sprawled out with their brains splattered."

"Do you own a gun, Jackson?"

Alarm on his face, Theo again looked to Drew, who took his cue. "Don't answer that. My client refuses to answer that question under the Fifth Amendment. Convicted felons cannot be required to register their guns because that would force them to confess to the crime of illegally owning a gun. With that understanding, have you recovered the murder weapon?"

"Hold on, Smith," Lowry said, "I'm asking the questions."

"No. You hold on. If you're fishing for some reason to hold my client under suspicion, forget it. He appeared here voluntarily to help solve this crime. I suggest you quit focusing on him and start looking for the real shooter."

Lowry clenched his jaw. "All right, I'll come right out and ask. Did you shoot your coworkers to death, make it look like a robbery, stash the money, dispose of the gun, then walk three blocks away to call the police?"

"No. I told you that yesterday, why would I do that? I cared for them." Theo's voice trembled. "They were like my own family, a part of my everyday life. I could never do that."

Drew placed a hand on Theo's forearm. "Theo has been through a lot the past twenty-four hours. He's not up to continually defending himself against false accusations. I assume we're here to go over his story, to try and find new evidence. If there are further accusations against my client, we're out of here. " Drew stood, lifting Theo by the elbow. "Is that clear?"

Lowry eased back in his chair and looked to an unresponsive Chief. The Lieutenant's frown intensified. "It's clear."

"Then we have an understanding." Drew and Theo sat back down. "So let's cut the bullshit and get down to business. You asked Theo to bring in the payroll records for the past three years. By accusing Theo, it's apparent you're approaching this crime as an inside operation. Maybe you have a conspiracy theory. Right?" Drew looked to the Chief. He smiled but said nothing.

"Keep talking," Lowry said.

"I propose we go through this list, focusing on the male employees eighteen to thirty-five, then run a NACI on each. Then we reduce the list further to those with criminal records and particularly robbery convictions."

"That includes your client," Lowry said.

"Theo, how old are you?"

"Thirty-seven."

"That does not include Theo. We can pare it down to a workable list, persons of interest. Theo can give us his own personal profile on each. I think that might be more productive than you sitting here browbeating my client. What do you say, Lowry?"

"We can go that route, only I don't believe that eliminates your client as a co-conspirator."

"Believe what you want. Just be prepared to prove it."

The conference proceeded, albeit less combatively. Theo repeated the same story he had the day before with no new details. He turned over the requested payroll ledger. After a secretary copied the document, the interview continued for another two hours. The police were meticulous and methodical in their questioning. Upon reviewing the payroll ledger, five names stood out. With no rap sheet, Gee—Nina's son, Gustavo Garcia—was eliminated.

The final list was narrowed to three men. Theo offered his impression of each man, his personality, and the circumstances surrounding each dismissal. One was fired for stealing tips, and another for no-call, no-show. The third, Jeffrey Legere, was fired because of his attitude and insubordination.

"What can you tell us about him?" Drew asked.

"He didn't last a full two weeks. Had a real attitude and difficulty following instructions. The chef couldn't work with him. He tried to intimidate the staff. I had to fire him." Theo's brow furrowed with an afterthought.

"What is it?" Lowry asked.

"Nothing."

"Did he go quietly?" Drew asked.

"Not hardly, called me a whole string of muthafuckas and made a bunch of threats."

It was decided Lowry would round up the three persons of interest and proceed from there. As the meeting broke, the Chief asked Drew for a moment of his time and dismissed the others. Drew walked Theo to the door and told him to wait outside.

"What's up, Chief?"

"The mayor is really leaning on me for some immediate re-sults. Your client is all we have to go on. We need help on this." Then he laughed. "I like the way you took control of that meet-ing."

"It's not the first time I've had to take Lowry to school. Any physical evidence?"

"Very little, a couple of bloody footprints. Jackson is the clos-est thing to a witness. We're waiting on ballistics. You know, you've represented a rogue's gallery of murder suspects and other violent felons. I suspect you're hooked into that grapevine."

"And?"

"Somebody saw something. We'll announce a reward soon. I guarantee somebody will be willing to talk. Listen out, let me know if you hear anything."

"I've defended a lot of criminals, and despite what you may think, that's not my social set. I'll keep my ears open, but maybe one of the victims knew the robber and he had to snuff them to avoid identification. You're wasting time focusing on Theo. Why would he rob and murder when he could have just skimmed money and cooked the books? It doesn't make sense. Focus on the former employees. Lowry needs to round up those persons of interest right away."

"How well do you know your client?"

"Very well, he's not a violent man."

"We're going to put him on the watch list and keep an eye on him for a while. I'd advise him not to leave town."

"Right. Now there's something I need from you. That conversation we had the other night about therapy?"

"You did hear me." The Chief smiled.

"I may not like what you're saying, but I listen. Gave your suggestion some thought, figure it couldn't do any harm. Can you recommend a therapist?"

"I know just the person. She helps us out from time to time when an officer needs grief counseling, posttraumatic-stress stuff."

"I hope it's not that serious. A woman, huh?"

"She's the best." The Chief said with a fatherly hand on Drew's shoulder walking him to the door. "I'll leave her number with your secretary."

"Appreciate it." Drew offered his hand. "We'll be in touch."

Drew joined Theo on the Municipal Building's front steps.

"Thanks, Drew, I feel better now that you got them to back off."

"That's what you're paying me for, and I am charging you for this."

"Not a problem."

"Now we're going to your place, and you're going to give me your gun. You do have a gun, don't you?"

Theo hesitated. "Yeah, I do."

"I'll keep it for you until this blows over. I just need to get it out of your possession. I don't trust these guys. They're just looking for a reason to lock somebody up to calm the public."

It wasn't uncommon for the average citizen to keep a gun in his home, for no other reason that to protect that home.

"And Theo, don't leave the area unless you check with me."

"Okay."

"I got the feeling you were withholding something from Lowry."

"No...it's just that when Jeffrey Legere's name came up. I hired him after Gee referred him, and we both later admitted it was a big mistake. But I remembered something else..."

"What? Come on, Theo."

"It just flashed in my mind. While I was running away, I got this image of Gee's car. Like maybe I saw it there that morning. I can't be sure. You know what I mean?"

"Maybe a similar model, just to make sure I'll ask Gee."

∞

Monday, August 7, 2:00 p.m.

On the Friday before the robbery, Gee had come to a decision about Tyrone and Jinx, and now he wished he had stuck with it. Waiting in the reception area, watching Mr. Smith's receptionist juggling the phone and typing on her computer, his stomach was queasy. He just wanted this meeting to be over. The attorney had called and asked if he had time to come talk to him about the Farragut, said he was representing Theo. Why would Theo need a lawyer? Gee hoped *he* didn't need one, and wished this all would go away. His secret weighed heavily on him. Could he tell Drew Smith? How much did Drew Smith already know? He should have stuck with the decision to stay away from Jinx and Tyrone.

∞

"Pleasant thoughts?" Drew asked.

Gee looked up as if startled. "Just thinking about Marie."

"She's enough to make any man dreamy. I enjoyed meeting her the other night. Come on in." Gee followed Drew into his office and was directed to have a seat in front of the desk.

Drew had watched him grow up. Julio and Chevy would often baby-sit, and Gee blended into Julio's brood. With the young man seated before him, Drew was reminded of Nina.

"I guess you're wondering why I asked you in. I hope you don't mind."

Gee looked about the office, apparently avoiding eye contact. "No problem, it's not like I had to go to work. The Farragut's closed this week. May not reopen for a couple of weeks. What do you want from me?"

"Just some information on a couple of your former co-workers. So far in the investigation, a couple of names surfaced. Police think it was an inside job, and the person responsible was someone who worked there and knew the setup. There are a couple of people of interest and I wanted to pick your brain."

"I'll try."

"Eddie Campbell, what do you know about him?"

"Not much, I know he went to Bell Vocational. He wasn't at the Farragut that long. Got caught lifting tips and was fired. I didn't know him at all. He only worked there two or three weeks."

"What about Sam Ellis?"

"Dude kept to himself a lot. Didn't talk much. He was probably there a couple of months."

"You ever have an opportunity to socialize with him?"

Gee shook his head.

"Now, this next guy, I understand you got him hired. Jeffrey Legere?"

Gee looked down at the floor. "Jinx."

"How do you know him?"

"Went to school together. He was expelled in the tenth grade. He had it rough. His mother was in and out of rehab or jail. Jinx and his sister were put in foster care. We go back to first grade and the playground. So about a year ago he found out I was working at the Farragut and asked me to hook him up. I recommended him to Theo. Boy, did I regret that. Jinx's got a bad attitude and a temper. He didn't like dishwashing. He'd always argue when Josh or Nadine asked him to do things."

"So he was fired?"

"Like I said, he had a real bad attitude."

"How did he feel about that, being fired?"

"We never talked about it. Wasn't much to say. I knew I'd never recommend him for a job again."

"Have you talked to him lately?"

Gee hesitated, then shook his head. "No."

"Theo thinks he saw your car near the Farragut that morning. Did he?"

Again Gee hesitated. "He might have, I left it around the corner overnight. Marie picked me up after work and we went out. We took her car."

"Why was it on the street and not in the parking lot?"

"I thought it would be safer in front of someone's house than a vacant parking lot."

"I see."

"Mr. Drew, why does Theo need a lawyer?"

"He doesn't really. Theo just wants to cover all his bases. Since he was there at the time of the robbery, the police aren't sure about his story."

"So he's going to be all right."

"I think so. You've answered my questions, Gee. Thanks for coming in. I hope I didn't take up too much of your time."

"Right now I've got plenty of time until school starts."

"How's that going?"

"Good, I graduate in May."

"Fantastic."

Drew walked the young man to the door and watched him disappear from his outer office. There was something about this kid he really liked. Maybe it was the fact that he was Nina's son, and because of that he had always kept his distance. But why was he lying?

Chapter 6

J ULIO CAME THROUGH the door grinning in his black uniform, his chauffeur's cap tucked under his arm. Julio owned a limousine fleet service and could better spend his time managing the office but left that to Chevy. Julio grew up on the streets and this was his preferred method of staying in the mix. Chevy was also the company's chief dispatcher and it was her way of keeping track of Julio throughout the day and providing her free reign in the day to day management of the family business.

"What brings you here?" Drew asked.

"Got a pickup around the corner in a half-hour, thought I'd pass the time."

"Glad you stopped by, got a call from Theo last night. You know his history, the police are working a conspiracy theory."

"They think Theo's the inside man." Julio dropped down on the sofa.

"You guessed it." Drew brought Julio up to date and suggested they check out the three on Lowry's list. "You game?"

"Should I bring my gun?"

"No guns. We come in peace."

"Wanna make sure we leave in peace. Isn't this a job for the police?"

"The lead investigator is Lowry."

"Uh-oh."

"Not exactly the type to share information, especially exculpatory evidence. Theo thinks he saw Gee's car nearby. I asked

Gee about it this afternoon. It was his car. I was more concerned with a job referral he made for one Jeffrey Legere. Guy's got a juvenile rap sheet as long as your limo, a number of distribution charges and auto theft, but nothing violent."

Julio shrugged. "Don't take much to graduate."

"Gee says he has a hot temper and a bad attitude. Let's see what he has to say about the Farragut. Around eight?"

"Have to be later, you're having dinner with us."

"I am?"

"Chevy's orders. And speaking of Gee, his mother needs your help."

"How so?"

"Hernando popped her last night. She and Candice showed up at our front door. It took both her and Chevy to keep me from going and letting him have it. She's miserable, you gotta help her."

"Help her? They've been married twenty years, and as my daddy used to say, you reap what you sow."

"Help her get out of that marriage."

"There are a thousand divorce lawyers in this city. I don't handle divorces."

"You can, though, can't you?"

"My mother used to say, don't get involved in other people's marriages. If she wants to talk to me, I'll help her find a good divorce lawyer. I'm not jumping into the middle of that. I was there once before, remember?"

"I'll tell her you want to talk to her."

"I want to talk to her? Hey, wait a minute. Chevy put you up to this, didn't she?"

"Uh…"

"I knew it."

Julio stood with a wicked grin. "Gotta go now." He made a beeline for the door.

"You just got here."

"Forgot something. Dinner's at eight. Don't be late." Julio snickered.

The door closed, and he was gone. Drew shook his head. He knew Chevy was up to something, but if it was that certain something--no way. His fiery passion for Nina had long since been snuffed.

Julio had introduced them. They'd hit it off and Drew soon fell in love. She puts off his proposals for five years before finally accepting his engagement ring. Her old man didn't take to the notion of his little girl marrying an African-American, and that was a major hurdle. Drew thought he had cleared it and planned their future by buying what was to be their first home. And then her old man hired Hernando to work for his home renovation business, a charming El Salvadorian, recent immigrant and skilled carpenter. Under Nina's supervision, the carpenter was soon banging more than nails and boards on the job. When the work was done, Hernando packed up his tools and swept away everything, including Nina. Drew's heart, too, it seemed.

Nina, a mestiza, had long dreamed of being carried off by a charming, handsome caballero. He came in carpenter's overalls, and her father's wishes held sway. Twenty years later, Nina and Hernando were not so happily married with two children, Gee and Candice. Drew never filled the void she left in his life and could never understand why life and love had to be so painful. What was the point? Nina was the right woman? Was there another? Would he find her?

❀

Monday, August 7, 8:00 p.m.

Julio dropped Drew off at the front door. "Go on in, man, I'll park."

Drew expected to be greeted by Julio's crew, but instead Chevy, Julio's attractive Filipina wife, met him at the front door. Julio hooked up with Chevy the day after he met Drew.

"Hey, cutie," she said, a customary greeting from the early days of their friendship. "Two visits in one week." She welcomed him with a firm embrace and a peck on the cheek. "We only see you when there's a crisis. Otherwise you'd be a stranger."

"Just because there's a crisis, you don't have to call me."

"You're our oldest and dearest friend, who else are we supposed to call?"

Arm in arm, they passed through the spacious living room with its eclectic blend of Asian and Latin-American décor. Like the boys she had borne, Chevy created a home with a handsome exotic blend of both their cultures. The boys had already eaten their grilled hotdogs and hamburgers and were on their way to the latest Harry Potter movie. Was their absence just coincidence or Chevy's design? She waved him toward the patio. "Go on out, we'll be right there."

Drew stepped out onto the patio and came face to face with Nina. Behind dark glasses, her forced smile seemed to mask uneasiness. He nodded, unable to return a smile. A decade or more had passed since they'd seen each other. In shorts and a sleeveless blouse, she was no longer the lithe young woman he once courted. Older, with a fuller figure, she was no less striking.

"Hello, Drew."

He sucked in his breath, summoning up courage. "Hi."

"It's been a while, you're aging well."

"So are you."

"You're being kind. You haven't gained a pound and I'm all fat now."

"I don't see that." He'd almost said that it had gone to all the right places. What he really wanted to say was that her mere presence still captivated him.

At dusk, the outside temperature had cooled comfortably enough for them to eat on the patio near the pool. Chevy brought out an informal platter of burgers, grilled potato wedges, and a garden salad, the remnants of the kids' earlier feast. In the uncomfortable silence, Chevy made small talk while preparing the table. Julio joined them, and when all four were seated and ready to eat, he said grace. His devout faith was one of the things Drew found most endearing and admirable. Raising the names of Gee, Nina, and Candice, he asked for a special divine consideration. Hernando was purposely omitted. After a unified amen, the table fell silent. For a group that in the distant past had often engaged in lively conversation, it was an awkward moment. Time had changed the dynamics, and each was keenly aware that this gathering had an agenda beyond breaking bread.

Chevy passed Drew a bottle of wine and a corkscrew. "We know you like wine with your dinner. Nina picked this. Cabernet."

Drew glanced at the label and smiled. "An old favorite." He looked at Nina. "You remembered."

Julio pouted. "I don't like wine, I want beer."

"You sound like Li'l Medhat," Chevy said. "You know where it is, get it yourself."

Julio muttered his displeasure at having to leave the table while Chevy gave him a defiant grin. He rolled his eyes at her. Drew found himself sharing a smile with Nina over the marital antics. In Julio's absence, a silence hung in the air. He soon returned with a frosty beer bottle and put it on the glass tabletop.

Chevy frowned. "Why didn't you get a glass and a coaster?"

"You know where it is. You get it."

Chevy gave him a look then slipped a folded paper napkin under the bottle. He leaned over and offered her a peck on the cheek. She accepted his apology with a smile. Drew poured the wine.

Julio patted Nina's arm. "Don't worry, Drew is going to get you that divorce."

Drew almost dropped the wine bottle. "Hold up, Julio, I never—"

"Not over dinner," Chevy said. "That's an attorney-client matter, and we're not privileged. Right, Drew?"

"I'm not her att—"

"So after dinner, we'll leave you two in private. But we're not having that discussion now."

"Why not?" Julio said. "I don't understand."

"I just told you why. It's private, between Drew and Nina."

"She'll tell you everything he says, and he'll tell me everything she says, and we'll tell each other. Might as well cut out all the bullshit right now."

"If Nina wants to confer with me," Drew said, "it'll be in private. I'm willing to talk after dinner."

She nodded. "I would like that, in private."

Chevy gave Julio another victorious smile. "That's that. Let's talk about something else. Drew, Julio tells me you're working on the Farragut robbery. What's up with that?"

"Nothing right now, a couple of leads but no real evidence. Is there anything Julio doesn't tell you?"

"I hope not." Everyone laughed.

Chevy, you had to love her. Her machinations were well planned and seemed to be working. At that moment, Drew couldn't figure who was her best puppet, he or Julio. She had them both on a string. They changed to lighter topics and the meal passed quickly. Julio and Chevy cleared the table and retreated inside, giving Drew and Nina their privacy.

Moonlight reflected off the still pool. A citronella candle flickered. Drew poured another half glass of wine and refreshed Nina's. "It's dark out here, take off those shades, I want to see your eyes."

"I'm too ashamed."

"Remember the time your father gave me a shiner and you and your mom had to break us up?"

She laughed. "How can I forget?"

"I refused to wear dark glasses. Remember why?"

"You said you'd proudly display it like a medal won in battle for my heart. I guess this is my payback. I'm not so proud."

Drew shrugged. "This isn't about us. I forgave you a long time ago. You had to go with your heart. I understand. When did you realize your marriage was in trouble?"

"Almost immediately after I said I do. I became his property. What he brought to the marriage was his, and what I brought to the marriage was his. He micromanaged everything. He took my paycheck and issued me a measly allowance I was supposed to manage the household from. We were always fighting over money."

"Did he...did you suffer physical abuse then?"

"This is the first time he's ever raised his hand to me, and for sure the last." She removed the dark glasses and shook her head. The swollen blue-black lump over her right eye made Drew cringe. He wanted to look away but forced himself not to.

"How did Gee react?

"He wasn't home when it happened. He doesn't know I'm gone. I plan to call him tonight. Candice and I came straight here."

"Why not your mom's?"

"I didn't want Hernando coming around upsetting her. He'll stay away from Julio."

"Will Gee confront Hernando?"

"I don't think so. Gee adores Hernando. I'll explain to him that I won't be coming back. Right now, he has so much to deal with, the Farragut and all."

While Drew calculated the legal considerations, they sat in silence.

"This isn't going to be a simple uncontested divorce from what you tell me, there may be grounds, mental cruelty and physical abuse."

"He's been seeing another woman. I've known for some time now."

"Infidelity." Drew took another moment to reflect. "How could you let this go on for so long? He doesn't deserve you."

"I loved him. I did what I had to do to keep him, but enough is enough. This isn't the life I want for me and my children. Gee will be out on his own soon. I'll take custody of Candice. I never wanted to be a single mom struggling to raise two children. I don't want them to hate their father. But his behavior is starting to affect them, especially Candice. Do you know what it's like for a child to fear and hate her father? He doesn't get it. His home is his castle and he rules. Well, he can rule it alone."

"I know a good divorce lawyer." Even in the growing darkness he could see the disappointment on her face.

"You mean you won't handle it?"

"We have a history. I'm not willing to get involved in what may seem like revenge, including to the judge."

"You're not capable of revenge. I trust you and he respects you."

"Respects me? By romancing you behind my back?" Drew shrugged. "But all is fair in love and war."

"I betrayed you. Don't hold it against Hernando."

"Let me think about it. I'll call you."

She offered a grateful smile. "Thanks, Drew."

"Let me ask you something about Gee."

She seemed to freeze with fear. "What is it?"

"The Farragut."

"Oh, it's terrible." She released a breath. "I don't want him to go back there."

"Do you know what time he got in Sunday morning?"

"No. Why?"

"Just curious."

"Gee's room is in the basement. He has a separate entrance. His father let him move down there so he could entertain his friends in private. I was against it."

Drew smiled. "I can imagine."

∞

Monday, August 7, 9:30 p.m.

Julio and Drew went to look up the three former Farragut workers. Eddie Campbell had moved out of state six months earlier. Sam Ellis, fired for stealing tips, a skinny little kid with an alibi, didn't look like much more than a meek sneak thief, certainly not like a killer. When they arrived at Jeffrey Legere's last known address, Lt. Lowry and Detective Blankenship were coming out of the house. Lowry's scowl tightened at the sight of them. On the sidewalk, he stepped into their path.

Drew smiled. "Hello, Lieutenant."

"Where do you think you're going?"

"To talk with Jeffrey Legere."

"Don't bother. He's not home."

"Then I'll talk to whomever's there."

Lowry put a fist on his hip, pushing his jacket back and exposing the handcuffs dangling from his belt. "I'm beginning to like this. You're interfering with a police investigation."

"Merely looking out for the interest of my client. Remember, you're the one accusing him."

"Back off, Smith."

"Fuck off, Lowry. Ever hear of the First Amendment?"

"Don't give me that legal mumbo-jumbo."

"It deals with free speech. Know what that means? I'll tell you—I can talk to whomever I chose and there's nothing you can do about it."

"Leave it alone, Smith. This is police business."

"What are you going to do? Arrest me? We did that dance once before, remember?"

"Tell me Smith, what do you know about Legere?"

"No more than you. And just like you, I'm going down the list. If I learn anything relevant, I'll let you know."

"You do that." Lowry stepped aside. Drew waited for them to drive off before knocking.

Moments later, Jean Legere appeared in the doorway. "What the hell do you— Oh..."

"Hello, I'm Drew Smith—"

"I know who you are." Suddenly smiling and batting her eyelashes, she made a vain attempt to smooth her hair. "The TV and newspapers don't do you justice. Who's your friend?"

"My associate, Julio Mejia."

Julio nodded. She looked him over before returning her appraisal to Drew. "What's this all about? The police just left here asking about my boy."

"You're Jeffery Legere's mother?"

She offered her hand. "Jean Legere, pleased to meet you. I'll tell you like I told the police, I haven't seen him since Saturday."

"Any idea where he might be?"

"No. You might check with his friends. He was with them the last time I saw him."

"Who are they?"

"A doofus named Tyrone Jones and this Spanish kid they call Gee."

"He was with them Saturday, you say?"

"That's what I said. You're a lawyer. Does my son need a lawyer? What did he do this time?"

"I just want to talk to him."

"What about?"

"The Farragut, I understand he worked there at one time."

Her expression grew sober. "The police didn't tell me that."

"Did you tell them about his friends?"

"Hell nah, I wasn't trying to tell that white man nothin', rolling up on me, bargin' in my house. Who's he think he is, coming up in here, looking all around, I didn't invite him in. He's supposed to have a search warrant. I didn't like the way he act."

"May I leave you my card? Let him know I'd like to speak with him."

"I'll keep it handy." She took the card, her fingers brushing his for a moment, and she smiled up at him. "Just in case I need a lawyer."

"Now why would a lady like you ever need a lawyer?" Drew cajoled hoping an added familiarity would loosen the flow of information.

"You never know, do you now?" Jean Legere said emboldened by flattery moving closer scanning the man from head to toe beckoning with a more sensuous volley.

Drew backed off. "Have a good night."

Amused Julio watched the woman employing her time tested skillful flirts. He could barely contain himself as they walked back to the car. "Miss Mama's was ready to eat you alive."

"Yeah...but something she said doesn't sit right."

"What's that?"

"I asked Gee this afternoon if he'd seen Jinx lately. He said no. According to her, they were together Saturday, the day before the robbery."

"Let's go talk to him."

"Not yet. It's probably nothing. Besides, I want to talk to the Chief first, see what he's come up with."

"Did you mean what you told Lowry, you'd let him know if you found out anything?"

"Hell nah, I ain't trying to tell that white man nothin', rollin' up on me." They shared a laugh as Drew checked his watch.

"What now?" Julio asked.

"I got a date. We'll talk tomorrow."

"A date. With that stripper?"

"Exotic dancer."

"Whatever. You need to be cool, man. The Chief called me Sunday. I wasn't going to say anything, but he told me about the fight at the Palais. He thinks you need help. I do too."

"You can help me by staying out of my business."

"You too old for that shit. You need a good woman."

"Shut up, Julio."

"Okay, okay, I'm not saying nothing else, except you need to get your head examined. Something's not right."

"If it'll get you off my back, I've decided to see a shrink. Okay? You satisfied?"

"Don't get mad." Julio broke into a triumphant grin. "You my boy, I gotta take care of you."

∞

Monday, August 7, 11:00 p.m.

Parking around Meridian Hill Park on 16th Street was impossible. Drew searched for twenty minutes before finally settling for an illegal spot in front of the Dorchester Apartments. On the seventh floor, he tapped on Angel's outer door. In the days before central air conditioning was common, the old building's lattice doors compromised privacy but promoted ventilation. With no answer, he tapped again.

"Who is it?"

"Drew."

"Oh, Drew." Angel stepped out and held the inner door ajar. His lust stirred at the sight of her perky breasts under a sheer negligee. Her eyes, pupils dilated, avoided his. She was high and didn't bother to ask him in. Over her shoulder, a movement caught his attention. The naked backside of a younger man with muscled shoulders and a narrow waist disappeared into the bathroom. He remembered the ponytail from the Palais and now noticed an ornate oriental tattoo covering his back, a colorful two-headed serpent. An unexpected pang of jealously struck him.

"Drew, I'm busy."

"Oh, I see." He backed up.

"I'm sorry."

"No, I understand."

"You really don't," she said. "I don't want to hurt you. Maybe we're making a mistake. You don't want to get involved with a woman like me. Somebody will get hurt."

"Who said anything about getting involved, we're just kicking it." He struggled to put on an indifferent face.

"Call me tomorrow, please."

"Sure thing." He faked another smile and returned to the elevator.

She had another partner for the night, another crackhead, at least they had something in common beaming up together. He winced in embarrassment about the Saturday night brawl. He wasn't her protector. So why did he feel rejected? Was he falling for her? There were things about her. Naked, she was as carefree as a child, laughing as the passion overtook them, joyous afterwards.

This was crazy. The Chief was right. Over the years he'd carefully fostered a public persona, his greatest marketing asset. It helped make him a wealthy man. He wasn't just a good lawyer, he was a great lawyer, and everybody knew it. He worked hard. What was he to do for personal entertainment? He liked the sexy young women who took his money, gave him pleasure, and made few demands. He had neither wife nor kids nor any need to be near hearth and home. He would frequent the hideaways purchasing his pleasure. What was the harm? None. And whose fault was it? Too many questions, and he had no answers.

∞

Monday, August 7, 11:00 p.m.

The late-model Crown Vic with tinted windows made its way uptown with Sam behind the wheel, Jojo riding shotgun, and Tyrone in the back seat searching the dark streets from an even darker interior. They stopped on 14th Street at the Barrel liquor store and picked up a fifth of Remy Martin. They'd just left the strip club and the parade of naked women had stimulated Tyrone's sexual urge.

"Sam, drive up to Arkansas Avenue. I hear the hos be out there. Maybe I can get a little oral action."

Sam looked across the seat to Jojo, who shrugged then glanced in his rearview mirror at Tyrone. "Damn man, you droppin' a lotta ducats. You bought the weed, the drinks, gave us money to tip the dancers. You hit the lotto?"

"Don't worry about it. That's my bidnis."

"Solid, don't mean to get into your *bidnis*. What's up with your boy Jinx? Ain't seen ya'll together lately."

"Cut 'im loose. Nigga's whacked."

"You just finding that out?" Jojo laughed, his gaze focused on his fingers rolling the blunt.

"Man, hurry up with that joint," Sam said.

"Be cool, you know I'm a perfectionist."

"Dawg, I ain't never known you to roll a perfect joint."

As they crossed the intersection of 13th and Arkansas, Tyrone sat up from the back seat and scanned the street. Near the corner, a Latina with a sensuous stroll meandered down the block. Tyrone rolled down the window. She smiled. From their vantage, the three men watched. Jojo completed his perfect joint and lit it.

"Pull over, let's check her out," Tyrone said. "Let me hit that joint." Sam handed the joint back to Tyrone, who sucked on it, filling his lungs, then passed it on to Jojo. A few seconds later he expelled the smoke with a cough. "Good stuff." He opened the back door and jumped out.

Minutes later Tyrone came out the alley and bounced up the street with a satisfied grin. He eased into the back seat.

"You get off?" Jojo asked.

"Sho nuff. Bitch can suck the chrome off a trailer hitch. You wanna go?"

"You paying?"

"Ain't no thing." Tyrone peeled off a twenty and handed it to Jojo, who pocketed it, got out, and headed down the street where the prostitute had resumed her stroll.

Sam passed the joint to Tyrone, then peered into the rear-view mirror and laughed. Tyrone looked out the back window. Jojo was returning to the car.

"Damn, that didn't take long," Sam said as Jojo got back into his seat.

"Man, something ain't right. Bitch got razor bumps."

"Drag queen?" Sam asked.

"That's what I'm talking 'bout," Jojo said.

Sam let out a belly laugh. "You like that fag action, huh, Tyrone?" Jojo joined in.

"What? I don't believe it," Tyrone said. The two hooted in the front seat. "Oh hell nah." Tyrone was out of the car.

"Where you goin'?" Jojo shouted. "Ain't gettin' your money back."

"Fuck de money. I ain't no faggot." Tyrone slammed the door. "I ain't no faggot!"

He ran down the block after the prostitute, who saw him coming and tried to bolt but wasn't fast enough to avoid being grabbed and thrown up against a wall. Tyrone pulled his gun. "Fuckin' freak!" Two shots, pop pop, one to the chest and the second to the head.

He stuffed the gun back in his waistband, looked up and saw the oncoming police cruiser. He spun and sprinted for the car, but it wasn't there. Mothafuckas! He cut across the school baseball field back toward Arkansas Avenue.

They gave chase, first from the car and then on foot. Tyrone ditched the gun then ran around the school searching desperately for a place to hide. Another cruiser was coming up Arkansas Avenue but hadn't yet seen him. He ducked down a stairwell leading to the school's furnace room. He tried the door but it was padlocked. He squirmed into the shadows.

The voices of the police grew closer. "See which way he went?"

"I didn't see anything."

A third officer with a flashlight approached the others. The light scanned the wall of the school then down into the stairwell. Tyrone pressed his back tightly against the door's recesses. The beam of light passed him by, then hesitated...and returned. He looked down to see, shining gloriously in the spotlight, the protruding toes of his bright white new Air Jordan Jumpman sneakers.

"Come out with your hands on your head."

Tyrone did as he was told.

Chapter 7

S TANDING IN A valley of knee-high grass, he sees her on a hilltop in a cloudy mist, a veiled woman in a diaphanous white abaya whipping with the wind, beckoning him to join her. There's something familiar about her. Curious, he walks up the hill. She turns toward a looming white granite mausoleum-like building. He pursues her but can't catch up. She stops on the threshold and again beckons him to follow. Shaking his head, he refuses. She's insistent but so is he. She hikes up her dress, exposing herself. Persuaded, smiling, he follows, though suspicious and cautious. When he comes close, again she takes off, running through a series of maze like rooms and corridors with stark white walls. She laughs and he chases like it's a game of tag.

Suddenly she stops in another doorway. He smiles and walks toward her. Then a man steps into the doorway beside her. It's Medhat with a welcoming smile. Drew stops, puzzled. Medhat's been dead for some time. It would be nice to talk with him, to hear his voice, to feel his touch. The woman tugs Medhat by the hand. He beckons Drew to follow. Drew wants to talk but not to follow.

"Medhat, don't go. I want to talk to you."

"Come on," Medhat shouts, and laughs as he chases the familiar woman. Who is she? They stop at the entrance of another room. Medhat faces the woman and pulls her close for a kiss, but first looks back to see if Drew is watching. She removes her veil and turns to face Drew. She has a gun. He's shocked with the recognition, turns and runs for his life, unable to escape.

He bolted up wide awake, unable to understand the nightmare. Its terror first grasped him right after Medhat was killed. Over the years it had come and gone, but lately the repetition was nightly. The dream pursued him, and he didn't know why. Today he would see a therapist.

∞

Tuesday, August 8, 10:00 a.m.

Gee greeted Marie at the basement door barefooted and still in his nightclothes, a pair of baggy nylon basketball shorts and a wife-beater undershirt. There was a hint of approval in the way she looked him over from head to toe. He knew the wife-beater hugged the contours of his upper torso, and his narrow waist accented the hard pectorals. The exposed fuzzy legs, bare shoulders, and the sinewy lines of his muscled shoulders and arms all cut an aesthetic figure. The door opened into the utility room, lit by a single bulb hanging from the ceiling. Once she was in, he took her hand, closed the door, then yanked the light's chain, pitching them into darkness.

She clutched his arm. "Ooo, its dark."

"Don't worry, I could walk this path blindfolded."

"I'll stick close." She said in a fearful whisper.

"Please." He chuckled.

He led her through the darkness, opened another door into a dimly lit, seldom used family room, and passed through it to his bedroom. It was a boy's room, cluttered with athletic paraphernalia and plastered with posters of Michael Jordan and Brazilian soccer stars Ronaldinho and Ronaldo. On the bureau, a mini-stereo played hip-hop. He grabbed the remote, switched to a mellow jazz sax, and turned the volume down low. He then fell onto the bed face down. His eyes avoided Marie's.

She stood over him. "It's ten o'clock in the morning. I know this Farragut thing's got you down, but life goes on. Please get up and shower. I thought we could go out for breakfast."

"I don't feel like it."

"Gee, you got to snap out of it."

He shrugged as his cell phone began to ring. Marie picked it up from the nightstand, glanced at its face, then handed it over. Gee checked caller ID, sent the call to voicemail, and tossed the phone aside.

"That was Drew Smith, why didn't you take it?"

Gee shrugged.

"What happened yesterday?"

Gee reluctantly sucked in his breath. "He asked me about a couple of guys who used to work there."

"Were you able to help him?"

"I don't know."

"What you knew mean, you don't know? What did he say? What did you tell him? How come you didn't take his call?"

"Why are you asking me all these questions? Will you shut up about that."

He caught her stunned expression. It was the first time he'd spoken a harsh word to her. He hurt her feelings. She was about to cry.

"I'm going now."

He leapt up and blocked the door. "Don't go. Please. I'm sorry. I don't mean to take it out on you. It's just that there's so much on my mind. I'm sorry, please don't go."

"I don't understand, what's wrong with you? It might help to talk about it. Maybe I can help." She tried to step away when he pulled her into his arms.

"Please, I'm just not ready to talk about it now. I'm sorry." He kissed her. "Give me fifteen minutes to shower and get dressed. We'll go to breakfast. Okay?"

"Okay."

In the shower, Gee debated whether to tell her. He wanted to confide in her. He found so much comfort just in her company. Maybe he should explain. She was his rock, he couldn't lose her now.

∞

Tuesday, August 8, Noon

Jinx got in after his mother went to bed and left before she rose. He caught the Georgia Avenue bus downtown to do some shopping, and bought a pair of black jeans, a t-shirt, a pair of black Reboks, and a prepaid cell phone. He spent wisely, bringing only five hundred dollars and returning with nearly three. To hit the road, he'd have to watch every penny of the remaining twenty-eight hundred dollars. Ten grand would take him somewhere else, maybe get a real job, punch the clock for a while. Things were too hot to stay in D.C. Another caper was necessary, alone this time. As for Tyrone, he was history, nigga was too shaky. He needed a target and a plan.

He got back in time to catch the noon news hoping for more on the Farragut. He tossed the shopping bags on the love seat, picked up the remote and turned on the TV. The reporter was just beginning the story when his mother appeared in the doorway, dressed to go out.

"Jeffrey—"

"Shush."

She stepped around and looked at the TV. A reporter stood in front of the Farragut. "That's the place you used to work—"

"Shut up, I'm tryin' to listen."

"Yesterday, just after dawn, four employees of the Farragut were busily preparing its legendary Sunday brunch. Within the hour, the police would arrive to find a bloody scene with three of them dead. Victims of an apparent robbery, all were shot to death execution style. One employee escaped through a second floor window."

"Damn, Theo—" Jinx caught himself and his mother's wayward glance.

"Among the dead..." The reporter continued as the pictures of the three victims flashed across the screen.

"Who could do such a horrible thing?" she said.

Jinx rolled his eyes. She went silent again. The reporter concluded by saying there were few clues and no suspects. His mother was staring at the shopping bags.

"What was you saying?" he asked.

"Looks like you been shopping. Where you get money to go shopping?"

"That's my bidniss. I don't ask you about your bidniss."

"Give me some money. I'm on my way right now to the food stamp office. I can't afford to lose those stamps. And the way you eat, you need to help me out."

"I help you out, so don't start."

"Then give me some money." She thrust an open palm in his face.

Jinx pulled out his $300 bankroll and peeled off two twenties. It was good the rest was stashed under his mattress. She'd be more demanding if she knew he had that kind of money. He'd never shut her up. She promptly transferred the two twenties to her other hand and shoved the same palm back into his face.

"What?"

"You can give me more than that. I got the electric, the phone, lights and food to pay for. And you use it all."

He shook his head and peeled off three more twenties, which she promptly snatched. "That's a hundred, now bye."

She folded the money with a smile, stuffed it into her bra, turned as if to leave, then glanced at the shopping bags again. "Where you get this money from?"

"You don't want to know."

She leveled a hard stare at him, and then stormed out the door.

⮾

Petite and attractive with a wild mane of curly black hair casually pinned up above a delicate face, Dr. Zoë Settles met him at the door. Her dark flawless complexion and fine features suggested a mixed ancestry.

"Drew Smith?"

In blue linen slacks and starched white blouse, peering over pince-nez half-glasses with an inviting smile, she had a smart air about her. She was a dark beauty with bright eyes and he couldn't help but stare.

"The one and only. Dr. Settles?" Their eyes met and her gaze lingered.

"Zoë. Come in, have a seat."

Surprised by her quick casual familiarity—weren't shrinks supposed to be stuffy and stuck-up?—he followed her into her office. He deliberately kept his eyes off her hips under the linen slacks.

"I'd recognize you anywhere." She offered him a chair before sitting behind her desk. The office reflected her femininity with bright colors and the walls were decorated with floral land-scapes. "I confess I've followed your career over the years and watched you grow into a local media personality." She began assembling forms on a clipboard. "Now, before we get started, there are some administrative details we have to tend to—insurance, patient information, you know the routine. If you have no objections, I'd like to tape our sessions. The tapes will be destroyed at the end of your treatment."

"No problem."

She handed Drew a clipboard and he completed the forms while she labeled a new tape and slipped it into the recorder on her desk. Moments later, he returned the clipboard.

She glanced at the forms then smiled up at him. "Okay, we're ready to begin. I had a cancellation and you were lucky to get an appointment so soon. Why the urgency?"

Drew cleared his throat. "Before we begin, may I ask some preliminary questions about your qualifications?"

"Certainly. B.S. in psychology from Howard, M.D. in psychia-try from Johns Hopkins."

"Where are you from?"

"D.C."

"A native Washingtonian?"

"Born at Freedman's and practically grew up on the Howard campus. My parents taught there."

"Married?" He search her hands for a ring.

"No." She looked at him quizzically consciously folding her hands hiding her ring finger.

"Are you seeing someone?"

"Just how is that relevant to my credentials and qualifications?"

He laughed. "I'm sorry, I guess it isn't. Just curious."

"What brought you to therapy?"

"Should I lie down or something? You got a nice big comfortable sofa over there. That's what it's for, isn't it? I better not, I might fall asleep. It's a little early for me to be sleeping with you." To his relief, this made her laugh. His jittery mouth was working faster than his brain.

"Mr. Smith, relax. You're fine right there. Let's get to know one another before we pull out the sleep sofa. Okay?"

Now she made him laugh. "Okay."

"Let's start again, what brought you to therapy?"

The easy humor made him feel comfortable and at ease. He dropped the clever mask. No longer feeling the need to be in complete control, he collected his thoughts.

"There's this recurrent dream I'm having, for one. My life is a mess, and my friends fear my reckless ways may be dangerous."

"What do you think?"

"I don't think about it."

"So you reject their advice?"

"Not really. Chief Washington suggested I get therapy. Maybe bring the recklessness under control."

He told her about the dream starring Medhat, the mausoleum, and the faceless woman. This had been his secret for years, and just sharing it with someone brought a sense of relief, as though unloading a heavy burden. She listened, and asked about Medhat. With fond recollection he recounted how he, Medhat, and Julio became friends. Tumultuous at first, the friendship evolved into a fraternity of loyalty and devotion. Medhat was a handsome young Egyptian of distinguished birth, and like many young men, he favored the party life of sex and drugs. With his looks and charm he took seduction to an art. Medhat was shot to death by a woman who betrayed him. He died in Drew's arms.

"You were close?"

"Very. Everyone loved Medhat. You couldn't help but love him. That was part of his problem. The loss was...I guess devastating is the word. I've never known such grief, not even when my father died. So what do you make of it? Do you believe people can come back to you in your dreams?"

"Dreams are sometimes a way for the subconscious to communicate with the conscious mind. Dreaming of something you're worried about can be the brain's way of helping you rehearse for a disaster before it occurs."

"So my dream is helping me to cope."

"Or somehow preparing you to."

Drew's brow furrowed. "I'm not anticipating any disasters."

"Maybe your subconscious is. Medhat disappears from the door just when you want to follow. But he doesn't wait, leaving you to your own judgment, a warning to keep you from the same fate. I need to know more about you and your history."

"What about the faceless woman?"

"Perhaps she represents the woman who killed him, or one who presents a danger to you. Hence she's faceless. Tell me, when did you first start having these dreams?"

"Right after Medhat's death, on and off since then."

The therapist paused in thought. "But they're more frequent at certain periods?"

"Yes."

"And are you seeing a particular woman on a steady basis right now?"

Drew hesitated. "I guess *yes* would be the answer to that question."

"You guess? Tell me about her."

"She's a dancer."

"Really?" Zoë sat up. "What kind, ballet, modern?"

"Exotic."

"Oh." He could see her try to cover it, but her disappointment was palpable. "What's her name?"

"Angelica Morales, stage name Angel."

Now she was biting her lip, restraining her amusement as she took notes.

"What's so funny?"

"Oh, nothing, I just pictured an angel in a scanty costume with feathered wings and ostrich plume fans."

"My secretary pictures her with horns and a pitchfork. No wings, no feathers, just a hot red tail."

They laughed together.

"Is this Angel someone you're serious about?"

"No, but she could be. Maybe I've reached a point where I'm willing to settle for Miss Right Now rather than continuing to wait for Miss Right."

"Why is she not Miss Right?"

"I'm not happy with her current lifestyle. She claims she'll change for me."

"What is it about her lifestyle that bothers you? The sex-oriented trade?"

"Plus she has a drug habit."

"I'm curious why a man of your caliber would be interested in a woman like that. You have so much to offer and it sounds like she has little. What do you get out of the relationship?"

"Sex. I don't have to work for it. It's instant gratification, no strings attached."

"And Angel, is that what she wants?"

"I thought so at first, but now she's sending mixed signals."

"Then is it fair to continue to mislead her into believing that someday you'll have a meaningful relationship?"

"I'm not misleading her." For forty-five minutes Drew defended his actions as the discussion moved from one relationship topic to another ending back where it started with Angel.

"Are you laying your cards on the table?" The therapist asked. "You've never been married, have you?"

"Almost, if that counts. I once had Miss Right. I thought she was the only woman for me. I lost her, but that's another story."

"We'll get to that. Over the next few sessions I'd like to explore your conscious personal philosophy."

"Freudian?"

"Not really. I believe a therapist should spend less time probing distant childhood experiences and concentrate instead on what's happening in people's lives now. People's conscious personal philosophies and beliefs—like the need to be appreciated or the fear of never finding anyone to love—often drives them to despair and distraction."

"Interesting... You think I'd benefit from that type of therapy?"

"I do." She looked at her watch. "But for now, our time is up. I'd like to see you the same time next week."

He stood up. "This has been interesting, I hate for it to end." It hit him that this was painfully true. When had he last really leveled with anyone about himself? Never with Angel. With Julio it was different, more buddy-buddy than serious talking. Not even, back in the day, with Nina. Was Medhat the last? "Would you be interested in having dinner with me tonight?"

She seemed taken aback. "Sounds fun, but that would be crossing a boundary."

He followed her to the door. "How so?"

"A deviation from traditional, strict, office-only, emotionally distant forms of therapy. Simply put, we can't get too close."

"So much for my nasty intentions, huh?"

This time she didn't laugh at his attempted joke. "I'm sorry, no dual relationships." She held the door open, waiting for him to step out.

"Sharing a meal may cross a boundary, but is that necessarily harmful?" Drew backed out. "I'm just talking about dinner."

"You're quick, Mr. Smith. That's what I'm afraid of. Yes, there are helpful boundary crossings. And as persuasive as you are, I don't think we should start out on a slippery slope. See you next week." She politely closed the door in his face.

∞

Tuesday, August 8, 9:30 p.m.

Plagued with insomnia for several nights, Jinx had fallen asleep on the sofa in front of the TV. He slept most of the day, unaware of his mother's coming in or going out early in the evening. It was well after dark when he woke. Nine-thirty according to his cell phone, time to hit the streets. With a job to do, he felt rested and up to the challenge. He had a particular target in mind and a plan to execute with the hope of pulling down at least two grand. Strange, he didn't feel the least bit nervous, not like the Farragut. Mistakes were made then, and he was determined no mistakes would be made this night.

He pulled himself up off the sofa and stretched, went to the kitchen to get a cold drink of water, and found the refrigerator well stocked. The old girl must have got her food stamps. She wasn't moving about, so was probably down at the Kenyon Bar and Grill doing her thing. After eating a bologna sandwich, he went upstairs, splashed some water on his face, and decided to wear something dark to blend in with the night.

In his bedroom, the smell of fabric softener and the stack of clean clothes and fresh bed linen set off a panic. He reached under the mattress, his arm searching the full length between the box spring, then pushed the mattress onto the floor. Disbelief swept over him. The money was gone. Only the gun lay where he left it. He knew who took the money.

He grabbed the gun, popped the clip, went to the closet for the extra clip he'd hidden in a shoebox, and snapped it into place. Then he refilled the other clip, which was still short the rounds he'd fired at the Farragut. He hefted the gun. Goddamn bitch. Good thing for her she was out, he'd deal with her later.

In his black jeans, he slipped into the new Reboks and laced them up. He looped the belt around his waist and buckled it with enough slack to secure the gun. In the bureau mirror he tried his hard, intimidating face and liked what he saw. He tucked the gun into his belt, covered it with his shirttail, and checked for visible signs. Stuffing his locks under a baseball cap, he was ready. He closed the bedroom door then glided down the steps and out the door into the night.

On Georgia Avenue, he took the 70 bus to U Street and transferred to the 90, riding through the busy 18th Street Adams Morgan nightlife to the end of the line at the Calvert Street Bridge. He walked back two blocks up toward the Adams Mill Road Exxon station. The evening traffic was light, his walk slow and deliberate.

Approaching the station, he paced each step, checking out each vehicle until he spotted the right one, a new Cadillac Escalade. The driver, a white man, fortyish in a business suit, was completing a gas purchase. As the man walked around the rear of the vehicle to the driver's side, Jinx met him face to face, displaying the gun. The man slowly raised his hands and stepped back. The attendant in his booth was occupied with a walk-up customer.

"Put your hands down, fool." The man complied. "Where are the keys?"

"In the ignition. Take it. I'm not looking for trouble."

Jinx pushed the man aside, jumped in behind the wheel, and left rubber as pulled into the traffic.

Jubilant, Jinx rolled down Rock Creek Parkway, bobbing to the radio's pumped-up volume of Gangsta's "Who's Hard?" The first stage of the night's operation had gone smooth. Twenty minutes to his destination through Alexandria to Hybla Valley in Fairfax County. In a musical haven, the ride was easy and comfortable. The acoustics of the Bose system blocked the blare of outside traffic and the rumble of the road. Great car, maybe one day he'd buy himself one.

Jinx ran his fingers over the packed dashboard. The small gold OnStar emblem sent a bolt of panic through him. The radio commercials said it could do all sorts of things—open doors remotely, dispatch help to accidents, and find stolen vehicles. He had to ditch the SUV. Ten minutes from his destination, every minute, every second counted. The authorities were closing in.

The dashboard clock read eleven-forty. Enough time. Jinx devised an alternative. He'd ditch the car in the shopping center across from the Hybla Valley Wendy's, hoping the police wouldn't pull him over before then. Jinx slid the gun from under his belt and laid it on the passenger seat. He was ready.

He parked the Escalade and quickly distanced himself from it. As though waiting, he watched from a nearby bus stop on Richmond Highway. Traffic whizzed by while in the distant parking lot, patrol cars flashing blue and red lights had surrounded the stolen vehicle. Out of cops' view, it was an ideal spot to watch and wait for the Wendy's to begin closing. Still, he had to be careful, so many cops this close. The Escalade owner could probably give them a good description. He tossed the baseball cap and shook loose his locks.

Jittery as the final minutes ticked off, Jinx crossed the highway and approached his target when his cell phone said it was two minutes before midnight. The dining room was empty. At the door, a cute blue-eyed teenager in her blue striped smock and the trademark Wendy's headscarf gave him a sweet welcoming smile. She was about to lock the door.

"This is your lucky night," she said. "You're the last customer."

"You got that right." Jinx stepped in, pointing the gun down low. The girl's mouth dropped open and her eyes widened with fear. "Now lock the door and no one will get hurt." She did as she was told. "Take me to the manager."

At the side entrance to the front line, she asked the cashier to open the door. Jinx followed her through. The front-line crew—two black teenage boys and two girls, a black and a Latina—were busy with their closing duties, cleaning the grill and breaking down the workstations. The boy on the grill, scooping up the dried burgers for tomorrow's chili, looked up at the stranger coming through the employee entrance.

"Hey, who's that? Why's he back here?"

Jinx showed his gun, answering all questions. "Get down on the floor!" They all silently complied. When one girl started to cry, the grill guy told her to shut up.

Jinx turned the corner at the Henny Penny chicken fryer, and straight ahead, seated behind a desk in a cramped office, the manager was counting the day's receipts. The skinny twenty-something with moussed hair looked up into the barrel of a gun. Jinx grinned in his face.

Less than four minutes after entering, Jinx made his exit, first ordering the employees to stay on the floor for five minutes. Nobody moved. Jinx calmly walked behind the restaurant, crossed the parking lot behind a Pizza Hut, and stopped a moment to watch the traffic entering and leaving the adjacent Gulf filling station. Feeling good yet again, he had to pace himself.

Phase two was now done, and no bloodshed. Sometimes you had to kill, but given the choice, he'd rather not.

The filling station setup was perfect. He didn't have much time before the police showed up at Wendy's, probably the same ones across the highway checking out the Escalade. This time, he'd skip anything high-tech.

He spotted his next victim, a young white female filling her Mustang GT, traveling alone, dressed like she was out for a night on the town. Jinx made his way toward the service island, trying to reach her before she got behind the wheel. Too late. Jinx double-timed it to the driver's side. Just as she hit the ignition, Jinx pressed the gun barrel against her skull.

"What? What?"

"Get out." Jinx took a step back.

"Oh my God, what are you doing? Please! Please! Don't hurt me!"

"Bitch, shut up and get out of the goddamn car."

She slowly reached to get her purse, then carefully unlocked the door and undid her seatbelt. Jinx transferred the gun to his left hand and yanked the door open.

"Please, please, I don't have any money!"

"Get out, goddamn it." He grabbed a handful of her hair and yanked her out of her seat. She screamed as Jinx dropkicked her out of his way and jumped behind the wheel. He threw the Mustang into gear and squealed out onto the highway.

At last, fate seemed to be coming over to Jinx's side. He slowed down to within five miles of the speed limit, making all the lights until he got in behind a slow van at the last light before the exit to the Beltway. He waited, watching the oncoming traffic turn across his path. He breathed little easier, seconds away from being out of Fairfax County. All he had to do was to cross the Wilson Bridge and he'd be home free.

Suddenly, in the rearview mirror, flashing blue and red lights were gaining on him. The sirens sounded closer. His impatience spiked toward panic as the lines of vehicles kept turning across his path. Fucking red light!

Jinx jerked the Mustang onto the shoulder, passed the van, and stomped the accelerator, barely missing the rear of a crossing vehicle. He floored it onto the cloverleaf. The vehicle hugged the curve onto Interstate 495 toward the Wilson Bridge connecting Virginia to Maryland. The two patrol cars were gaining on him now joined by two more on the Interstate. With four Virginia police vehicles on his tail in hot pursuit, Jinx crossed the Bridge. At the state line, the police vehicles slowed to a halt, disappearing from Jinx's view as he took the I-295/Maryland 210 exit.

He was going too fast. Jinx tried to slow but lost control coming out of the cloverleaf, smashed into the guardrail, then veered back onto the median. He struggled to bring the Mustang back to the road, but he was no stunt driver. It spun out of control, flipped onto its side, then turned over and over before coming to rest. Rubbernecking drivers gawked and traffic slowed in both directions while Jinx struggled to extricate himself from the wreckage. People had begun to get out of their vehicles by the time he dusted off the pebbles of broken glass, reached back in to grab his backpack, then took off up the steep hill into the woods.

Jinx hiked through the woods, constantly looking over his shoulder, and followed the road about three miles until the lights of Alabama Avenue and Good Hope Road came into view. He caught a Metrobus to Branch Avenue and transferred to the Green Line train back uptown to Georgia Avenue.

At his porch steps, his mother was seeing off one of her johns. The man spoke, Jinx didn't. He pushed his way past his mother and into the house.

"Where's your manners, boy? I didn't raise you like that."

"I told you, you didn't raise me." Jinx mounted the steps two at a time. Dumping the contents of his backpack on the bed, he laughed with glee at the sight of all the bills in various denominations. His mother's footsteps sounded on the stairs. He waited for her door to close. He'd deal with her later, first he had to count the night's take.

Fifteen minutes later the count was complete, five thousand six hundred fifty-six dollars, better than the Farragut. He stepped down the hall to his mother's room. No signs of light from under the door. She was hiding, not sleeping. After a knock, he tried the knob. It was locked.

"Ma."

"What?"

"Open up, I need to talk to you."

"Talk to me in the morning. I need my sleep."

"Ma, you got my money?"

"What money?"

"The money you stole from under my mattress."

There was a long silence.

"Ma, open up."

Still she didn't answer.

"I know you ain't asleep, open the door."

After a moment Jinx stepped back and with a good swift kick sent the door flying open to slam against the wall. He hit the light switch. Terror filled his mother's face.

"What the hell? Jeffrey, what's gotten into you?" She pulled herself up from under the sheet.

"I want my money."

"I put it in the bank."

"You're lyin'."

"After the police came here looking for you."

"The police? What they want?"

"They didn't say. And Drew Smith was here."

"The lawyer?"

"Wanted to ask about the Farragut."

"What'd you say?"

"That you wasn't here. The police said they'd be back tomorrow. You better leave."

"Soon as you give me my money."

"You killed those people at the Farragut, didn't you?"

"Why you say that?"

"I figured it out. You and Tyrone robbed that place. You better get out of here now, before I call the police."

"Where's my money?"

"I told you, in the bank."

Jinx went back to his room and reappeared moments later with the gun. As she reached for the phone on the nightstand he snatched it from her grasp and yanked the wires from the wall.

"I want my money."

"I told you, I put it in the bank. The police are coming back here tomorrow and I betcha they have a search warrant. I put it away for safekeeping."

"Show me the deposit slip."

"What?"

"You heard me. You're lyin'. Where is my money?"

"Jeffrey Legere, I want you out of my house, right now. I'm calling the police."

He raised the gun and struck her head with just enough force to unleash a flood of terror. She screamed and flailed her hands to shield her head from more blows.

"Get up!"

"How can you do this to your mother?" she whimpered. "I brought you into this world."

"Yeah, and left me to fend for myself. You didn't care if you ever saw me again. You never wanted me."

"That's not true. I-I-I love you, Jeffrey. I couldn't always take care of you and your sister." She cried uncontrollably.

"You were too busy drinkin' and druggin'. Yeah, you gave me life, a life of misery. Where's my money?" He raised the gun again.

"Oh no! I'll get it. I'll get it."

"Where is it?"

"Downstairs in the kitchen, hid in a cereal box in case the police came and searched the place."

"Get it."

The gun waved her to the door. On shaky legs, Jean Legere got up off the bed. Jinx pushed her into the hall. She took a few steps towards the stairs then stopped and glared back at her son.

"Pull a gun on your mother, boy, you ain't right. Crazy. Just plain crazy."

He pushed her forward, close on her heels, the gun aimed straight at her back. She took one step down and again turned to face him.

"Would you kill your mother?" Suddenly she shoved both hands into his chest. Caught off-balance, Jinx fell back. She leapt down the steps, grappled with the deadbolt on the front door and flung it open. Jinx crashed down the stairs, and just as Jean Legere crossed the threshold onto the porch, he grabbed the nape of the neck and pulled her back in. He shoved her down on the hall floor and slammed the door shut.

She began to scream hysterically. He bolted the door and stared down at the pitiful woman. But he felt no pity.

"Where's my money?"

"To hell with you." She resumed her screaming.

"Shut up!"

But she continued to scream.

A single bullet to the head silenced her forever.

Chapter 8

T OGETHER THEY ACHIEVED a moment of ecstasy. Drew rolled off Angel, energy drained, taking deeps breaths, laughing at their abandoned performance.

"I like it better this way." He exhaled.

"Like what?" Angel shifted on her side away from the damp spot in the sheets and closer into Drew's embrace.

"When we get down and you're not under the influence."

"I'm giving it up for you. Marry me, Drew, take me away from this life."

"You chose that life."

"I never had any choices. Marry me?"

"I'll think about it." He answered with indifference.

"I'm in love with you. You can give me the life I want. Do you love me?"

"Yeah baby, I love you."

"So marry me, or are you saying that to shut me up?"

"You're serious about this?"

"I'll leave the drugs alone. I can go back to school, get a good job. I need your help."

"I'll help you, but don't think I'm going to jump up and march down the aisle just because you abstain for a few days."

"I'm giving the Palais two weeks notice. I need you to help me find a job."

"What kind of job?"

"I can type and answer phones. I did temporary work. I've got computer skills. Why don't you give me a job in your office?"

"Oh no, that won't do. With you around all day, I'll never get anything done."

"Will you help me get a job?"

"I'll ask around."

"When are we getting married?"

Drew's eyebrows raised.

"You don't want to marry me." She pouted. "You just want to keep me hanging on."

"I said I'd think about it. Come on." He pulled himself up out of the bed. "Let's go have a snack. You worked up my appetite. We have some talking to do."

"There's nothing to talk about. I know you don't want to marry me."

"The other night you told me it was a mistake for us to continue to see each other. Now you're talking marriage. I don't think you know what you want." He pulled her up off the bed into his embrace. They kissed.

She broke away. "Go ahead. I'll be down, I need to freshen up."

"Don't get too fresh, we're not done. Just hit the vital parts."

"Oh, shut up."

His eyes followed her into the bathroom. She closed the door.

He poured a glass of white wine and started making sandwiches while he waited for Angel. He hated conversations like that one. With Nina, love was simple. There was never any doubt about marriage, not the kind of doubts he was having with Angel. To thine own self be true. At least he could convey his true feelings to Dr. Settles. The truth was, he wasn't in love with Angel and could never marry her. But his therapist was right: it was wrong to lead Angel on. He had to tell her. She deserved better.

Hair still tousled, Angel strolled in wearing the red mesh teddy. None of her other lingerie excited him as much, and he didn't know why. Maybe it was the way the color complemented her complexion. She knew he liked it. In it she always looked like a woman and eager to please and be pleased.

"What are you eating?"

"Ham sandwich. I made you one."

She tossed her hair and eased up onto the stool across from him. She had his complete attention when their eyes locked. He winked. She ignored his come-on and inspected the sandwich with a grimace.

"What's wrong?"

"You put mayonnaise on it. I don't eat mayonnaise."

"I never knew that."

"It's all right. I'll scrape it off. Where's the mustard?"

"On the fridge door. There's a lot about you I don't know."

"That's all right. You'll learn."

He released a breath. "I've been thinking."

"What about?"

"Us. It's not going to work. Except sex, we don't have much in common. I don't think we could build a life together. I can't marry you."

She froze for a moment then slowly closed the refrigerator door.

"Why didn't you tell me that before you fucked me? What was it, the final lay, one for the road?"

"No. I was hoping for many more. That was never my intention. I told you I'd think about it. I did my thinking, that's my decision. I'm trying to be upfront and honest. I don't want to marry you. The only kind of relationship I'm interested in is sexual."

"So that's it, maybe we can just continue like this, having sex a couple of times a week. No strings attached."

"That's how we started, remember? You changed the rules. But yes, that's what I want. That's what I'll pay for. I'll even pay for you to go to school."

"I won't be your whore, Drew Smith. You're just like all the rest. You're just a dog."

"You don't want to be my bitch anymore?"

"It's not funny." Angel broke down and wept. Drew wanted to comfort her, but he didn't know how. He had no words to sooth her anguish.

"You son of a bitch, Drew Smith. You were supposed to be my savior. You were the one who was going to help me turn my life around." She launched herself at him in all-out physical attack, flailing with both fists. He wrestled to subdue her, but she fought hard, and it took a minute or two and much effort to bring her under control in a bear hug. She surrendered, crying in his arms. Then quietly, with the serenity of acceptance, as sudden her rage appeared, it vanished.

"Oh Drew, I love you. All we need is time. I'll be good to you. I promise. All we need is time." She wrapped her arms around his back. He returned the embrace, her wet cheek against his. Her softness through the red teddy and the heat of her body sparked an urge. She was clinging to him the way she made love. He felt himself growing, wanting her one more time, and then a chill swept through him. It was unsettling the way she suddenly switched her emotions on and off like hot and cold water.

"You're my savior, Drew Smith."

But who would save him from her?

His desire waned. He couldn't encourage her, no matter how good a lay. It had to end, once and for all. He broke away from their embrace.

"Get dressed. I'll take you home."

"I don't want to go home. I'll stay the night."

"Maybe you should sleep in the guestroom."

"If that's what you want."

"It's best."

She left him at the kitchen island. Full of mixed feelings, his appetite gone, he finished the glass of wine alone and returned to bed. Angel wasn't there, but shut away in the guestroom down the hall. He considered looking in on her, but decided against it. After some effort, he fell asleep, but it didn't last long. The dream returned and this time the mysterious woman had a face. It was Angel. He rose early to find her gone. Just as well, he could do without the drama.

Suited up and ready for work, Drew walked to his Mercedes in the driveway. The sports sedan was sitting unusually low—the tires had been slashed. His first thought was getting to court. It was eight o'clock so he had plenty of time to catch a cab on 16th Street.

By the time the cab dropped him off at the courthouse, his anger had calmed. Angel was bad news. He'd made the right decision to cut her loose. One thing he didn't need in his life was a psycho crackhead, a crazy and deranged ho, and to think he'd considered marriage. Four tires were a small price to pay to get off that hook.

Before entering the courthouse, where he'd have to turn off his cell phone, he stopped to make a call. "What's up, Julio? I need a favor. My tires were slashed last night, all four. Can you get it towed to your company garage and put on four new tires?"

"Oh, man, you know who did it?"

"Tell you about it later, I'm due in court. You know where I keep the spare car key. See you this afternoon."

∞

Wednesday, August 9, 12:30 p.m.

Past noon, and Gee still lay in bed, resisting rising, showering, and getting on with life. It was difficult facing the reality of his involvement in the death of three co-workers. He couldn't erase from his mind the memories, their faces, their laughter. He wished Marie were still lying beside him. She was a distraction from the haunting thoughts. At dawn, she'd left him alone to wrestle with his conscience. He didn't know what to do, but if he didn't do something soon, he feared he would implode from anxiety and fear. On top of all that, his mother had left, taking Candice. Now it was just him and his father in the house. They were having problems. He hoped they could work it out, but it didn't look like it. Papi angered him sometimes with his craziness, but he loved his father, and didn't want to see his mother go.

His cell phone rang. "Hey, Marie."

"Gee, have you seen today's paper?"

"Something on the robbery?"

"No, it's your friend Tyrone."

Gee sat up. "What?"

"He shot a prostitute."

"When?"

"The other night."

"Damn." He was up on his feet, pacing.

"He was one of your boys at Coolidge. Aren't you glad you don't hang with that crowd anymore? And there was that other creep who fought a lot, Jinx."

"What's it say?"

"Let's see...'Police arrested and charged Tyrone Jones of no fixed address with the shooting death of Marc Sanchez, a transgender also known as Maria Santos...' blah, blah, blah...'Jones attempted to flee the scene but was immediately apprehended and the weapon recovered...' Gee, you there?"

He sighed. "Marie, I need to talk to you. Can you come now?"

"You sound scary. I'll be right over."

∞

Wednesday, August 9, 2:00 p.m.

Jinx stood over his mother's corpse, shaking his finger, pointing the blame. She made him do it. All night he had paced about, blaming her for his miserable childhood and the state of his life. It was all her fault and she'd got what she deserved. At dawn's light, physically and mentally exhausted, he took a seat on the sofa, surrendering his griefless anger and falling into a deep sleep.

Awakened by a mid-afternoon knock at the door, he started up but froze at the sight of his mother's corpse lying at the door. The night before played out in his mind—the carjacking, the robbery, and his mother expressionless face below the bloody hole in her forehead. The knock was hard and steady. Then it stopped.

Footsteps retreated from the front porch. Jinx peeped through the blinds. Two plainclothes cops were heading back to their unmarked car. What was going on? He'd have to leave soon, they'd keep coming back. But first he needed a plan. Tattoo's warning and offer came to mind. And his sister. With his mother's death, he suddenly wanted to see his sister.

"Why'd you make me do it?" He tucked the gun in his belt and lifted the corpse, now stiff with rigor mortis, by its shoulders, and dragged the dead weight up the steps to her bedroom. He was going to leave her on the floor, then considered putting her in the bed, and finally stuffed the corpse in the closet out of his sight.

The money she took had to be around the house somewhere. He began his search. The house was hot, close, and shut up. The afternoon sun had peaked. He didn't dare open a window for fear his movements would be seen or heard from the street. He ransacked her room until there was nothing more to search. Standing in the middle of the room sweating profusely, Jinx mumbled more curses at his dead mother. Where was the money? And then he remembered.

He plodded down the steps to the kitchen, pausing a moment at the foot of the stairs before stepped over the bloodstain. He cursed her once again. He slid a chair to the refrigerator, stood on it to reach into the highest cabinet, and immediately spotted the oatmeal box. He dug through the flakes and found the bankroll. Just like she said.

Again, heavy and urgent, a knock at the door. Listening intently, he eased down off the chair, brushed the oats off his sweaty hands, and pulled the gun from his belt. Frozen with fear, he waited for the knocking to stop.

∞

Drew returned to his office late in the afternoon. Shirley had left a pile of messages on his desk. One was marked urgent. He dialed the number, and was immediately put through to the Chief.

"Yes sir, your message said it was urgent."

"The ballistics report showed a match with the Farragut and another shooting Monday night."

"You got a shooter?"

"I have a suspect in custody. There were two shooters at the Farragut. The suspect's not talking."

"Who is he?"

"A creep named Tyrone Jones, petty street dealer. He shot a prostitute the other night, a transvestite. I want to run something by you."

"I'm on my way." Drew hung up. Jean Legere's voice echoed in his mind, "a doofus named Tyrone Jones."

Julio barged through the door. "Dude, we got a problem."

"What's the problem?" Drew rose from behind his desk grabbing his jacket.

"Hernando. He showed up at Nina's job today. She wouldn't see him, and security had him removed. We need to talk to him."

"To say what? And why is this my problem?"

"Tell him to stay away from Nina and Candice, or else."

"Or else what?"

"I'll figure that out when I'm in his face. You goin' to do this with me or what?"

"Slow down, chill out for a moment. We may have a bigger problem. I just got a call from the Chief. Ballistics got a match on the Farragut shooter. And they apprehended a suspect."

"Who is it?"

"A doofus named Tyrone Jones."

Julio hesitated. "Not the same Tyrone Jones who was supposedly with Gee on Saturday."

"The Chief wants to see me. I want you to come along. Then, I'm all for going to talk to Hernando, but we have some business with Gee to clear up as well."

"Let's roll."

⸎

From his vantage next to Julio on the sofa, Drew could see the fatigue in the Chief's face. The mayor was obviously coming down hard on him and he was pulling late hours and losing sleep. Tyrone Jones was the first real lead, but with the suspect invoking his right to remain silent, the police had run into a brick wall.

"Ballistics extracted a single shot from Naomi Sims. It was fired from Jones's gun, and it didn't kill her. The second shooter had better aim."

"The second shooter killed them all?" Drew asked.

The Chief nodded.

"What do you know about Jones?" Drew asked.

"Not much, he had a couple of distribution charges and a couple of grand theft auto arrests. Never the driver. Incarcerated for a couple of stints, nothing long-term. Tell you the truth, he's a squirrelly-looking kid, doesn't act like a cold-blooded killer, but he definitely shot down that prostitute. And he was known to keep company with Jeffrey Legere."

"I spoke with his mother," Drew said. "Right after Lowry was there. Has he done any follow-up?"

"Can't seem to catch up with her. The neighbors haven't seen her in a couple of days. I'm working on a warrant. We'll go in first thing in the morning. One thing is certain, Legere's the man we're looking for."

"Which proves my client is innocent."

"Not necessarily, but I have a theory about that single bullet. What do you think happened?"

"Jones got off one shot but couldn't kill her, so his accomplice finished the job."

"Jones didn't have any trouble killing the prostitute."

"That happened a day later. He had time to build up nerve and prove himself. Who knows the psyche of a killer?"

"You heard anything on Legere?" the Chief asked.

Drew shifted in his seat. "Is that why you wanted to see me?" Both Julio's and the Chief's eyes were set on Drew.

"Close to the chest. Is that how you want to play this?" The Chief switched his gaze to Julio's blank expression.

Drew shook his head. "I haven't heard a thing. I plan to visit his mother again and I'll let you know what I get."

"Maybe you'll have better luck than my men. I got a team periodically checking the house. If they give you any trouble, call me."

∞

Marie listened to Gee's confession and for hours tried to convince him to go to the police. He couldn't really argue against her reasoning that it was the right thing to do, but fear of consequences kept him immobilized. Lying there on the bed, he once again felt like the timid schoolboy she once didn't bother to talk to.

"Gee, you can't just sit here and do nothing. What are you afraid of—Jinx? He could be behind bars by now."

"I'm not afraid of Jinx, I'm afraid for my family. If I go to the police, they'll lock me up. They see me as just another thug. Who'll believe me? It'll sound like a lie."

"What if—" Marie paused mid-sentence. "What if you go to Drew Smith? He'll see that you get fair treatment."

"I thought about that."

She fished her cell phone out of her purse.

"What are you doing?" Gee asked.

"Calling Drew Smith. He'll understand."

"Don't." He grabbed her hand.

"Why?" She jerked free. "He'll know what to do."

"I'm not ready to deal with it."

"This is a matter of life and death. You'll have to face up to it sooner or later. The longer you wait the worse it gets. The time is now." Marie dialed 411 and was connected to the office of Drew Smith, Attorney and Counselor at Law. After several rings the call rolled over into voicemail.

"Mr. Smith, this is Marie. I wanted to thank you for the wonderful evening and dinner Friday. That's not really why I'm calling. I—I mean we, Gee and I—need your help and would like to see you as soon as possible. It's very important. Could you call me as soon as you get this message?" She left her number and ended the call.

"Why did you do that?"

"'Cause I want to help you, Gee, even if you won't help yourself."

"Why?"

She seemed to struggle with herself for a moment. "I think I'm...we've only just gotten together. I don't want to lose you. Not now." She broke down and wept.

He wrapped his arms around her. "I don't want to lose you either. I'm glad you're here. And I know I love you."

She wiped away her tears and gave him a peck on the lips. "We'll go see Mr. Smith first thing in the morning, okay?"

"Okay."

Her eyes still brimming, she forced another smile. "I hope it's not too late."

"What do you mean?"

"Four people are dead. Who knows what Jinx is doing? You said so yourself, he's dangerous. I hope no one else dies. With Tyrone in jail, you think Jinx'll come after you?"

"I don't know what he'll do, he's crazy." Gee stood up. "I already feel like I'm in jail, let's get out of here, go to the park or get something to eat. I got to get out of here."

⚭

The working-class neighborhood was made up of modest, well-kept homes with manicured lawns. Nina married a carpenter, a man who made an honest living with his hands. Comparing their house to his, Drew was convinced she married for love over money. Yet money was one of the problems that tore at the seams of their marriage.

Drew and Julio headed for the front door. He looked around with an eerie feeling, and found himself under a neighbor's watchful gaze from a second-floor window across the street—all the more reason to keep Julio under control. He wanted no witnesses to an altercation.

"Remember, let me do the talking. I wish you would just let me handle this. I don't want you acting up. I'd feel more comfortable if you'd wait in the car."

"Hell, no. I want to see his face, and I want him to see mine just before I make him look like Nina."

Drew rang the doorbell. "I'm not looking for a fight. I'm not here to kick his ass."

"Well, I am."

"In that case, let's go." Drew began walking back to the car.

"Okay, okay, okay, I promise to act right." Julio's expression showed more cunning than sincerity, and "acting right" was whatever the circumstances required.

"I'm not playing, Julio. Let's go. We'll talk to Gee first, then we'll confront Hernando."

"Whatever."

A front light came on and Julio stepped into the shadows out of sight from the door. Drew sighed and walked back to the house. Hernando opened the door, brow furrowed.

"Drew?

"Hernando." It had been a while. Drew was taken aback by the man's appearance. He had a weathered complexion, a graying mustache, and thin creases about the eyes, and an added fifty pounds. No wonder Nina complimented Drew on how well he had aged.

"What can I do for you?" Hernando didn't ask him in.

"I'd like to speak to Gee. I have some questions on the Farragut investigation."

"He not here. Just left with his girlfriend."

"So much for that." Drew looked to Julio hidden in the shadows. "There's another matter. Nina asked me to talk to you."

"Where is she?"

"She's safe."

"What you mean?" Rage was growing in Hernando's eyes. "Why you come here? She fucking you again? I knew it."

"She wants a divorce."

"You had your chance. Never, I never divorce. She's my wife for life. Over my dead body."

Before Drew could respond, Julio stepped into the light. "I can arrange that."

"You." Hernando turned his stare back on Drew.

Julio stepped forward. "If you ever lay a hand on Nina again, I'll cut it off."

Heated Spanish flew back and forth, sending off sparks of emotive intent as the two men delivered threats and counter-threats. Drew stepped between the two shouting men. For a moment the three were so closely enmeshed that a single blow or mere false move would have exploded into a melee, which Drew knew he could get the short end of by trying to separate the two. He turned his back on Hernando and pushed Julio away, ordering him to return to the car. Julio backed down. Drew returned to face Hernando.

"You don't have to consent to a divorce. You've given her adequate grounds. I'm filing papers for a restraining order. You'll refrain from any contact with both her and your daughter."

"You can't do that."

"Disobey the protective order and I'll have you in jail before you know it. I suggest you start looking for a good lawyer. Let's not make this more difficult than it has to be."

"Fuck you," he shouted as Drew turned and walked back away. He joined Julio at the car. "Come on, let's pay Jean Legere another call."

❧

Jinx gripped the gun, holding it close slightly parting the drawn curtains of his mother's front bedroom window peeping. The two cops stopped knocking and returned to their car. Parked in front, it didn't look like it was moving any time soon. Probably waiting for his mother but most likely him. Not good, they wouldn't wait forever. How long before they'd force their way in? It was dark and time to go.

He slunk down the hall to his room and looked out the window. The alley looked clear. He tucked the gun into his belt and pulled a duffle bag from his closet. Good thing he had clean clothes to travel with. At least his mother had done one good thing. He stuffed the bag with t-shirts and underwear, then changed into a pair of cargo pants. Half the bankroll went into a pocket, the rest into the duffle bag.

He sat on the edge of the bed. Where would he go? How would he get out of the city? Time was running out, and so was he.

❧

Julio's limousine turned off Georgia Avenue and headed east on Missouri. The Legere house was the only one on the block shut up and dark on this hot and humid evening. At sundown, few neighbors sat on their porches, most preferring the air conditioning inside. Drew spotted a police vehicle parked in front.

"Drive around the block, let's take a stroll through the alley."

"What you got in mind?"

"I got a funny feeling. After the police talked to his mother, they haven't seen her since. What's up with that?"

Julio parked in the alley near the house. "This guy is strapped. We're not."

"I thought about that. So be careful."

Julio leveled a hard stare at Drew. "Ay! Estas loco?"

Drew scanned the house. "You go knock on the door. I'll stand back in the alley, get a clear view, and see if someone peeps out the window."

"I got a better idea, you go knock, and I'll watch from the road."

Drew laughed. "What's the matter, you scared?"

"No man, I just ain't no fool."

Drew opened the chain-link gate while dogs barked from two houses down. Trashcans stood empty at the gate. No one had put the out the garbage lately. He stepped up onto the back porch, opened a rickety screen door, and knocked. The house was in desperate need of repair.

Drew looked back at Julio, who saw no movement from the upper floor window and shook his head. He tried the doorknob. It turned freely. Waiting a few moments, he repeated the knock, and with no response, he signaled Julio over. Julio grabbed a flashlight from the glove compartment and joined Drew at the door.

"It's open?" Julio asked.

"Somebody left in a hurry."

They stepped in. Julio quickly skimmed the flashlight beam around the kitchen. The place was a mess. Only the dripping faucet's metronomic rhythm disturbed the silence. Dirty dishes filled the sink. Julio peeped into the well-stocked refrigerator.

"Nobody's starving."

Drew was more concerned with the possible presence of another in the house. Floorboards creaked underfoot as they continued up the hallway to the front door. "Keep the flashlight away from the windows." Nothing of interest stood out except the air. A stench seeped into the stuffy room. Julio began whistling.

"What are you doing?" Drew asked.

"Making some noise. This place is as dead as a cemetery. Nobody here. It stinks."

Listening intently, they slowly climbed the steps.

"What's that smell?" Julio asked.

"I hope it's not what I think."

At the top of the stairs, the bathroom and a bedroom were open and empty. The door to the master bedroom was closed. They stepped into the open bedroom. The room was somewhat more orderly than the downstairs. A scattering of men's clothing and sneakers lay on the bed and floor.

"Must be Jinx's room," Julio said.

Drew picked up some cell phone packaging from the bed and inspected the box and receipt with the flashlight.

"New cell phone?" Julio asked.

"Pay-as-you-go, virtually untraceable, bought the day before yesterday." He read the receipt while Julio looked over his shoulder. "Got a pen and paper?"

"So he was here." Julio pulled a pen and pad from his breast pocket.

"Somebody was. Write this down." Drew dictated the cell phone number from the receipt, then laid the receipt back on the bed alongside the packaging.

"Come on." Drew returned to the hallway and stepped to the closed door of the master bedroom across the hall. It opened easily with a slight push. The overwhelming stench flooded the air.

"Damn." Julio covered his nose with a handkerchief. Drew did the same. "Did someone die in here?"

The room was ransacked. Stepping over the scattered debris, searching the room with his flashlight, Drew went to the closet door as though drawn to some hidden treasure. When he opened it, a twisted bundle fell out at his feet.

"Turn on the light, Julio."

"The police will see it and come running."

"Turn it on."

Julio hit the wall switch and stepped to Drew's side. "What is it? A dead body?"

"Jean Legere."

"Wow. This place *is* a cemetery."

"At least a temporary one, no telling how long she's been dead. The heat and humidity accelerate decomposition. The body's gone into rigor mortis and come back out again. Putrefaction has set in."

"You think? Let's get out of here."

Suddenly, banging on the front door. The two uniformed officers were stunned to see Julio and Drew open it.

"Come in, officers. I suggest you call the morgue immediately. There's a rotting corpse upstairs."

"Drew Smith, what are you doing here?" an officer asked.

"Looking for Jeffrey Legere."

"How did you get in?"

"The back door was open."

"Can you wait outside?" He opened his cell phone. Drew watched the two head up the stairs then stepped outside. The city's polluted air was refreshing. Moments later the officer returned with a grim expression. "Lt. Lowry asked me to hold you here. He's on his way."

"No problem, we'll stay."

"Mind waiting in the squad car?"

"You mean we're being detained?"

The officer hesitated. "Lt. Lowry's orders."

Julio and Drew found themselves locked in the back of a squad car.

"They're arresting us?" Julio asked.

"Not yet, but maybe before the night's over. Lowry's not one of my biggest fans." Drew dug out his cell phone to give the Chief a heads up. Within minutes, Lowry was on the scene, focused more on Drew Smith than the crime scene investigation.

"What in the hell are you doing here, Smith? Tampering with a crime scene, obstruction of justice, breaking and entering. I'm charging you and your friend."

"Look, Captain Lowry—"

"It's Lieutenant, shitface."

"Okay, Lieutenant Shitface. Maybe you should close this case before you start creating other crimes. Legere murdered his mother. I haven't committed any crime."

"Breaking and entering's a crime," the red-faced lieutenant shouted.

"There was no forced entry," the officer told him.

"Who the fuck asked you?" Lowry's cell phone rang. He yanked it from his breast pocket. "Yes, Chief?... Shot with a single bullet to the head. It appears to be Legere's mother... I haven't fully assessed the crime scene... But... Yes, sir."

Lowry put away his phone. "Where the hell's medical examiner?" He shouted at his awaiting uniformed officers.

"Lieutenant, are we free to go?" Drew asked.

Lowry didn't look back. "Get out of here, Smith."

Drew and Julio walked back to the limo.

"I don't know who's more loco," Julio said, "the cops or the crooks."

"Both, equally. That's how they balance one another."

"But cops man," Julio shook his head, "they're the worst kind of thugs."

∞

Six blocks away, the approaching squad car's flashing lights and wailing siren sent Jinx a bolt of distress and adrenalin. He stopped and watched the speeding vehicle pass. He sucked in a breath. He had to get off the street as soon as possible. He could catch a Greyhound to Richmond, the Silver Spring stop out front of the Holiday Inn was perfect—no terminal, cashiers, or lines, decreasing his chances of being recognized or remembered.

He stepped into the street and hailed a northbound cab. Jinx fretfully tried the back door. It was locked. Looking Jinx over, the driver made no attempt to unlock it.

"Yah man, where you going?"

"Holiday Inn in Silver Spring." Jinx yanked on the locked door handle. "Open the muthafuckin' door."

The driver's suspicious eyes swept over his face and the duffle bag before he released the lock. As Jinx settled into the back seat, he sensed being watched from the rearview mirror. The driver made a notation on his manifest.

"Goin' outta town?"

"What do you think?"

"No problem." The driver said something else in Jamaican patois, and put the car in gear. Jinx didn't understand the patois, but knew an insult when he heard one. Turning up his reggae, the driver merged into traffic, taking North Capitol Street to Blair Road. It was a fifteen-minute ride. Ten minutes later, after they turned onto Georgia Avenue in Silver Spring, Jinx ordered the driver to pull over.

"This is not the Holiday Inn."

"I'll walk from here."

"Seven dollars."

Jinx pulled out his gun and stuck it to the back of the driver's head. "Now what was that you said back there?"

"I didn't say nothing, man. What's your problem?"

"Pull over and give me your money."

The driver pulled over out of traffic, all the while looking in his rearview mirror. "The fare is seven dollars."

"You got a hearing problem—"

The driver turned in his seat and grabbed the gun barrel. As the two struggled, he accidentally stepped on the accelerator. The car careened onto the sidewalk. An elderly couple was caught in its path. The old man jumped, the woman didn't. Jinx yanked on the gun and a sudden flash-bang filled the taxi. The driver slouched over in his seat. In a panicked frenzy, Jinx stripped the driver of his watch and money, and as traffic stopped and a crowd began to gather, he leapt from the cab and disappeared into the night.

∞

Drew was in bed early but couldn't sleep, tossing and turning with a lot on his mind. Did Gee really lie to him, and why? As for his father Hernando, Drew's threat to file papers and handle Nina's divorce was just that, a threat and nothing more. He once hated Hernando, and the thought of representing Nina in a divorce held a dark appeal, like triangulating some love affair in a soap opera, playing out a diabolical scheme of revenge. They both had left so much pain in his life, and now they were back.

After two hours of sleeplessness, he got up, put on his robe, and went down to the study. Wakefulness drove him to work. When he turned on his computer, several files came up as recovered, including his bank statements. Normally, documents were only recovered if the computer was improperly shut down or the system had crashed, neither of which happened last time he was on it.

The phone rang. At two a.m., who could it be? When he answered, whoever was on the other end didn't speak. He hung up, must have been a wrong number. Thirty minutes later it rang again and the caller still refused to speak. He checked the caller ID, but the number was blocked. Twenty minutes later, same thing. Only this time he didn't answer it, but turned off the ringer. He also turned off his cell phone.

∞

Thursday, August 10, 9:00 a.m.

"You're late." Shirley greeted him like a displeased boss rather than his secretary. "Rough night?"

"Sort of."

"You have messages on your desk. One from Chief Washington, says it's urgent. Also, a young couple's waiting in the conference room. They've been here more than an hour. Seem really nervous."

"Who are they?"

"A very pretty girl named Marie and a young man who goes by the name of Gee."

"Gee, good, he must have got my message."

"And you have hers. She left a message yesterday, said it was important."

Shirley followed Drew into his office, pen and steno pad clutched to her bosom. She stood in front of the desk as he dropped his briefcase and began thumbing through the messages. She was older than him by a decade and had been with Drew for about as long. Mature and motherly, not to mention competent, she ran his business like a partner, often offering unsolicited advice on personal matters.

"Okay, let me call the Chief, then I'll see them. And—"

"I know, coffee."

He gave her an appreciative smile.

"Drew, I don't mean to get into your business—"

"Then don't." He continued thumbing through the messages, in no mood to listen to Shirley voice her disapproval of the company he was keeping. She left the office.

Drew was promptly put through.

"Chief, your message said it was urgent."

"There's a problem with your client Theo Jackson."

"What now?"

"He's been arrested."

"How's that?"

"I'll tell you when you get here, and there's more developing on Legere."

"I'll be there in an hour." As Drew hung up, the receptionist announced Angel was on the line. He debated whether to take the call, but couldn't resist the urge to give her an earful. "What do you want, Angel?"

"Are you free for dinner?"

"For you? Never. I'm warning you Angel. Stay away from my house, my car and me. I'm pressing charges against you."

"For what, sweetheart? I haven't done anything. You got any witnesses?"

"Don't play with me. You're looking at big trouble."

"Trouble, huh. Mister big shot lawyer, let me tell you one thing. You haven't seen trouble. Just wait until I get done with you—"

"You sick bitch, I'm warning you—"

"Watch your back." The line went dead.

Drew hung up as Shirley placed a steaming mug of coffee in front of him. Nettled, his thoughts were elsewhere as he mechanically picked up the mug and took a sip. Shirley cleared her throat.

"Oh, thank you," he said.

"Are you ready?"

"For what?"

"The couple, Marie and Gee."

"I'm sorry, show them in."

"That Angel needs to give you a break. Forgive me for saying it, but Angel's a she-devil."

"I forgive you. Now I need you to reschedule my appointments this morning."

"But you have two new clients coming in."

"Can't help it. The Chief calls, I run."

Shirley expelled a frustrated breath. "And when will you be back?"

"Not sure."

"At my church, there are some nice professional women I could introduce you—"

"Gee and Marie, now, Shirley."

She twisted her mouth and sucked her teeth, then left the office. Seconds later, Marie and Gee entered.

"Come in." Drew pointed to the two chairs in front of his desk.

"Good morning, Mr. Smith," Marie said. Gee nodded.

"It's Drew. You make me feel old."

"Yes, Drew." Marie led Gee by the hand. An image from years ago popped into Drew's mind, a shy little boy hiding behind his mother's skirt. "I hope you don't mind our showing up like this without an appointment."

"No problem. I got your message. Now what's this about?"

Marie looked at Gee, but he only stared at the floor. Marie's gaze was attentive, caring, even protective, much as Gee's gaze at her had been that night at the Farragut. In a few short days they'd fallen in love. Drew had an urge to protect them, too. Not from each other, he hoped.

Marie gave up waiting for Gee and looked at Drew. "Gee may be in trouble and needs your help. Desperately."

"Okay, Gee, what's the problem?"

He squirmed boyishly in his seat, his eyes still cast down. "I know what happened at the Farragut."

"What can you tell me?"

"I lied to you. I know who did it. I was there."

"So Theo did see your car?"

"Probably. My two friends—ex-friends—robbed the place. They forced me to drive them there."

"Forced?"

"With a gun."

"Who are these friends?"

"Tyrone Jones and Jeffrey Legere, goes by the name Jinx."

Drew sighed. It was a fear he'd been struggling with. "And you were at the Legere house on Saturday?"

"How did you know?"

"His mother told me. That's when I knew you lied. I wish you hadn't done that. Tell me everything that happened—the truth."

Gee relayed an abundance of detail surrounding that morning. With limited past interaction, Drew had insufficient insight into Gee's personality to gauge how he might have been swayed to act or not to. Gee had been a mystery to Drew since birth, and whether he was telling the whole truth remained in question.

"You waited?"

"Yeah."

"Why didn't you leave and get help? Why stick around?"

"He threatened to hurt my family. He had a gun and he said he would hunt me down. You don't know him."

"Why did you wait so long to tell someone? You could have saved a life."

"I don't know. I guess I was too afraid for my family."

"I wish you'd come to me sooner." Drew sat back and took a moment to think. They watched him.

"Marie, you go home," he finally said.

It was apparent from her expression that his order had struck her like a slap to the face. "You've done well," Drew said. "I'll call you later. This is going to take some time with the police. There's nothing you can do now. Thanks for encouraging Gee to come in. You may have saved him from bigger trouble. And Gee, you and I are going to talk to the Chief of Police. I hope I can keep you out of jail."

"Jail? I didn't do nothing. Am I an accessory? That's what Jinx said, an accessory."

"The police may consider you an accessory, especially since your long silence hindered the investigation. It's been what, four days. I want you two to step out and ask my secretary to come in. I need to make some calls. I'll be with you shortly." He watched the couple leave the room. This time it was Gee leading Marie by the hand.

Drew placed a call to Julio, hoping to get word to Nina and Hernando. It rolled to voice mail, and Drew hung up. On second thought, just as well. Gee was twenty and of majority. It wasn't Drew's place to tell his parents. He dropped his head into his palms and wished he'd had more sleep. It was going to be one of those days.

∞

Drew was told to go right in to the Chief's inner sanctum. He instructed Gee to have a seat outside. Gee appeared more relaxed and confident now that he'd entrusted his fate into Drew's hands. Drew straightened his back and took a deep breath before strolling in.

"Come on in, Drew, have a seat. Like I said, there have been some new developments. You won't be happy."

"I'm already unhappy. What's happening?"

"Your client Theo Jackson was just picked up at the Reagan National Airport. He had a one-way ticket to the Bahamas and ten thousand in cash."

"What?" Drew dropped into a chair in front of the Chief's desk. "So where is he now?"

"Airport police are holding him. I've just dispatched a team to transport him here. I'm sure the U.S. Attorney's going to want us to hold him on suspicion. Even if Jackson is innocent, he's not helping his case."

"I'm sure there's a reasonable explanation."

"A one-way ticket and ten grand looks like he was planning an extended stay."

"I'll deal with him later. What about Legere?"

"He hijacked a cab last night. We got the images. He apparently robbed a Wendy's and hijacked a couple of other vehicles the night before."

"I think I can shed more light on the situation."

"How's that?"

"There's a young man, Gustavo Garcia, waiting outside that door. He's Nina's son and a waiter at the Farragut. Tyrone Jones was a buddy, along with a Jeffrey Legere, a.k.a. Jinx, also a former employee of the Farragut. Gustavo, they call him Gee, says they forced him at gunpoint to drive the getaway car."

"Likely story. When did you find this out?"

"The kid came to me an hour ago. I understand your skepticism. He's scared. You'll change your mind once you hear his story."

"Why didn't he come forward sooner?"

"The mastermind, Jinx, threatened to harm his family if he talked."

"This doesn't bode well for either of your clients, Drew. The boy is your client?"

"Only at this point in the proceedings until I can find someone to represent him. Right now, Theo's my primary client, and I don't want to get into any conflict of interest. I'll speak with his parents, help them find a good lawyer."

The Chief dialed the U.S. Attorney's office and explained he had a witness to the Farragut robbery and was planning to videotape the interview. They said someone would be there within the hour.

"Right now, Drew, I need to speak with my staff."

"We'll go next door to the courthouse and get a cup of coffee."

"Be back in an hour."

Drew stepped out of the office and Gee was nowhere in sight. Close to panic, Drew asked the clerk of his whereabouts. She shrugged. Drew rushed out the door, down the hall, and around the corner to the elevator. He sighed in relief when he found Gee bent over a water fountain.

"I told you to stay put."

"I just got a drink of water. I'm sorry, Mr. Drew, I was thirsty."

Drew pinched the bridge of his nose. Even though he once saw Gee as Nina's little boy, he was now a man and entitled to that respect.

"I'm sorry, Gee."

"Everything all right?"

"No. They picked up Theo at the airport headed for the Bahamas. He was under orders not to leave the area. They think he was making a run for it. They'll probably hold him under suspicion."

"But he didn't do it."

"And neither did you. But now it looks like a four-man conspiracy. Unless... Come on, let's go get some coffee. They're going to videotape your statement, I need to prep you."

"Then what?"

"Then we'll just have to see what the U.S. Attorney plans to do. But there's one thing that may be a problem. You told me that after the robbery, Jinx was driving, and you told him to take North Capitol Street if he was going to speed."

"Right."

"Why?"

"I didn't want a ticket. The camera would capture my car."

"Do yourself a favor. Forget you ever said that, and whatever you do, don't offer it in the interview. It's called an interview, but trust me, it'll turn into an interrogation."

"Sure."

"Do you know why I told you to forget it?"

"It'll look like I was helping Jinx."

The correct answer made Drew smile.

"Mr. Drew, I want to thank you for doing this. I don't know how I'll pay."

"Right now, Theo is my client. Taking you on would be a conflict of interest. I can't represent you both. I'll help your parents find a good lawyer. Okay?"

Drew felt the hurt in the boy's eyes as his shoulders slumped with disappointment.

"Okay," Gee said in a harsh whisper.

Chapter 9

AFTER GEE HANDED over his wallet, keys, and cell phone to Drew, two uniformed officers handcuffed him. He gave Drew a farewell nod as they led him away.

"There goes another one," Drew whispered. Another young man of color being jailed. Too many like Gee were incarcerated, their innocence stolen, and many would never return to a real life.

With unquestionable sincerity, Gee had told his story to the camera, the U. S. Attorney, Lt. Lowry, and the Chief. For two hours, Gee withstood a barrage of questions with truth, his only defense. But it wasn't enough to keep him out of jail. Only Lt. Lowry questioned his veracity. It was common knowledge that Lowry was on a mission to make a name for himself. Producing a suspect—any suspect—would serve his need to quell the criticism of the Department and particularly of his unit for their abysmal statistics of unsolved homicides and cold cases. The police were doing little to stem the rising tide of homicides, which every day claimed the lives of young men in the city. Had Lowry been on top off things, Gee and all the Farragut employees would have been interviewed immediately after the crime. Lowry was going about the investigation ass-backwards. Tomorrow the newspapers would float a false banner headline, "Robber Caught," claiming it was good police work.

"Mr. Smith."

It took Drew a moment to realize that Dan Gaines, the Assistant U.S. Attorney, was addressing him. Gaines had sat in on the interrogation and made the final decision to jail Gee. Gaines appeared to be right out of some Ivy League law school, self-assured, probably with political ambitions, and this job was a starting point. He had no idea what Drew was feeling, no idea what it was like to be a man of color in a racist society. Offering a handshake, the preppy AUSA displayed a toothy grin, a fresh tan, and lots of blond hair, swept back.

"Why are you holding him?" Drew grudgingly shook his hand. "You heard his story."

"Lt. Lowry doesn't buy it. I acted on his recommendation, and he believes there was probable cause for the arrest. He is, after all, in charge of this investigation."

"Lowry wouldn't know probable cause from his asshole."

"I'm sorry, Drew. You don't mind me calling you Drew, do you?"

In no mood for civility, Drew didn't respond.

"I believe there are facts in issue and there is probable cause."

"How long have you been an Assistant U.S. Attorney?"

"A year."

"You heard Garcia's story. There wasn't a crack in it. He's telling the truth. He has no priors."

"Like I said, Lt. Lowry believes there's sufficient evidence to support a conspiracy, especially with Jackson's attempt to flee. They'll both be arraigned tomorrow morning. We'll consider bail."

"Is that a promise?"

"A promise to consider. We'll talk." With a final smirk, he wheeled and headed out the door.

At the entrance to the inner office, Lowry spoke to the Chief in whispers. Trying to ignore Lowry's gloating grin, Drew interrupted to ask the Chief for a minute of his time.

"So what do you think of your innocent client Jackson now?" Lowry said.

"My thoughts haven't changed."

"Only a guilty man runs."

"There is no evidence he was running. Under our law, a man's presumed innocent until proven guilty. Haven't you heard?"

"Not even a crooked-ass shyster like you can get that one off. Jackson, his amigo Garcia, and the other two were all in it together."

Drew sucked in his breath and looked to the Chief. It was more than he could take. Drew surprised himself, and the Chief, but most of all Lowry when his fist impacted the man's chin. The cop buckled to his knees.

"God damn it, Smith, get in my office and shut the door." The Chief stepped between the two men and helped Lowry to his feet. Others in the suite looked stunned or amused. Drew obeyed the Chief's order. "The rest of you, get back to work."

Moments later, the Chief marched into his office and slammed the door. "Smith, what the hell's gotten into you? You're a loose cannon."

Drew slouched on the couch. "He had it coming. You heard what he said."

"That's what I told him. But you're a lawyer and not a street fighter—although some may claim you're that too—and as a member of the bar you're held to a higher standard. Expect repercussions. He may bring you up before the bar."

"Let him. Whatever censure or reprimand they hand down will be worth it. I'd do it again. Lowry brings out the worst in me. He sees himself as a rising star and hates the idea of sharing the limelight."

"Did you call that therapist?"

"I met with her."

The Chief smiled and raised an eyebrow, probably waiting for a crack about Dr. Settles's beauty. Drew didn't oblige. "Well, good," the Chief said. "What are you going to do about Theo Jackson?"

"I'd like to see him now. Can you arrange it?"

"No problem. He should be downstairs by now. The U.S. Attorney will arraign all three tomorrow morning, Jackson, Garcia, and Jones."

"You know as well as I do, he'll never be able to prove they were acting in concert."

"I know, but let Lowry learn the hard way. That's how you handle men like that. Let him fall on his face."

"I'd rather rearrange his face—"

"You just tried, I advise you not to do it again."

"You got two white men out there deciding how to deal with blacks and Latinos. Their only solution is jail."

"Get a grip, Smith."

Drew scowled for a moment then stood to leave.

"So Garcia is Nina's boy." Chief eyed Drew closely. "Who's the father?"

"A guy named Hernando Garcia."

"Kid reminds me of you, back in the day."

"You sound like Lowry. We all look alike."

Drew didn't wait around for an explanation.

∞

Theo was being held at police headquarters and hadn't yet been transported to the D.C. jail. Drew spoke to him through the bars of the holding cell.

"What the hell were you thinking? Didn't I tell you not to leave the area without checking with me?"

"I'm sorry, Drew, I thought it was a formality. I didn't know they were watching my every move. What for? The press kept calling my house, knocking on my door. They even followed me to the grocery store. We had to get away."

"Gail was with you?"

"Yes."

"And the ten thousand dollars, why so much money?"

"I don't have credit cards. We were planning to do some gambling. That was from my savings."

"Can you prove it was your money?"

"What do you mean?"

Drew sighed with impatience. "Do you have a withdrawal slip? Bank statements?"

"Yes."

"I'll need them to prove the source of the money."

"Gail can get them to you."

"With that I could probably argue for your freedom. Theo, this couldn't have come at a worse time. You should have called me."

"I didn't think it was a big deal."

"We now know who did the robberies."

"Who?"

"Jeffrey Legere and Tyrone Jones."

"Jinx. I should have known."

"And Gee."

"Gee?"

"They forced him at gunpoint to drive the getaway car. That's why your little jaunt couldn't have come at a worst time. It looks like an inside job gone wrong. Maybe you let the robbers in and tried to cover your involvement by jumping out the window, and Gee drove the getaway car. But something went wrong, and three people died. That's how the prosecutor sees it and they plan to arraign you, Gee, and Jones tomorrow morning."

"They can't prove that. Can they?"

"I don't know what they can prove. We'll have to wait and see."

∞

Drew got the supporting documents from Theo's wife and spent a good part of the afternoon back and forth on the phone with Gaines explaining Theo's mistake, even faxing the banks statements. Gaines was too low-level to make any final decisions, leaving Drew in limbo on Theo's charges.

He and Julio decided to break the news to Nina together. As always, just being in her presence stirred longings in Drew, but this was no time for such thoughts. She insisted on returning to her home with them to tell Hernando.

Hernando appeared stunned when he opened the door to find Nina standing between Drew and Julio.

"Nina," he said. "I knew you'd come back. Why you make me worry?"

Nina looked away.

"Nina, please come in."

Instead of moving, she looked to Drew.

"What do you want?" Hernando said to Drew. "I don't want you in my house. Go. Now."

Nina stamped her foot. "Hernando!" His eyes widened and his mouth dropped open. "Gee. He's in trouble."

"Trouble?" he said. "What you mean?"

"Gee is in jail, Hernando," Drew said.

"Jail? I no understand."

Drew stepped forward. "May we come in?"

Nina sat in the Mediterranean armchair. Drew recalled her fondness for the style and how she'd considered it for the décor of their planned home. She'd scaled back her plans to basics for her home with Hernando. It was a modest house, more evidence she'd married for love over money. Was she ever happy? He could have given her so much more.

Gee's arrest left both parents shocked and frightened. Hernando paced like an expectant father. Abruptly, he stopped in front of Drew. "Why he come to you, not me?"

A couple of biting answers sprang to mind, but right now he needed to cobble together a united front from this contentious coalition. "Gee's a grown man. He didn't want to run to his parents with his troubles. He was trying to handle it on his own."

Nina seemed to catch on, almost reading his thoughts, just as in years past. "He's always been independent." Hernando nodded, a hint of pride returning to his face. Nina could twist Hernando's thoughts and emotions around her little finger too. "But what I don't understand is how this could happen," she said. That was like her too, to blame herself and search for a specific neglect. "Gee was never in any trouble. This is so unlike him."

"How much you cost to be his lawyer?" Hernando didn't so much ask as demand. Drew resented his tone but tried to make allowances for the father's stress. Drew was again struck with how little Hernando resembled the young man he recalled, the memory of him shirtless in overalls, exposing the sparse hair on his chest and a workman's beefy muscles. Years and the sun had taken their toll, leaving a dried complexion, premature lines, and a perpetual frown. The crown of wavy black hair was now thinning and almost white, and the sculpted facial features had eroded to a softness that matched his growing paunch. The son of a bitch was beginning to annoy Drew.

"I can't represent Gee. I already have a client in this matter, the manager, Theo. I can refer you to a couple of good attorneys."

"What do you mean?" Nina said. He'd seen that fear in her eyes before.

"I no understand," said Hernando. "You be Gustavo's lawyer. We pay."

Nina leaned forward and clutched Drew's arm. Hernando's deepening frown added to the little burst of pleasure. "But Drew," she said, "everyone knows you're the best criminal lawyer in the city. You must do this."

"This is all at the preliminary stage, and I've already agreed to represent Theo. It presents a conflict of interest and it would be unethical for me to take on Gee as a client."

"But you said Theo wasn't involved."

"That has to be proven. He may be charged, and I have to defend him."

"But they won't. You know they won't."

"Is it the money?" Hernando asked. "We pay. We mortgage the house if we have too. You represent Gustavo. You have to."

"I don't have to do anything." Drew stood and walked to the door. "And it's not the money. I'm finished here, you coming, Julio?"

"Wait," Nina said, "I'll walk you to the door."

"I'll be with you in a second, Drew." Julio then spoke to Hernando in Spanish. This time, Drew didn't care if Julio popped him one. At the door, Nina stepped in front of him, blocking his exit, and stood with one hand on the knob looking up at Drew with teary eyes.

"Drew, please help my boy."

"I'll do all I can, but my hands are tied." He waited for her to open the door, her lost expression tearing at his heart. He wanted to take her into his arms, to hold and comfort her. He knew then that he'd never stopped loving her. He wanted to steal her away from Hernando, privately assure her everything would be all right...

But that was her husband's duty. He turned the knob under her hand and walked out. At Julio's limousine, he turned to find her still watching him. Even from the distance he could see the pain on her face. Finally, Julio emerged and gave her a hug.

With Drew riding shotgun, they were two blocks away before a word was spoken. Drew turned to watch Julio's expression. "What was that all about?"

"What?"

"That conversation you were having with Hernando. When did you two get to be such buddies?"

"Hey, man, if one of my boys got into that kind of trouble, I'd be crazy with worry. Gee's always been like one of my boys. I told him not to worry. I just tried to make him feel good, and..."

"And what?"

"I told him I'd make sure you'll get Gee out of this mess."

"Don't go giving them false hopes. It doesn't look good. Anyway, I don't want to get involved, especially not with them."

"Why not?"

"Why should I? There are other lawyers, and besides, I don't want their money. What happens if I fail and that boy goes to jail for thirty years? I don't want them blaming me."

"We can do this—we can clear him."

"We? Since when did you argue a motion or prepare a brief."

"I've helped you investigate other cases. I'll help you with this one. Forget about Nina and Hernando. Think about the boy."

"That's all I got to say on the subject."

"But—"

"Julio."

"Just think about Gee. That's all I'm asking. Just think about Gee."

❧

Drew had been back in his office for an hour calling colleagues trying to find a capable attorney to enter an appearance on Gee's behalf. It was the eleventh hour. With each request, once he gave the case background, interest waned. Prior commitments were suddenly remembered. Attorneys were less inclined to take on a high-profile criminal case with political ramifications if big money weren't in the offing, it just wasn't worth the trouble.

To hell with it. Theo was his client. If Gee appeared without counsel, the court would appoint a lawyer, and in these high-profile cases, defendants were sometimes appointed a higher caliber of legal representation.

Still, Julio was right, this shouldn't be about Nina and Hernando. Drew had no particular loyalty to Gee, to whom his only connection, a painful one, was Nina. It was Julio who over the years had served as surrogate uncle. Although there was something endearing about the boy, his well-spoken manner, quick mind, and bright smile. The boy's youthful shyness reminded him of his own. Gee's only crime was naïve indiscretion and keeping bad company. As for keeping bad company, Drew was guilty of the same.

Chapter 10

D REW ARRIVED AT the court with his mind made up. Let the court appoint Gee's lawyer. It was the most ethical and safest thing for him to do. As he was about to enter the courtroom, a voice called out from behind. It was Dan Gaines.

"Drew, I need to discuss the matter of Theo Jackson."

"What's up?"

"We've decided to hold off charging him. Based on the information you provided, my superiors want to see how the investigation pans out."

"Is he still in custody?"

"We released him on his own recognizance."

"But you're saying he's still not off the hook."

"No one's off the hook, but for right now, we're only proceeding against Garcia and Jones. Are you representing Garcia?"

"No."

"I'll let you know on Jackson."

Gaines walked into the courtroom, and through the opening door, Drew caught a glimpse of the overflowing gallery waiting for the judge to take the bench. Gee was corralled amongst the other detainees in the jurors' booth. Nina, sitting next to Hernando, was looking anxiously toward the door but Drew didn't think she spotted him. The door closed. Silently wishing Gee well, Drew turned and made his way to the escalator.

He didn't need this case, nor did he want it. A victory would somehow be yet another triumph for Hernando. Too bad, for it was the type of case he found most challenging: an innocent young man up against insurmountable odds. An acquittal was the equivalent to saving a life.

As he stepped off the escalator and walked toward the Indiana Avenue exit, Marie was clearing the security scan. She saw him and came running. "Mr. Smith, what happened? Did I miss it? Is Gee going to be all right? Is it over?"

Momentarily speechless, Drew took her arm and led her to a quiet spot. "I was looking for you," he said. "I need to explain what's happening."

∞

The media was well represented among the courtroom spectators. The news was out: the Farragut robbers were being arraigned. A bulletproof shield protected the courtroom players from the gallery. The detainees were under the watch of young, unarmed, but well-muscled U.S. Marshals in t-shirts who looked ready and itching for hand-to-hand combat.

The door near the bench opened, the bailiff announced "all rise," and a black-robed relatively young black man took the bench. As the gallery reseated, the judge got right into the pro forma proceedings, reviewing the file jacket handed up by the clerk. The more serious cases were handled first.

The clerk announced, "District of Columbia vs. Tyrone Jones and Gustavo Garcia." The two were directed to the defendant's table. Between them stood Tracy Connors, Tyrone's court-appointed counsel.

"Tracy Connors for defendant Tyrone Jones."

Relying on Smith, Gee hadn't requested appointment of counsel. Gaines stood at the prosecutor's table. Gee turned his head toward the gallery, searching about. Tyrone fidgeted nervously, looking more dunce than desperado, hardly tough enough to fight his own shadow.

"Mr. Garcia, have you retained an attorney in this matter?"

Gee looked around again.

"Drew Smith, appearing on behalf of defendant Garcia. I apologize for my tardiness, your honor. I would like to enter a limited appearance on behalf of defendant, Gustavo Garcia."

Heads turned and necks craned to watch Drew make his way forward. The gallery stirred and a rising volume of murmurs and whispers competed with the judge's gavel. Once order was restored, the judge looked down over his glasses.

"Very well, Mr. Smith."

By permitting a limited appearance, the judge allowed Drew to withdraw his representation at any time. Drew was now standing next to Gee, who looked very relieved.

The proceedings were brief. Drew declined a reading of the charges. Not-guilty pleas were entered, and on Gee's behalf Drew motioned for bail. The U.S. Attorney objected vigorously, citing the nature of the crime and the statute requiring a five-day hold. The motion was denied. The strategy was simply to go on record, and the motion a mere formality. Drew requested an expedited preliminary hearing, arguing that an innocent man, a victim in fact, was in custody and wrongly accused. The judge set a preliminary hearing date a week away. Drew would then again motion for bail. With an assuring hand on Gee's shoulder as he was escorted away, Drew promised to visit soon.

With the Farragut case, the main event had ended, and media representatives flooded the aisle vying for statements from the attorneys. Drew pushed his way through, offering no comment, and led the parents down the hall until he found an empty witness room. Marie stood with them. They all looked uneasy. He sensed Nina was still punishing herself but he had no words of comfort to offer.

Hernando scowled at him. "I thought you no represent Gustavo."

"We were hoping you would change your mind," Nina quickly said.

"I haven't changed my mind. I wasn't able to find anyone on such short notice. There's a preliminary hearing in a week. The court will determine whether there's probable cause to hold Gee over for trial."

"Then they let my boy go."

"Possibly." But very unlikely. "At that time, the judge will consider bail."

"Why so long?" Nina asked. "I'm worried about him. Gee's never been in jail."

"It's a capital offense. The law requires a minimum five-day hold. Even after that, it's pretty much up to the judge's discretion whether to release a defendant on bail. Try not to worry, Gee can take care of himself."

"You make them free him?" Hernando in his ill-fitting suit, demanding tone, and awkward language came off as if ordering one of his laborers. Drew was tempted to remind him that he'd once worked for Drew and that relationship would never, ever be reversed. Still, the man was clearly scared and desperate for his son, and his failure to learn decent English after all these years must add humiliation to his plight. Drew struggled to make Gee's welfare his primary concern.

"I have to go now."

"Drew, wait," Nina said. "Can we speak in private?"

Glowering, Hernando escorted Marie into the hall. The door closed behind them.

"I knew you wouldn't let us down."

"I didn't want to let Gee down."

"That's one of your qualities I've missed. Hernando never had your compassion and consideration."

"So you actually missed me?"

"You'll continue to represent Gee?"

"Not if I find someone else. And next time, show your appreciation in front of your husband. I don't want to have to answer for this later. If you have any questions, call me, I'll be in my office after four." He left the room, passing Marie and Hernando in the hallway without a word.

∞

From the courthouse, Drew went to the Chief's office. He couldn't just drop the damn case. Something was driving him in a direction he didn't want to go. It was Marie who persuaded him to return to the courtroom, not Gee's parents. And until he found another lawyer, he was required to provide zealous representation and find out all he could to hand over to the next attorney.

"What's the word on Jinx?" Drew eased down onto the Chief's sofa.

"No new developments. So you're representing Garcia?"

"For the moment. Lowry's wasting resources. You and I both know that boy can't be held accountable for the robbery."

"Perhaps, but I don't want to interfere too much in Lowry's investigation. He's a big boy now, he can be responsible for his own mistakes. If your client is innocent, I trust justice will prevail."

"I've worked in this system long enough to know not to trust, especially when dealing with people like Lowry and Gaines."

"That's the world we live in. But I remember when I walked in Lowry's shoes. I made similar decisions, no one ever called me a racist."

"You wanted to do a good job, you were twice as capable as Lowry, and you had a legal education that gave you some respect for constitutional rights. Lowry has his own ideas about law and order."

"You do a good job with your legal education, your client will be all right. Besides, you need something to keep you out of trouble. How's it going with Dr. Settles?" That smile again.

"Very funny. You didn't tell me she was fine."

"That she is. Something told me that might be a problem."

"Not at all. I'm getting all the problems I need from this dancer at the Palais. She flipped out last night and slashed my tires. I need your help."

"What do you want from me?"

"Run a background check on her."

"Can you get me a Social Security number and date of birth?"

"I'll see. Thanks." Drew headed for the door.

"What made you reconsider representing Garcia?"

"His girlfriend, I couldn't say no to those pretty eyes."

"Women must find you real easy."

"My weakness—to a point."

∞

Hernando and Nina showed up at the office without an appointment. She appeared burdened with worry, and Hernando, still too anxious to sit, stood behind her. They'd come directly from the jail after a brief visit with Gee.

"I don't know if I can tell you any more than I already have," Drew said. "You have to be patient. There's an expression, the wheels of justice grind exceedingly slow."

"Gee wants you to represent him," Nina said. "We want you to continue to represent him. It doesn't look like Theo Jackson is going to be indicted. Doesn't that free you to represent Gee?" The look in her eyes beckoned and after all these years she could still draw him in.

"I don't have time for this type of case. Too many exigent forces are at work here."

"What's that?" Hernando asked.

"The press is watching, the public, and especially the politicians. Crime is a political hot potato in this city. Whoever makes the loudest noise figures he can get the most votes. The public's crying out for blood." Not that he'd ever shied away from controversy, publicity, or a fight.

Nina said, "Drew, we need you."

"You must," Hernando said, "you must—"

"Why?" Drew shot to his feet.

Hernando cut Nina a look. "Because—"

"No, Hernando." Nina shook her head. "Let's go."

"God damn it, if you've got something to say, spit it out. Because what?"

"Because he's your son." The words spilled from Hernando's mouth.

The statement hit like a cannonball to the chest. Drew dropped into his chair. Nina's head was bowed and she didn't meet his gaze.

"Nina?"

She nodded and began to weep. "I'm sorry, Drew. This is all my fault. He's our son. I should have told you long ago."

Rage, frustration, and an inexplicable grief flooded into the vacuum left by the shock. He swiveled his chair to turn his back to them. "Out. I want you two out of my office. Now."

"Drew, I can explain," Hernando said.

"Out!" Drew stood up and pointed a shaking finger at the door. "Out!"

"Oh, Drew!" Nina cried.

"I have to explain," Hernando said. "Listen to me."

Drew stepped around his desk to face Hernando. "What's to explain? You are one devious son of a bitch."

"You listen to me!"

Drew landed a solid blow to the man's chin. Hernando fell back onto his butt and looked up, stunned.

"I've been wanting to do that for twenty years. Get up!"

Drew was about to pounce on him when Nina screamed, "No, Drew!" and pushed him back.

Shirley came through the door as Nina struggled to lift her husband. Hernando gently disentangled himself from her grip and rose to his feet.

"Let's go, Nina. There are other lawyers."

"Get the fuck out my office!"

Shirley ushered them out and closed the door, leaving Drew alone with his anger.

⸎

Within the hour of being told he was a father, Drew was at the jailhouse fulfilling his court promise. He'd planned to apologize and explain why he couldn't continue as Gee's attorney. This new complication changed things, moreover an added reason to refuse going forward as Gee's counsel.

Gee was escorted into the cramped consultation room where Drew sat waiting. He watched the guard remove the handcuffs, and as never before the sight of this young man had a calming affect. Years of suspicion finally put to rest and the fellow known as Gustavo Garcia was indeed his son. The guard left them taking up his post outside the door.

"How are you, Gee?"

"I'm all right. Better when this is all over." The sudden wry twist at the corner of his mouth—Drew's father had that tic, so did he, and now his son. "Mom and Papi were here, and Marie. At first I thought they wouldn't like her because she's black, but it didn't seem to make any difference, they really like her."

"Your parents aren't racists."

"I thought that's why they didn't like you."

"What do you mean, they didn't like me?"

"Tia"—Chevy—"told me that a long time ago you were all good friends, but every time I saw you on the news or mentioned your name they acted like they didn't want to talk about you. What happened, Mr. Drew?"

"Friends grow apart, something you'll understand one day. And please, for once and for all, stop calling me Mr. Drew."

"I know what you mean about friends. Tyrone and Jinx used to be my friends when we were kids. We've grown apart, I wish I could have realized it earlier."

"Speaking of Jinx, let me give you the latest. He's still on the loose and two more people are dead, one of which is his mother."

"Oh, man, he's crazier than I thought."

Gee had transformed from a skinny, bookish little boy into a broad-shouldered, slim, good-looking man with an easy, confident air—much like he himself had done years ago.

"What do you know about Jinx?" Drew asked.

"Not much to know. His mother pretty much abandoned him when she kept getting locked up or was in rehab. Social services put him and his sister Tamika in foster homes. Jinx was always in trouble and ended up in a group home then juvenile detention. His sister was adopted by an older couple."

"Where is she now?"

"Richmond last I heard. Jinx was always talking about moving there to be with her."

Drew pulled out a pen and pad. "Tamika Legere?"

"She took her adopted family's name, Hicks."

Their conversation turned to other subjects. Drew wanted to know everything going on in Gee's life. Maybe some of it would turn out to be relevant to the case, but Drew was curious about it all. Their discussion was an easy exchange covering school, Marie, and Gee's plans for the future. Drew spent more time with Gee than he intended, until other pressing business forced him to end the meeting.

As the guard was about to handcuff Gee, Drew held out his hand. "You're officially my client now. I don't know how it's going to work out with Theo, but you can count on me from here on out."

Gee smiled with relief. Drew resisted the urge to clasp the young man's shoulders in a fatherly embrace and settled instead for the manly handshake.

∞

Another muggy August workday was coming to an end. Drew stood at his office window watching the thinning rush hour traffic down on K Street. Unable to work, he refused all calls. Distracted and haunted by the image of Gustavo Agusto Garcia behind bars, he contemplated Hernando's revelation with mixed emotions. It hadn't fallen out of the blue, but followed a long-held but unspoken suspicion he'd refused to consider. Now he had to face his biggest fear, that a young man with so much potential—his son—was about to be crushed by the criminal justice system. Could he possibly provide adequate representation? Yet there was no one else in whom to entrust this responsibility.

Julio bounced in the door. "Hotter'n hell out there. How's Gee?"

"Still locked up. Preliminary hearing's in a week."

"Poor kid, never been locked up before. Hope he's all right. Have you decided?"

"I had a visit from Nina and Hernando earlier. You knew and you never told me."

"Told you what?" Julio looked baffled.

"Don't play stupid. You betrayed me too."

"What are you talking about?"

"Gee. I'm his father."

"Oh." Julio relaxed down onto the sofa. "I didn't know. I suspected. We suspected. Remember? When the boy was born, we counted off the months. Nina left you in February, the kid was born in November. We thought it was a possibility, but we knew Nina couldn't do that, not tell you. So Hernando had to be the father. At that time, she probably didn't even know."

"She must have told Chevy."

"If she did, Chevy never told me. And Chevy tells me everything. Of course we had our suspicions, but it wasn't my place to ask. I didn't betray you, I've been with you all the way. Over the years I could see he was becoming a lot like you, but it wasn't my place. I guess that's why they finally told you. God makes things happen for a reason. What did you tell them?"

"Kicked them out of my office. After I punched Hernando."

"And you were worried about me?"

"I couldn't help it."

"You got to talk to them. At least let them explain."

"They've had twenty damn years to explain. It was bad enough she left me for another man. I forgave her for that. But then to have my child and keep it from me? To let another man raise my son? That's unforgivable."

"Let her explain. You can forgive her again. You got a good heart."

"I need time to think."

"And I need you to come with me now."

"Where?"

"Chevy wants to talk to you. She told me to bring you there right away. She wouldn't say why, but now I think I know."

He could have resisted the summons, but Julio would have caught hell. Drew secretly believed Chevy was queen and ruler of some pacific island in a past life. It was the only explanation how one little Asian woman could rule over so many males. He went willingly, hoping Chevy with her mother wit could offer words of comfort. Besides, the prospect of sitting amid a family in itself offered solace.

∞

Drew expected to be greeted by Julio's crew. Instead, they found Nina and Chevy out on the patio. When Drew turned to leave, Julio stood in his way.

"Go ahead," Julio said. "You're going to have to face her sooner or later. Do it now. I'll get us a couple of beers."

Drew stepped out onto the patio. Nina looked startled, and Chevy eased the tension with a warm smile. "Drew, come sit down with us."

Moments later, Julio placed a frosty bottle in front of Drew.

"Nina was just telling me what happened," Chevy said. "Maybe we should leave you two alone."

"No, stay," Nina said. "Julio, have a seat. I owe all of you an apology. We used to be inseparable. I changed all that. Now I need you to forgive me, especially you, Drew. I kept this secret too long. It all happened so fast. When I left you, I was sure it was Hernando's baby. I wasn't thinking straight. I found out I was pregnant, and made the second mistake. The first was cheating on you. Instead of telling you first, I told Hernando."

"I could understand if you loved another man," Drew said. "I can't understand why—"

"Please, let me finish. I should have told you, I wanted to tell you, but Hernando persuaded me not to. I was pregnant and all mixed up. We were so convinced the baby was his. He said we should get married right away. That's why I left you the way I did. My father really liked Hernando, which made it a little easier. I thought everything would be all right. I know I hurt you, but I thought it was best. I will always love you, no matter what you think of me. I'm sorry Drew."

"How do you know he's mine? I haven't submitted to any DNA test."

"Every time I look at him I see you."

"That doesn't—"

"I know because Hernando, Candice and me, we all have O positive blood. Gee's A positive. It's impossible for two O's to produce an A. What's your blood type?"

"I'm not sure."

"It's the same as G's. It's impossible for Hernando to be Gee's father. Even though that hasn't stopped him. He promised—no matter what—to love our son as his own. He's never strayed from that promise."

Drew sat back in his chair. The table was silent.

"Are you going to tell Gee?" Julio asked.

"I don't know. I don't want any more secrets, but I'm afraid he won't understand. He may never forgive me. Things will never be the same. Drew, do you want me to tell him?"

"Don't put that decision on me. I was never privy to the decision to keep it from anyone."

"Drew, please, I beg you to understand. Don't be bitter. I beg you, don't let your feelings toward Hernando keep you from helping Gee."

"Suddenly he's my son, and I'm supposed to save his life. Up until now you decided I wasn't a necessary part of his life. Do you really expect me to forget the past and rise to the occasion?"

There was a long silence.

"Are you going to tell him?" Julio asked again.

"Not now," she said. "Gee may never understand, either way I could lose him. Drew, I pray you'll represent him."

Drew turned to Julio and Chevy. "Can we have a moment alone?"

"Take all the time you need," Chevy said. The two disappeared into the house.

Drew waited to hear the click of patio's sliding glass door close behind Julio and Chevy. "Let me tell you why I'm so damn mad. Not only did I lose you, I now find out I lost my only son."

"Oh Drew, I'm so sorry. I never meant to hurt you. Hate me if you want, but don't take it out on Gee."

"Hate you? Nina, I still love you. I never stopped loving you."

Nina looked stunned.

Drew took her hand. "Leave Hernando, come live with me. I'll take care of you, Candice and Gee. Tell Gee he's my son."

"Oh Drew, do you know what you're asking? That's crazy we can't just pick up again--"

"We had a life together once. We can again. As a family."

"Don't do this to me." She began to weep.

Drew stood and left her alone with her tears.

∞

Drew took the long way home, driving along Georgia Avenue, past Walter Reed Army Medical Center, and onto Arkansas Avenue. At the 14th Street intersection, a group of young bruthas were hanging out, smoking marijuana. The young urban male— his son Gustavo Garcia was included in their number, and so was the murderous Jeffrey Legere, still terrorizing the streets. What kind of sociopath would off his own mother? What was Gee capable of, if push came to shove?

He parked his Mercedes with its new tires in the garage. When he entered the kitchen from the garage, he heard music coming from upstairs. He grabbed a butcher knife from the kitchen drawer and cautiously made his way up the stairs. Too bad his revolver was locked away.

At the threshold of his bedroom, fear turned to anger. Angel lounged on the bed in her red mesh teddy thumbing through a magazine and sipping champagne.

"Hey, baby, I've been waiting for you." She ignored his scowl and raised a champagne flute. "Have some champagne. It's time we made up. No fighting tonight. Just sweet you-know-what."

"How did you get in here?" He laid his briefcase on the bureau with the knife underneath.

"Is that anyway to greet your fiancée?"

"How did you get in here?"

"You're late. Were you out with her again tonight?"

"Bitch, I asked you how you got in here. I'm not going to ask you again. I'm calling the police."

She hesitated. "The other day when you let me sleep over—"

"You put the key back under the flowerpot, I have it. So you had another made."

"I was planning to tell you."

"Uh-uh, you know I don't want you to have a key. And after what you did last night, I don't want you around here."

"Can we talk?" Angel pulled herself up off the bed with a coquettish smirk.

"Hell, no. Get your ass outta here. Now!" He grabbed the clutch purse from the armchair where her clothes were draped.

"Why are you like this?" She wrapped her arms around his neck. "Still mad about last night? I was angry, please understand. You do that to me. All I want is to love you."

"I don't want anything to do with you." He pushed her away. "The drugs make you crazy. Look at you, like you just beamed up to Mars. Get some help. Give up the cocaine. But first get out of here."

"That has nothing to do with you and me."

"It has everything do with me and who I choose to be with. You waltz in here and make yourself comfortable like nothing happened. You really are crazy. You slashed my tires. You done lost your mind."

"I'm sorry. I'll pay for it."

"Just get the hell out of here." He snapped open her purse and riffled through it.

"What are you doing?" she screamed.

"Getting my key."

She threw herself at him and tried to grab her purse. He pushed her back with such force she landed on the bed.

"Why are you doing this?" Tears flowed, and she began to sob. "All I want to do is love you."

"You're crazy." He turned his back and dug into the purse. He found the key, but kept looking until he also spotted her driver's license. He stuffed both into his pocket, then faced her again and threw the purse onto the bed, followed by her clothes.. "Get dressed and get out of here. Now."

She pulled herself together, gathered her clothes, and started for the bathroom.

Drew stepped into her path. "Change out here where I can keep an eye on you."

Angry eyes glared as she stood with pursed lips and began to dress.

"I'll call a cab for you."

"Don't bother."

He followed her down the steps to the door and locked it behind her. He returned to the bedroom and dropped the key and her license in the nightstand drawer.

A shattering of glass startled him. He raced downstairs and found a gaping hole in the living room picture window and glass shards everywhere. A rock sat in the middle of the floor. He looked out the door, but she was nowhere in sight. Then he called the police.

Twenty minutes later two officers arrived. He signed a complaint for property damage, listing the broken windows and slashed tires, identifying Angel, and giving her home and work addresses. They gave him a police report number and told him to file a formal complaint at the police precinct.

Chapter 11

I T WAS TWO hours before the emergency glass repairman arrived to install a new picture window. Drew stopped at the police precinct on his way to work and filed a formal complaint against Angel. Shirley greeted him with a cautioning eye directed to the waiting area. In his carpenter's overalls, Hernando sat wringing his baseball cap.

"Drew." He stood up.

"I told him he needed an appointment," Shirley said. "He insisted on waiting."

"Please, I need to talk to you." He looked distressed and desperate.

"It's all right, Shirley. Come on in, Hernando."

Drew closed the door and pointed Hernando to a chair in front of his desk, not bothering to hide his wary resentment. "Why are you here?"

"You heard Nina's side, now I want you to hear me. After all these years, I owe you a reason."

"You have five minutes. I have work to do."

"We should have talked a long time ago. But I wanted nothing to do with you. I was jealous, afraid, you had so many blessings, and I had none until Nina. For the past days I looked in my heart and know I am a very selfish man. Today I have many blessings, more than a man like me should have. I pray God and you will forgive me. I love Nina with all my heart, and I love the two children, Gustavo as much as Candice."

Drew stood, walked over to the window, and with his back to Hernando, stared down on the street.

"We knew right after Gustavo was born, you were his true father. I said not to tell you. I was afraid she go back to you. You had so much more—more money, big house, security for a woman. I told her that you would never know. That it was our secret. But I was wrong. Some secrets are bad. A boy should know his true father. I so sorry. Please, so sorry."

Drew didn't know what to say and so avoided the sight of the man.

"I love my family, I lay down my life for Gustavo. Blame me, but don't blame Gustavo." The big pitiful man was crying.

Drew had heard enough. He'd already decided to represent Gee and his decision not to tell Hernando had come from spite. The man had not suffered enough. But the groveling was beginning to annoy him.

"I accept your apology. I've decided to be Gee's lawyer. Let's not talk about the past any longer. I'll meet with you and Nina sometime this week to go over our strategy." Drew turned to face the weeping man.

"Thank you," Hernando whispered. He pulled out his handkerchief and dried his eyes and blew his nose. On the way to the door, the misty eyed carpenter suddenly turned and grabbed Drew in a bear hug.

"Okay, okay," Drew said. "Let's not get carried away."

"One more thing."

"What's that?"

"This talk of divorce. I don't want a divorce, I want my Nina back. When this is over, she plans to go through with it. She still has feelings for you."

"Hernando, if I could, I would destroy your marriage. But you seem to be doing that all by yourself."

"If she leaves me, I'll never get her back. Her love means so much to me. Please don't take that away from me."

Drew blew out a breath. He had no words for Hernando, and without giving any assurances, watched the man leave.

Drew's forgiveness hadn't washed away the residue of bitterness and resentment that festered at the bottom of his heart. At least the tension between the two men had eased. He had no choice but to represent his son, and to do no harm would be one standard of his representation. Suddenly, he asked the powers that be to order his steps. Then he picked up the phone and dialed.

"Zoë, Drew Smith here."

"Drew, how are you?"

"I'm not sure right about now."

"What's wrong?"

"I got some news that rocked my world off its axis. I need to talk to you."

"You haven't told me what this is about."

"It's not the kind of thing I can express over the phone."

"I'm sorry, my calendar is full today."

"How about dinner? You do eat dinner don't you? I understand your boundary restrictions, but this can only be one of those helpful boundary situations. Please. I need to see you."

"No dinner. I'll see you at five in my office. I have to go now, a patient's waiting." She hung up.

Drew grimaced. Suddenly the father of a grown man, he didn't know how to deal with it.

❦

Tracy Connors, Tyrone's lawyer, was a well-respected public defender and a good attorney known for her hard-nosed lawyering. Together they sat in the consultation room waiting for Tyrone Jones to be delivered.

"Thanks for allowing me to talk to your client," Drew said.

"Anything that'll help me. He's hopelessly deluded."

"How does he plan to plead?"

"Not guilty. I told him the gun was linked to the Farragut. He claims he took it off the prostitute who tried to rob him. He claims the killing was self-defense. I told him that sounded like a lie."

"My client claims Jones and a third party kidnapped him and forced him at gunpoint to drive them to the Farragut. He didn't go inside."

"You believe him?"

"You know as well as I do, what I believe isn't important. I've known the boy all of his life. I'd like to think he's telling me the truth."

"The prosecutor seems pretty sure with his evidence. There's really no point in taking Jones to trial."

"I agree. Maybe your client can give a sworn statement exonerating my client."

"That's tantamount to a confession. I don't see that happening."

"They were once good friends. Maybe Jones has a conscience."

"He doesn't even have a brain, besides the prosecutors may not move on this until Legere's in custody. You're asking for bail?"

"I'll motion again at the preliminary."

"Good luck with that."

Tyrone was escorted into the conference room and took a seat. "What he doing here? Ain't he Gee's lawyer?"

"Since you and Garcia are codefendants, we want to coordinate our defense strategy. I believe it would be in your interest to speak with Mr. Smith and to cooperate."

"Got any cigarettes?"

"No," she said.

Drew reached into his valise and tossed a pack of Newports across the table.

"Dey ain't open."

"The pack is for you."

"Thanks."

"Mr. Smith would like to ask you some questions. You don't have to answer if you don't want."

"A'ight. What you wanna know?"

"What happened at the Farragut that Sunday morning?"

"Don't know nothin' 'bout dat."

Tracy smiled at Drew.

"The gun they found on you was used to shoot Naomi Sims," he said.

"Who dat?"

"The cook at the Farragut, the one you shot."

"I ain't shoot nobody."

"They say you shot Marc Sanchez, killed him in cold blood."

"Freak had it coming."

"And Naomi, what did she ever do to you?"

"Don't know no Naomi."

"You shot her once, but you couldn't kill her. So Jinx made you step aside and finished them all."

Tyrone's eyes widened with fear. Drew had struck a nerve. His guess based on the ballistic report was right on point.

"Why should you spend the rest of your life in jail? You didn't kill them. Jinx did."

"What are you trying to do?"

"Now is the time to help Gee and to help yourself."

"What Gee saying?"

"He says that you and Jinx showed up at his door Sunday morning and with a gun to his head forced him to drive to the Farragut. He tried to fight you, and feared for his life. He had no choice but to go along."

"He lyin'."

"He said you pulled the gun on him."

"Jinx pulled the gun on him. I didn't."

Tracy held up a cautionary hand. "Tyrone."

"Nah, Gee lyin'—"

"I advise you not to say anything more."

"But he lyin'. He think he can pin it on me and Jinx. Well he's wrong. He was in on it. He picked us up in fact, me and Jinx, at Jinx's house. He was there when we planned the job the day before. Now what you got to say 'bout dat?"

"What was his share of the take?" Drew asked.

"What?"

"What was his share? How much did he get?"

Tyrone hesitated. "I don't know."

"Did he get a third? Or did you and Jinx divide it in half?"

"I don't know."

"Must have been a lot of money for you."

Tyrone relaxed back in his chair. "I ain't saying no more. My lawyer says I ain't got to talk to you no more." He looked to Tracy for backup, but she'd already thrown in the towel.

She looked at him and rolled her eyes. "It's a little late for you to shut up now."

"So it's your story that Gee was in on it as much as you and Jinx?" Drew asked.

"Right." Tyrone cocked his head, defiant in his answer,

"And yet he still talks," Tracy said.

"You're mad at Gee. You want him to go down too. He's not your friend anymore. So this is your payback."

"I ain't saying no more. I wanna go. Can I go now?"

"Sure, Tyrone. But if you change your mind, the judge will go easier on you if you enter a guilty plea. I'm sure Ms. Connors has told you that. If you change your mind and want to help Gee, let her know. We'll talk again."

"You want your cigarettes back?"

"You keep them."

Tracy stood and knocked on the door. The guard reentered, handcuffed Tyrone, and led him away.

Tracy waited for the door to close. "Well? You think he's telling the truth about Garcia's involvement?"

"Do you think he took that gun off Marc Sanchez? Too many holes in his story."

"Let's hope he changes his plea before we go to trial. I don't have a defense for him."

"Too bad stupidity isn't a defense."

"Insanity is, but unfortunately Jones is only crazy. Getting bail for Garcia won't be easy. Politics—the mayor, City Council, and Congress are all watching for just one misstep. No one wants to be seen as soft on crime and get pilloried by the press."

Drew sighed and closed his valise. "Tell me about it."

"I'm not one for trying the case in the press, but your client could use some favorable media coverage. It might help. There's no gag order—yet."

A momentary silence passed between them.

"There's something Jones said that bothers me," Drew said.

"What's that?"

"I'm wondering what really went down at that Saturday meeting. Did Garcia pick them up? Or did they pick him up?"

"Who do you believe?"

"I better act like I believe my client."

∞

"Drew Smith, this better be good. Two sessions in one week, I hope it's an emergency." Zoë eased down in her chair.

"Whether it's good, I'll let you be the judge. I'm working on the Farragut case. My client is a young man—"

"I read about it in the morning paper. Gustavo Garcia."

"Except he should be called Gustavo Smith."

"What are you saying?"

"I just found out he's my son."

Zoë's jaw dropped. "Oh, my. Are you sure?" She smiled then caught herself. "This *is* good. I mean—"

"I know what you mean."

"I'm sorry, I don't mean to be flippant. It must be a shock. Tell me how this came to be."

Drew made a long story short. He confessed how difficult it was for him to come to terms with this revelation, and how it weighed on the representation he felt forced to undertake.

"As a therapist, I've been told many amazing histories, and yet each time I hear stories like yours I'm still surprised. Do you plan to accept this man as your son? And he is a man, so I suspect there'll be some adjustment problems."

"If given the chance, I'd welcome him with open arms. But that's a big if. The most painful thing, and it hurts—" For the first time since being delivered the news, Drew found himself getting choked up. His voice quivered as he tried to regain control. "All the lost opportunities to watch him grow, the soccer games, the birthdays, graduations and all those little milestones. I wasn't there." Drew stopped talking. Zoë waited while he withdrew to his innermost core. The moment passed. "I'm sorry," he said.

"I understand. Do you still have feelings for Nina?"

"And that's another thing. She asked me to handle her divorce."

"Do you see yourself going back to her?"

"I want her back."

"Does she know?"

"I told her."

Now Zoë withdrew for a moment before speaking.

"Obviously you two need to work that out. Though I must tell you, it's usually very hard for two people to recapture what made them fall in love in the first place. As far as your son is concerned, I'm sure you can make up for lost time. Does she plan to tell him?"

"I'm not sure what she'll do. I can't speculate on what she's capable of." He snorted a bitter laugh. "I found that out the hard way years ago. As if Gee doesn't already have enough to cope with. She's afraid he'll turn on her and her husband. Right now he's struggling with his own future. I don't think he should get hit with being told his parents have been lying to him all his life. At least not until this case is over."

"Children are often more resilient and accepting of life's changes than adults. Granted you're both grown men, it's very important that you put aside your bitterness. I'm not sure how to counsel you about dealing with it. The two of you may need counseling together. But you'll cross that bridge when you get to it."

"I always liked the kid and watching him grow. He was always hanging out with Julio's boys, they're like my nephews."

"And how was he to you?"

"I kept him at a distance. I wish I hadn't."

"It's not too late to change all that. I don't mean to change the subject, but have you had any dreams lately?"

"That's another reason I wanted to talk to you. This time she had a face."

"Who was she?"

"Angel."

"But you were having the dream before you met Angel, right? Over twenty years if I'm not mistaken? They couldn't have all been about Angel. So Angel is symbolic, your subconscious put a face on the problem or fear."

"If you say so, but—"

"What kind of women would you say you dated in the past?"

"What do you mean?"

"I mean were they all strippers?"

"Exotic dancers." Her mouth twitched into a smile for a split second. "I wouldn't say all," he said, "but they were mostly party girls. I've done a lot of dating."

"Let me put it this way. Did you ever have these dreams while sleeping with some of these women?"

"I've disturbed more than one bedmate by bolting up from a deep sleep in a cold sweat."

"Are you drawn to Latin women?"

"I confess I am. Julio says I got the Señorita Sickness."

"So you prefer them?"

"I love women, all women. It's just that I have a special thing for the señoritas. What's wrong with that?"

"Who says there's anything wrong with it? Some brothers like women with big butts, or big breasts. Some sisters prefer the darkest brothers, while others only look at the light-skinned ones. And you have the Senorita Sickness. You seem to feel guilty over your preference."

She was right. He was guilty, but it wasn't the preference so much as what he preferred to do with them. He couldn't tell her about that. She'd recoil in disgust. Some things weren't meant to be told.

"You pay them money to satisfy your desires. Doesn't that debase them?"

Drew shook his head. "I rent them."

She almost looked offended. "Could it be that your debasement exacts revenge for the one that got away, the woman who would never give her heart to you in marriage?" She paused, apparently reluctant to push on, and Drew didn't want to go there either.

"There's something you're not telling me."

Stone-faced, Drew didn't respond. Now she was reading his mind? Of course she was, that's why he was there.

"You're only as sick as your secret," she said.

Well, she wouldn't hear it from him.

"I have a theory," she said. "Were you ever in a serious relationship with any of these women?" Drew hesitated. "Or were you using them all for sex?"

"Why couldn't they have been using me for sex?"

"They may well have been, but I'm talking about your intentions, your motives. This is the probable scenario: After a while they get comfortable and even a little demanding, wanting more of your time. The relationship turns rocky, and you begin your withdrawal. Sometimes suddenly, others slowly, whichever causes the least conflict."

"Okay, okay, I've heard enough. You're good, you know that?"

"I know."

"There's something else. I broke it off with Angel."

"Because of the dream?"

"Because she's crazy, and the dream was a warning. Now she's stalking me, slashed my tires and threw a brick through my picture window."

Zoë managed to suppress a laugh but not a smirk. "I'm sorry," she said, "it really isn't funny, and it may be dangerous."

"That's what I'm afraid of. So what do I do?"

"That's a legal question. The best I can offer is to get her into therapy. But all this confirms my theory. The dream is a warning, this type of woman or relationship isn't good for you. I would venture to say that once you become involved in a more stable long-term relationship with a woman you care about, that dream will stop."

"You're saying find a good woman, settle down."

"What do you think?"

"I wish it were that easy."

"Apparently you and Nina were compatible. What drew her to Hernando?"

"Do we have to talk about him?"

"Not if you don't want to. What is it about him you don't like?"

"He betrayed me by romancing my fiancée behind my back. This was after I already liked him, trusted him. He was probably what she always wanted. Her father approved of him and not me. I'm not Latino."

"But he's still a likeable guy?"

"He's not my problem, Angel is."

"What do you know about her background?"

"Not much. She came here a few months ago from New York. She doesn't talk much about her life there."

"What brought her here?"

"I don't know. I'm looking into her background now."

"You're the lawyer, but as a psychiatrist I can tell you one thing. Delusional stalkers almost always come from an emotionally barren or severely abusive background. They grow up with a very poor sense of their own identities. This, coupled with a predisposition toward psychosis, leads them to strive for satisfaction through another, yearning to merge with someone who is almost always perceived to be of a higher status—doctors, lawyers, teachers, or celebrities."

"Makes sense, but so what? Wait—you mean she's probably done this before?"

"Very possibly. But I want to get back to where we started, the Garcia matter. You seem anxious and angry—on edge. How's he reacting to being arrested."

"He's a little stoic. He believes in me. I'm not sure I can help him." Drew retreated into his thoughts under Zoë's watchful gaze. "Sometimes I think I chose the wrong profession. At least if I were a medical doctor I could see the positive results of my work, an occasional patient healed. Being a black lawyer in a racist criminal justice system, I feel like I'm just spinning my wheels while the system is spinning that revolving door. Blacks just want a level playing field. But all too often we're slapped in the face. All they want to do is lock up the brothers. That's the last thing Gee needs. He has so much potential. I'm afraid he may be lost—that I'll fail him, yes, but even worse, that he'll be lost."

Zoë said nothing and waited for Drew to continue.

"If you've got money, you can get a good criminal lawyer. If O.J. had been a poor black man, he'd still be locked up. Robert Blake got out on bail. O.J. stayed locked up. For O.J., it was a metamorphosis. He was the chosen black man. And yet whites were so shocked when the system said, "Beyond a reasonable doubt." Blacks reveled when Johnnie Cochran beat the system. Nobody was cheering for O.J., he was irrelevant. L.A. has been notorious in dealing with black folk, but is D.C. any better?" Drew fell silent again.

"You seem very hard on yourself," Zoë said, her voice soft and soothing. "Others might think you've done more than your share of healing, that you underestimate the value of your work."

"When you see the waste of so many black men, broken families, lousy schools, lack of opportunity, when I think about all those young brothers behind bars—why can't we break the cycle?"

"So you feel inadequate in your work."

"Yes."

"But you've had so many successes. The press is full of them."

"That's different."

"How so, you have a successful practice? Why do you feel inadequate?"

"Right now, I find your counsel very frustrating."

"That's good. It means we're breaking ground. But our time's up, let's continue with our regularly scheduled Wednesday session. Okay? And next time I want to take up your feelings of inadequacy."

"Okay, but I'm not feeling any better about myself. I have a headache and I'm hungry. You sure you don't want to grab some dinner?"

"You don't give up, do you?" There was no hint of humor in her response.

"Not easily."

"No means no. Have you ever heard that from a woman?"

"Not often. But it's good you're annoyed, it means we're breaking ground." Still no smile. Drew stood up to leave. "Look, I just wanted to continue this discussion in a more relaxed environment. I thought we were onto something and I hate leaving things loose-ended like this."

"I'm sorry, Drew, I didn't mean to be curt. Your treatment can't be completed over dinner or in a few quick sessions. Meanwhile, we need to keep this relationship on a professional rather than social level."

"Next week, then."

❦

Drew returned home that evening with a persistent headache. He popped three aspirins and sat down with his pad at the desk. If Jinx and Tyrone had broached the idea of the robbery, as Tyrone claimed, then Gee wouldn't have been so surprised when they showed up that Sunday morning. But if—

The phone rang. The caller didn't give him a chance to speak and he recognized her unmistakable voice.

"Drew."

"What do you want, Angel? I asked you not to call me anymore."

"I'm calling because I think I can help you. I read in the paper this morning you're representing Garcia."

"And just how can you help?"

"Maybe I know where Jinx is."

"Where is he?" Drew heard a man's voice calling her.

"Can't talk now, call you back."

"Wait a minute, Angel—"

The line went dead. He started to dial her right back, but stopped to think. Did Angel really know where to find Jinx? And she called him by his nickname, Jinx, not Jeffrey Legere, as the press referred to him. She might actually know something. And what did he know about Angel? Not enough. He went to the bedroom to get her ID.

Drew had another thought. If Jinx was out of the area, he'd want to know what was going on, and he could no longer call Tyrone—or for that matter, his mother. Might Jinx try to contact Gee? Drew had Gee's cell phone.

Chapter 12

A FTER A GOOD NIGHT'S sleep, finally, Drew arrived at his office anxious to work. From his desk drawer he pulled out Gee's cell phone that lay alongside his keys and wallet. He had intended to turn them over to Nina, but with all the activity and high anxiety, he somehow forgot. He checked the list of missed calls against the number he'd jotted down from the receipt in the Legere house, and bingo, Jinx's cell phone number appeared twice. Drew pressed callback and let it ring. No one answered. Damn.

He slipped the phone back into his desk drawer, debated whether to share the info with the Chief, and decided to wait until he tried again later.

He had less than a week to prepare for Gee's preliminary hearing. This was his priority among a half-dozen other cases he had to juggle. Thank God there were no trials on his calendar.

The city had recently suffered a wave of high-profile crimes. Among them, the robbing and killing of a young white man returning from a movie in Georgetown with his girlfriend, a spree of nighttime robberies on the national mall, and the fatal street robbery of a *New York Times* correspondent. Pressure was on the mayor and City Council to curtail crime, and they reacted by enacting an emergency crime bill that invoked a teen curfew, suspended certain statutory bail requirements, and expanded existing restrictions. How this might affect Gee's case? As Drew logged onto the computer to start his research, Shirley came over the intercom to announce that Angel was on the line.

"I'll get rid of her," Shirley said. "Just give me the go-ahead."

"I'll take it."

Shirley let out a deep sigh and put Angel through.

"Good morning, Drew. Sleep well without me?"

"Like a baby. What do want?"

"The question is, what do you want?"

"I want you to stop calling me."

"What about Jinx? Do you want him? I hear there's a reward."

"So why are you calling me? Call the police."

"Nobody can know. I'm not a snitch."

Drew hesitated a moment. "Do you really know where he is?"

"I do."

"Where is he? And you better not be lying."

"I'll tell you if you help me get the reward. Come to the Palais around five, before it gets busy."

"Not a good idea."

"You want Jinx or not?" She hung up the phone.

Was she telling the truth, or just running another scam to bait him back into her crazy web? Drew fished her ID out his briefcase and called the Chief.

"Chief, anything on Legere?"

"Nothing. I'm afraid he may have left the area."

"I got a call this morning, someone inquiring about the reward."

"Oh?" Drew pictured him rising up in his chair. "Who?"

"I'm not at liberty to say, but suppose that person provides you, through me, with information leading to the arrest and prosecution of Jeffrey Legere. Can they collect the reward?"

"Sure, but there's an easier way."

"You mean the Tip Line."

"Right."

The Tip Line was anonymous and manned twenty-four hours. Once the tip is given, a code number is assigned. The informant files a claim, and after a successful arrest and prosecution, an anonymous cash drop is made—no questions asked.

"So who is this informant and where is Legere?"

"I don't know yet. I'll suggest they call the Tip Line. I'm not sure how reliable this person is."

"Smith, you make sure we get that tip, reliable or not. So far we have nothing."

"I'm with you, Chief. Another thing, remember my stalker?"

"Your crazy stripper pal."

"Exotic—look, I have her Social Security and date of birth."

The Chief took down the numbers and promised to get back to him before the end of the day.

"It's possible she's done this kind of thing before," Drew said. "That's what we need to dig up."

As Drew hung up, Shirley walked in and closed the door behind her. "Why do they keep showing up without appointments? Don't they know you're busy?"

"Who?

"Mrs. Garcia. I know you. There's something going on between you and that boy's mother. Out with it."

"Shirley, we'll talk. In the meantime, you're my confidential secretary. Remember that."

"Then you need to start confiding."

"You don't need to know everything, but I'm sure you will, eventually."

"Should I send her in? Order her flowers?"

"Just send her in." Drew took Gee's belongings from his top drawer, then on second thought, put them back. Nina walked in and Drew directed her to the sofa.

"Drew, I know you're busy, and I don't want to take up too much of your time. Hernando called me and told you were going to represent Gee. I wanted to thank you in person."

"He called you? I thought this thing with Gee would have brought you two back together." He eased down beside her. "You know Hernando loves you more than life itself. You've given him twenty years, why leave him now?"

"I have my reasons. Living with that man has grown dull, monotonous, and routine. While he's out and about, I'm caring for his children, working and managing his home. The love is gone. I'm tired of it all."

"Try counseling before you go further with the divorce. I'll set it up, a sit-down between you two. At least discuss it."

"My mind is made up."

"Why, after twenty years?"

"Twenty years is enough."

Drew took a deep breath and let it out. "Why did you leave me, Nina?"

She froze for a moment, then picked up her purse. "I shouldn't have come. It was a mistake."

"Just tell me why."

She stood and walked to the window. "Your love was suffocating. It scared me. You had it all figured out. You planned the rest of my life—till death do us part—the house, where we would live, the number of children. I'd be a stay-at-home mom. You never once ask what I wanted."

"That's not true. I would have given you anything you wanted. You could have said you didn't want to marry me..." He steeled himself for the reply he suddenly realized would come.

"I did say it. For five years. You wouldn't accept it. Give me what I wanted? You never even asked what I wanted. Like Hernando, you would have given me what you thought I needed. You were in control. Your career was taking off and everything was falling into place. I wasn't your equal—an educated professional. I felt limited, almost lost in your world. It was your life. I would have been going along for the ride."

"That's your same complaint now, with Hernando. What did he have that I didn't?"

"That was a mistake. Hernando was just a convenient alternative. His kind's a dime a dozen, a macho pretty-boy. I probably would have broken it off with you anyway. The pregnancy just complicated things."

"Maybe we could try again. People do it all the time."

"Drew, don't. If you knew how often I've thought of you, longed to be with you. Things are more complicated now. I need time—"

"What about our son?"

"Our son is a grown man. I want a divorce, Drew, not another husband. I want my freedom, to make my own decisions and not have them made for me."

"I want you back—as my wife, not as your lover."

"Haven't I hurt you enough?"

"So you still love him. You still love Hernando."

The two sat in silence. It was Drew's way of demanding a response and Nina's way of refusing.

"I'll arrange a meeting for you two to discuss counseling," Drew finally said. "If that doesn't work, we'll start divorce proceedings."

Nina picked up her purse and walked out.

Drew felt the same loss as twenty years ago, but now there was something different. For some reason, the pain was gone.

He dismissed her from his thoughts, pulled Gee's phone out, and hit redial. The low-battery alarm sounded as the call connected.

"Yo, Gee, what up?"

"What's up with you, Jinx?"

After a moment, "This ain't Gee. Who dis?"

"Drew Smith."

"What you want? Why you calling me?"

"We need to talk."

"What about?"

"Gee. You don't want to take him down with you?"

"I don't care about Gee, or anybody else."

"Not even your mother?"

Jinx was silent.

"Why don't we get together? I can arrange for you to turn yourself in. I'll make sure you get a fair shake. If you keep going like this, you won't live long."

"I don't give a fuck."

"Where are you, Jinx?"

Jinx ended the call.

∞

Staring out the window at the K Street rush-hour traffic below, Drew watched pedestrians scurrying home to evening routines. Jeffery Legere seemed to have disappeared. No one knew where he was, or even if he was still in the area. The police were stymied and the investigation had come to a halt. Nobody knew the inner workings of Jeffrey Legere's mind or his ethics of murder and money. Probably not even Legere himself could sort it all out. His twenty years of life offered a limited view of the world. Surrounded by wealth, opportunity, security, and comforts which the more fortunate took for granted, but lacking the skills and wherewithal to honestly acquire them, maybe Jinx thought he could have it all with nothing but guts and a gun.

Drew longed to be homeward bound, like the commuters below, to some imagined wife and kids. Zoë came to mind. What had set off her hostility? Was she P-M-S-ing? Or was he really a male chauvinist pig? The door swung open, jolting him out of his reverie.

"Yo."

"What's up, Julio?"

"Nada. Anything new on the Farragut case?"

"Talked to Tyrone Jones today. He won't be any help. Also talked to Jinx."

"Say what?"

"He tried to contact Gee on his cell phone. I called back."

"Where is he?"

"I don't know, but someone might be able to help us. You and I are meeting with a tipster in an hour. By the way, I had the house locks changed." He handed Julio the spare key. "That's the front door. Get rid of the old one, and I changed the security code."

"DREW was easy to remember."

"The new one is easier. W-E-R-D, Drew backwards."

"Word up, I can remember that."

"And remember, if the security company can't reach me, they'll call you. You're my backup."

"I know, I know. Hey, your stripper friend, she been acting up anymore?"

"She's an exotic dancer, who also happens to be our tipster."

"Hold up, the crazy ho? How she fit in?"

"That's what she's going to tell us."

∞∞∞

It was early, and unlike late-night business, the strip club was nearly empty. Perched on barstools, Julio and Drew sat back to back. Julio was captivated by a particular busty sistah strutting her stuff and jiggling her healthy bottom, while Drew focused on the staircase, waiting for Angel to appear. Moments later she came down the staircase, and despite her recent behavior, she still exited him.

He nudged Julio. "Here she comes."

"Who?" Julio asked with eyes still glued on the dancer.

"Angel. Pay attention. You're a witness now."

"What?" Julio swung around on the barstool to catch Angel making her way toward them. "Oh, mami, that's her?"

"Now you see why."

"I see, I see. But she don't look so crazy." Julio spoke under his breath, smiling as she came nearer.

"What does crazy look like?" Drew slid down off the barstool.

"Hey, baby." Angel took his hand. "I miss you."

Drew pulled his hand back. "Do we need to talk in private?"

"We can move to that booth over there." Julio followed the two to a corner table. She looked him over with suspicion. "Who's your friend?"

"Julio, meet Angel."

"Hola." Julio beamed a bright smile.

"Why is he here?"

"I need a witness. It's in your best interest if you want that reward."

She looked back at Julio then slowly turned her gaze to Drew. "I can trust you two?"

"Where is Jinx?"

"He left town."

"How do you know that?"

"Don't worry about it. Just make sure he's arrested and prosecuted."

"Only thing you've told me is he's out of town. That's not much to go on."

"He's at his sister's for a couple of days."

"Again, how do you know this?"

"Let's just say I overheard a telephone conversation. Now how do I collect the reward?"

"As soon we walk out that door, you go call the Tip Line. Tell them the same thing you just told me."

"Is that it?"

"That's it. It's anonymous. You'll get a claim number." Drew stood. "Let's go, Julio."

Drew raced back to the car, with Julio on his heels. "Where we going?"

"Back to my office to get my gun, and then to Richmond. Where's yours?"

"Under the seat. Where in Richmond?"

"You have Wi-Fi on that notebook?" Drew pulled the dashboard computer to face his way. "How do I log on?"

Unleashing the limo's array of high-tech equipment, Drew quickly checked the online white pages and found a Tamika Hicks residing in Richmond, Virginia, then programmed the address into the GPS navigational system. Ninety minutes later, as the sun was going down, they pulled up in front of a small bungalow on the south side of Richmond near Virginia Union University.

Julio confirmed the address. "What do we do now?"

"Knock on the door."

"If he's there, do we shoot him?"

"Not unless you have to. I need him alive. Just keep your defenses up. Let him draw down first. Okay?"

Julio pulled his revolver from under the seat and snapped a clip into place.

The two walked to the front door sizing up the house, looking for signs of life, and searching for possible escape routes. When Drew knocked, Julio stepped aside, out of view, his hand ready on his shoulder holster. Drew knocked again.

An attractive woman resembling a young Jean Legere but without the attitude appeared in the doorway.

"Tamika Hicks?" Drew asked.

"Yes. Who are you?"

"My name is Drew Smith, I'm an attorney."

"I've heard of you. It's my brother, Jinx, isn't it? What did he do?"

"Have you seen him?"

"Yes, but what—"

"Is he here now?"

"No, but why—"

"May we come in?"

"What is this all about?" She stepped aside to let them in.

Her puzzlement seemed genuine and Drew decided she was telling the truth. He had apparently left soon after the phone conversation with Drew.

"Did he say where he was going, what he planned to do?"

She sighed. "He was sure of one thing, he needed to go away, start a new life."

"Did he say where?"

"Atlanta."

"Why Atlanta? Do you have family there?"

"Not that I know of."

"Friends?"

"My brother doesn't have many friends. What's he done?"

"Are you familiar with the Farragut Tavern?""

"I grew up in D.C. I read about the recent...oh, no. My brother was involved in that?"

"We think so."

She seemed close to tears. Drew led her to a chair. "He seemed so different, I knew something must have happened."

"How so?"

"He put on this happy face. My brother's not a happy person. I know him too well, better than anyone else. He wasn't himself, too fake...and nervous, like he needed to be somewhere else. Oh God... How did my mother take the news?"

"I honestly don't know." She would find out the rest of the news soon enough.

Drew left his card and wished her well. She promised to call Drew if she heard from her brother. "But whatever he's done, I don't want him hurt, all right?"

As Drew and Julio stepped down off the porch, Lowry and several Richmond PD vehicles pulled up to the curb.

"What the hell are you doing here, Smith?"

"I came to talk to Legere's sister."

"You knew he was here?" Lowry looked suspiciously at the bulge in Drew's jacket just under his left armpit.

"No. I came to talk to his sister."

"Where is he?"

"Not here. Let's go, Julio."

"Does she know about her mother?"

"No, but I bet you'll be glad to break the news?"

"Where are you going Smith? What's your hurry?"

Drew and Julio walked away leaving Lowry to his exasperated anger.

They returned to Washington as evening turned to night. It was after eight, and the temperature had cooled.

"Think Lowry will pick up his trail?" Julio asked.

"Maybe. But he's on the lam, he wouldn't want anyone knowing his plans. He probably lied to his sister. I wonder how Angel knew he was going to his sister's, and what else she knows. I'm beginning to feel like Wile E. Coyote."

"Who?"

"Road Runner cartoons."

"Oh, yeah, beep beep."

"The Road Runner never leaves the road, there's no dialogue, and the Road Runner never does anything to hurt the coyote."

"He's up the road going beep beep when the coyote blows himself up."

"Let's go back and talk to Angel."

"Beep, beep." Julio smiled.

∝∞∾

At the Palais, Angel was just starting her act, and they grabbed seats at the stage apron. Julio couldn't take his eyes off her and was almost drooling.

"Cheez, man, you really gonna give up hittin' that..."

"We're here on business. Do I have to call Chevy on you?"

The Friday evening crowd had grown, and the strip club was moving into full swing. This time, the sight of Drew and Julio seemed to spook her. She avoided their end of the stage, giving every other man some play while ignoring Drew. He slipped a fifty from his money clip and held it up between two fingers. Still she ignored him.

"Hey," he called out. "You go'n let my arm fall off."

With a theatrical smile, she pranced toward them without meeting Drew's gaze, her eyes darting about while he threaded the bill through her garter. He grabbed her hand and whispered, "This is the only reward you're getting."

"What happened?"

"We need to talk. Where did he go?"

"I don't know. Go away." She pulled her hand back and strutted to the other end of the stage.

"She's afraid to talk." Drew looked around to see who was watching, but recognized no one. Angel finished her act and they left.

The city dwellers had settled into another sultry summer night, ending one day and preparing for the next. Most had retreated into air-conditioned homes, bars, and restaurants. Comfortable in their silence, Julio and Drew strolled toward the car, which was parked off the main drag on a quiet back street, empty except for them. Having to deal with a woman he was trying to get rid of was annoying, but if it could help Gee's case—

Suddenly, just as they stepped off the curb, headlights flashed across them, tires squealed, and a car sped toward them. Drew was slow to react. Julio grabbed Drew's jacket, jerked him forward, and slammed his body down onto the pavement between parked cars. As Drew lay pressed under Julio's weight, gunfire sprayed overhead.

Tires screeched again as the vehicle turned the corner and raced away. A moment of fearful silence passed with Julio laying over Drew's back only the sound of their rapid breathing.

"You might like rough sex," Drew said, "but I don't take it up the ass."

"Better me up there than that car's hood ornament." Julio's laugh released their nervous energy. "Who was that?"

"You can get off me now."

"You know you like it when I dominate." Julio kissed him on the head then eased up off Drew's back and cautiously peered over the hood of the parked car. "Friends of yours?"

"No idea." Drew stood and brushed himself off.

Julio stood all the way up now. "Were they trying to kill us?"

"If they were, they need some shooting lessons."

"Looks like you've made some enemies."

"Over the years, plenty. You?"

"Everybody loves Julio."

The houses across the street began to light up. Some residents peeped through blinds while the braver ones spilled out onto the sidewalk to investigate.

"Somebody saw us leave the Palais," Drew said. "Let's get out of here."

"Shouldn't we call the police? Make a report or something."

"Did you see anything?"

"An SUV with tinted windows coming at us with the barrel of an Uzi sticking out."

"License plate?"

"No."

"That's not a lot to report. I think the police have enough to deal with."

Drew arrived back home feeling zapped. He went directly upstairs, undressed, and got into bed. Throughout the night he tossed restlessly in some twilight between sleep and waking. But when the phone rang, startling him, he realized that at last he had fallen asleep.

"Hello?... Hello?... Angel, is that you?" The line was dead. He dialed *69 but the number was blocked. What the hell was she up to?

The day's events still tossed and turned on his mind. With one day to prepare for Gee's preliminary hearing, he had nothing. He tried to dismiss the shooting as some young gang-bangers out on a lark pulling random drive-bys for kicks. He wished he believed that. He should have been on the ball enough to have gotten a license plate or the make on the SUV.

Drew put on his robe and went down to the study, where he started reviewing cases on severing conspiracy defendants. The phone rang again. He ignored it to focus on his work. The first legal hurdles were securing bond, overcoming the political histrionics, and persuading the judge that his client didn't pose a threat to the community. A nagging question repeatedly surfaced. What was Angel's connection? Uncover that and it might lead him to Jinx. It had to be drugs—Jinx was a street dealer, she was a user.

∞

Drew dragged himself into the office around ten a.m. Shirley looked him up and down, peered into his face, and frowned. "Wild night?" Drew ignored her and walked into his office. "Then I guess you also don't want to hear that the Chief called."

He immediately returned the call. "Morning, Chief, what's up?"

"Smith, why didn't you call me after you spoke with your informant?"

"I advised the informant to call the Tip Line."

"And then you raced Lowry to Richmond."

Drew grinned, at a loss for words.

"Stand by your fax machine, I'm sending Angelica Morales' rap sheet."

"Anything jump out at you?"

"I've seen so many of these, Angelica Morales looks pretty tame, a couple of possession charges, and one harassment charge, but it looks like it was dismissed."

"No details?"

"Federal rap sheet, abbreviated. You could probably get more by checking with the local jurisdiction."

"Thanks, Chief. One more thing. Any recent reports of random drive-bys?

"No. Why?"

"Last night, downtown, somebody took a couple of shots at me and Julio."

"Where?"

"Near the Palais."

"What were you doing there?"

"Having dinner nearby, if you must know."

"Nothing's passed over my desk, but I'll check with my precinct captain. Did you file a report?"

"No."

"Why not?"

"Nothing to report, it happened so fast we didn't see anything except the trash in the gutter we dove into."

"You know crime reports help to glean patterns and promote early intervention. Come on, help us out here."

"Next time somebody takes a shot at me, I'll be sure to report it."

Within seconds, Drew was pulling the NCIC report off the fax machine. There was no mistake as far as Angel's identity, right down to the rose tattoo on her left breast.

Drew picked up the phone and called a local private investigator with New York connections. He ended the call as Shirley appeared at the door.

"Angel's on the phone. She insists on speaking with you. She's called several times. Should I tell her to take a flying leap?"

He knew what Zoë would advise him to say, but Gee's future was at stake.

"I'll take it." He lifted the receiver.

"What happened, Drew?"

"He wasn't there. Supposedly he's on his way to Atlanta. Do you know how to contact him?"

"I told you all I know."

"And how did you come to know that? We need to talk."

"No, I can't see you." She ended the call.

A knock on the door, and Julio entered.

"What's up?"

"Couldn't sleep last night." Julio plopped down on the sofa.

"The shooting?"

Julio sighed and nodded.

"Remember my fight with the two amigos? Another man was with them. He's involved with Angel."

"Was he there last night?"

"I didn't see him. Damn."

"Damn what?"

"Tracking those two down might not be easy. No arrest records... Who could they be?" Suddenly he smiled and snapped his fingers.

"What?"

"They both went to the ER that night."

Julio jumped up. "Let's go."

∞∞

For a weekday morning, the emergency room was busy. After the mayor shut down D.C. General, Howard Hospital became the last resort for the city's homeless and uninsured. Most of the ill waited quietly, suffering their pain and discomfort, while others complained loudly. Drew and Julio passed a gray-haired alcoholic lying on a gurney suffering a fit of the DTs moaning, groaning, and muttering obscenities while the paramedics who had parked him there dealt with the admitting clerk. Drew and Julio waited in line behind the paramedics. Once the paramedics were done, they wheeled the yammering disaster into the treatment area.

The bubbly receptionist smiled up at Drew. "Hi." The brown-skinned girl had bright eyes and the whitest smile. Her hospital-issued scrubs did little to hide her ample figure. "May I help you?" Before Drew could get a word in, she said, "Oh, oh, I know you! You're that lawyer. I know, I know, it's, it's—"

"Perry Mason."

"No, silly," she giggled. "Drew Smith, that's who you are. Are you sick? I mean, you look fine." She let out another girlish giggle.

"We need some patient information."

"The information desk is in the main lobby."

"Not current patient information. I'm trying to contact two men who were treated here in the ER two weeks ago Friday."

"Sorry, I can't help you."

"Because it's confidential?"

"I don't have access to that data up on my computer. You should check with Medical Records." She pointed the way, and Drew thanked her.

"Let's hope the records clerk is as excited to see you as she was," Julio said.

The clerk turned out to be a young Hispanic man with a slight build but a taut, ripped body. He obviously spent too much time in the gym. Both ears were pierced and his long dark hair curled over his ears.

"I'll let you handle our new amigo," Drew said.

Julio smiled. He didn't have a homophobic bone in his body. He still had the commanding presence of his youth, and with his unassuming character, boyish charm, and good looks, he could ingratiate himself into the company of most anyone. He approached the clerk and glanced at his badge.

"José."

"Si?" The young man took one look at Julio and grinned.

They conversed in Spanish, their smiles getting easier and their heads getting closer. The extended conversation seemed to take it's sweet time in getting to the point.

"Hey, Drew, when was that again?"

Drew gave Julio the date of the brawl, José tapped it into his computer, and moments later his printer spit out a list of names. The clerk scribbled on the paper before handing it over. Julio grinned and the two men shook hands before Julio followed Drew out.

"You two sure did hit it off."

"He's Nicaraguan like me. I asked if he wanted to get together for a drink sometime." Julio handed Drew the slip of paper with José's number scrawled across the top.

Drew laughed. "I hope it don't break his heart when you don't call."

"Who says I won't call?" Julio looked at the sheet. "So what do you think?"

"He's cute." Drew ribbed Julio.

"No, the names."

Drew smiling skimmed the list. "Here we go, Oscar Torres, treated for a broken jaw. And this must be the other, Adan

Mendoza, injury to the groin. Oscar's occupation is construction laborer, 1460 Irving Street."

"Columbia Heights. Let's go see him."

"This'll have to wait till tomorrow evening. I need to get back to meet with a client. It'll keep."

"You sure?" Julio pulled the sheet from Drew's hand.

"I'm sure, besides, I need to prepare for court tomorrow." Drew snatched the paper back from Julio. "Tomorrow, both of us, and I don't want you going up there alone. Tomorrow, together, understand?"

"Si, jefe, comprendo."

"Uh-uh. Whenever you resort to Spanish I know you're thinking so far ahead your English can't keep up. Promise me you won't act on this without me."

Julio frowned. "Promise."

Chapter 13

D REW ARRIVED AT the Superior Court well prepared for his two cases. First, the preliminary hearing on Gee's indictment, and later, to testify against Angel on the stalking charge. Earlier that morning, he received a fax from the New York investigator. The court documents were incomplete and raised more questions. A Manhattan dentist had filed similar stalking charges against her, but the case was dismissed for failure to prosecute. Drew had no time to check it out further before his court appearance.

The preliminary hearing on the indictment of Gustavo Garcia and Tyrone Jones was scheduled for 11:00 a.m. Drew arrived shortly before the judge was to take the bench. Nina, Hernando, and Marie were waiting outside the courtroom. He felt powerless to calm their anxious fears, and could barely contain his own. Freeing Gee on bail was near impossible.

"What's going to happen?" Hernando asked.

"The grand jury found probable cause with sufficient evidence to return an indictment. I'll enter a not-guilty plea. The judge will set a trial date, and a hearing date for pretrial motions. Finally, I'll motion for bail. If things go well, he'll be free this afternoon. But don't count on it."

"How much?" Hernando asked.

"Not sure. Considering the severity of the crime, it'll be high. Whatever is set, you'll have to come up with ten percent. My estimate is two hundred and fifty thousand dollars."

"How much?" Hernando looked to Nina.

"We'll have to raise twenty-five thousand dollars." She repeated the number in Spanish.

Hernando nodded. Apparently, it was doable.

Drew turned his attention to Marie. "How are you?"

"Scared."

"Tell you the truth, so am I."

Marie looked up at Drew with hopeful eyes.

Judge Margaret Upton took the bench. The Caucasian woman's graying hair was pulled back in a tight bun and a pair of reading glasses sat perched on the bridge of her nose. She gave the severe appearance of a stern, no-nonsense woman. Around the courthouse, they called her Judge Judy for her abrasive, intolerant style. Once, after a very contentious trial, Drew had her reversed on appeal, and both had since held a mutual disdain and respect for one another. One slip, and she'd be all over him.

Drew was seated at the defendant's table with Gee to his right and Tracy Connors on his left. Next to her sat Tyrone Jones. Gee wore a dark suit with a blue tie knotted against a crisp white collar. Drew had provided a pair of fake tortoise-shell glasses to give Gee a more studious air, especially compared to Tyrone, slouching in his jail-issued orange jumpsuit.

With the judge on the bench, the clerk called the first case on the docket. Dan Gaines was seated alone at the prosecutor's table. Without co-counsel, he would perhaps be trying the case solo. This was unusual for a high-profile case. Dan Gaines might be a bright and rising star, but the young man was no match for the two more experienced attorneys. It may have been considered a mere routine hearing, hence Gaines was dispatched alone, but it was Drew's plan to make it anything but routine.

"Are all the parties present?" Judge Upton peered down as the attorneys stood with their clients.

"Yes, your honor, Dan Gaines for the government."

"Tracy Connors for defendant Tyrone Jones."

"Drew Smith for defendant Gustavo Garcia. Your honor, co-counsel for defense and I have agreed to suspend with a reading of the indictment."

"Very well." Judge Upton perused the file. "Do we have a plea agreement?"

"No agreement has been offered, your honor," Tracy Connors said. "I assume because my client has another pending charge. Until one is forthcoming, Tyrone Jones pleads not guilty."

"And your client, Mr. Smith?"

"My client pleads not guilty."

The parties proceeded to pin down a trial date. Expecting it to run at least two weeks, they finally agreed to the judge setting a trial date six months away, the first week of February, with pretrial motions to be heard two months before. The judge then asked if there were any other preliminary matters. Drew renewed his motion for bail.

Judge Upton removed her glasses then clasped her hands under her chin. Her expression mingled skepticism with curiosity. "Bail for a capital offense such as this with three people murdered is highly unusual, Mr. Smith. What makes your client worthy of this departure from standard procedures?"

"Your honor, Gustavo Garcia isn't the usual defendant and therefore usual standards cannot apply. My client doesn't pose a threat to the community. He has no record of violence, indeed no priors at all. Gustavo Garcia is as much a victim as those three dead restaurant workers. Only, he—"

"Your honor." Gaines rose to his feet. "Gustavo Garcia is a close associate of the gunmen. They conspired to commit this heinous crime—"

"There's no proof of that—"

Judge Upton slammed the gavel. "Mr. Gaines, I'm listening to Mr. Smith right now." Gaines grimaced and eased back down into his chair. "Continue, Mr. Smith."

"Your honor, the Bail Reform Act, Title 18—"

"I'm familiar with the statute, Mr. Smith. What's your point?"

"The statue requires that the defendant be detained prior to trial if there's clear and convincing evidence no condition placed on his release would reasonably assure the safety of the community. Gustavo Garcia is in no way a danger to the community."

"Your honor." Gaines was on his feet again. "The court must look to whether the offense is a crime of violence—"

"In the case at bar—"

Judge Upton slammed her gavel again. "Mr. Gaines, you'll have your opportunity. I don't want to remind you again. Continue, Mr. Smith."

"Your honor, in the case at bar, the court has considered no evidence that defendant Garcia is violent or a danger to the community—"

"Okay, stop right there. Mr. Gaines, how do you respond? Do you have evidence to proffer?" She folded her hands and looked down at Gaines.

He hesitated a moment. "This isn't an evidentiary hearing, and even assuming it were, the indictment handed down by the grand jury is prima facie evidence."

A weak answer. Drew suspected the judge knew where he was going and Gaines didn't.

"So," Judge Upton said, "your argument is that the indictment is sufficient. Mr. Smith?"

"Your honor, in *U.S. v. Dillon*, the government presented the indictment to show there was probable cause to believe the defendant had committed a drug offense punishable by a maximum sentence of ten years or more. The court held that the indictment alone was enough to raise a rebuttable presumption. The burden has shifted, and under *U.S. v. Simpkins*, due process entitles my client to an evidentiary hearing."

Presumably amused by Drew's gutting of the young upstart, the judge smiled. "Mr. Gaines, have you any other evidence to proffer?"

"Well, I didn't, if I'd...not at this time, your honor."

"Very well, I'll give you some time. I'll schedule a de novo detention hearing for Monday morning, written briefs are to be filed. Mr. Smith, you have twenty-four hours to file your brief. Is that time sufficient?"

"It is, your honor." Drew smiled at Gaines.

"And the government's reply brief is due in forty-eight hours." The judge slammed her gavel and ordered the clerk to call the next case.

"What happened?" Gee asked.

"You'll get a full-fledged hearing on bail. Think you can stand to be locked up for five more days?"

"Do I have a choice?" A marshal was at his side waiting to escort him away.

"I'll come see you Friday," Drew said, and Gee was whisked through the door out of the courtroom.

Drew found Hernando, Nina and Marie waiting outside in the hallway. He checked his watch—he was due in another courtroom. He stopped to brief them. They all sensed the hearing went well, and for the first time since he broke the news to Nina, she seemed hopeful, no longer lost in some distant pain. Her eyes fixed on him. It was the look he remembered from their past, a lingering gaze that always sparked his passion. He explained there'd be another chance at bail, then hurried down the hall.

Saul Lieberman snagged him in the vestibule. A short balding man with a potbelly and a coffee-stained tie, Lieberman was a courthouse fixture who usually picked up his clients on the courthouse steps the day of trial.

"Judge Locke has another hearing going on right now. We're up next. I'm representing Angelica Morales. Can I have a word with you outside? Just for a minute." Drew followed him back into the hall. Angel was nowhere in sight. He'd wanted to talk to her. "Mr. Smith, I only spoke with Ms. Morales this morning, and I haven't had time to prepare for this hearing. She's ill today, and I'm asking for a continuance."

"I'll consent to a continuance, but I'm still asking for a TRO. Ms. Morales has to cease her harassment and damaging my property."

"A restraining order—even a temporary one—requires an evidentiary hearing."

"I'm prepared."

"Ms. Morales denies that she's done the things you allege, slashed tires and the broken window. Did you see her do it?"

"No, but I have evidence of prior conduct that would lead me to reasonably believe she's responsible."

Lieberman paused a moment to think. "Why don't we stipulate to a continuance for one week. At that time, we'll argue your restraining order."

This would give him a week. Angel had no intention of confessing her guilt, and a restraining order could complicate his search for Jinx. Drew had no idea what Angel was capable of, but because she might be able to lead him to Jinx, he had to stay in communication. The case had been dumped in Lieberman's lap at the last minute, and the judge would be forced to grant a continuance. The upside, it presented an opportunity to speak with the New York dentist.

"Agreed."

∞⊗⊙

Thursday, August 16, Noon.

"I hate to add to your problems, but this came in the morning mail." Shirley handed over a letter.

A complaint had been filed against Drew with the Grievance Committee of the D.C. Bar Association. The letter set forth allegations of professional misconduct in the interference of a police investigation. The Grievance Committee controlled the entrance, exit, and timeouts for those practicing law in the city. Drew had thirty days to respond to allegations lodged by Lt. Lowry. The committee would investigate, and if facts warranted, set a hearing.

"Withholding evidence and obstruction of justice can get you disbarred," Shirley said. "Did you really slug that cop?"

"I did. Put this in the suspense file for ten days." He handed back the letter.

"You have thirty days to respond."

"I want to be reminded in ten."

Only the assault allegation was serious enough to raise his concern. Drew would argue it was provoked. But Lowry had made a procedural error by not filing a complaint with his own department, or if he had, it was never served on Drew. Without prosecution, the claim carried little or no weight. Putting the cart before the donkey, Lowry was ass-backwards as usual. Drew would respond, but he had no time to think about it now, not with Gee in jail and unanswered questions about Angel.

"Your alarm company called," Shirley said. "There was a false alarm at your house. The police checked it out. Didn't find anything, the alarm was reset. And you didn't forget your shrink appointment, did you?"

"No."

The burglary alarm raised some concern, but he had a brief to write. First, though, he fished through his briefcase for the fax from the New York investigator. After a brief Internet search, he picked up the phone and punched in the number.

"Hello, this is Drew Smith, a Washington attorney. I'd like to speak to Dr. Malik Khalid, please. It's in regard to Angelica Morales." After a lengthy wait, a man came on the line.

"Hello, this is Dr. Khalid. Who is this?"

Drew introduced himself. "You filed a harassment charge against Angel two years ago but didn't prosecute."

"How can I help you?"

"Dr. Khalid, she's stalking me. I'd like to know more about her."

The dentist paused as though mulling of his words then spoke. "I'm not comfortable discussing this over the phone. If you're who you say you are, I'll be glad to meet with you in person."

"I can be there this evening, say around seven."

"I'll be in my office."

Drew hung up, glanced at his watch, then called Zoë to push his appointment back an hour. She agreed.

He had already done his research for the brief, and the writing went quickly. After a couple of hours of focused work, refusing to take calls, he pulled it all together. Drew saved the document, grabbed his jacket, instructed Shirley to format the brief, check the case cites, and to prepare the certificate of service for his signature in the morning, and he was out the door.

∞

Wednesday, August 16, 3:00 p.m.

"It's been a week since our last session," Zoë said. "Have you had any more dreams?"

"No."

"Good. Let's talk about that inadequacy we ended on last week."

"Okay, why do I feel inadequate?"

"That's my question. You have to answer it."

Drew eased back and took in a deep breath. "It's frustrating. Everybody expects me to be the answer man. I'm not a miracle worker. Do you know what it's like, always trying to come up with the right answers?" He laughed. "Actually, you do know, and now I'm doing it to you."

"But you seem to thrive in conditions of competition and conflict."

"Why is that?"

"You tell me. It's not uncommon." Zoë paused for a moment, her brow knit. "Do you feel driven to prove something? Competition can stem from a belief that you have to prove something, which in turn can mean that down deep, you don't think you're worthy. This insecurity, if not understood as coming from an internal belief, can get you thinking that it's other people who don't believe you're good enough. So you rebel against this perceived unfairness, but the anger turns against yourself, and you become self-destructive.

"Then why do I swing from bulging with overconfidence one moment to feeling inadequate and depressed the next? Why can't I just stay on an even keel?"

"Not even ships stay on an even keel all the time. We experience storms in our lives, times of pressure and stress. The question is, how do we handle the stress? In normal constructive ways or with self-destructive behavior?"

"How do I handle it?"

"Often it's reflected in how one handles his interpersonal relations. Which brings us back to our discussion last week and your preference for pretty young Latinas."

"I never characterized them as pretty and young."

"Am I wrong?"

"No, you got the right picture." Except for Nina, who was no longer young, but still had that effect on him. "It's just that I didn't say it."

"It's what you're not saying I'd like to get at. Do you prefer young women who respond to your money?" Zoë waited for Drew to respond. He didn't.

"Do they make you feel loved? Or is it only a brief fleeting love?" She waited again. "Somehow it seems you're confusing lust with love."

Drew remained silent.

"You're not responding."

"Did you ask a question? Sounded like a statement."

"I want your reaction to my analysis."

"I'm not going to sit here and let you pry into the details of my sex life."

"You're angry. I'm not prying into the details of your sex life, I've been trying to get at your love life. Are you afraid of what you'll find? Each time I ask, I get a different answer as to what's going on, as if your energy is leading me around this crisis instead of to it."

Drew looked at his watch. "Can we cut this session short? I have a plane to catch."

"Where are you going?"

"New York, to talk with another one of Angel's stalking victims. I'm sorry, I should have cancelled this session."

"I'm glad you didn't. And I'm sorry you have to leave. We seemed to be on the verge of something."

"It'll have to wait." Drew was out of his chair, heading for the door.

"Drew, wait."

He stopped. "Yes."

"You have my home number. If you find yourself back on that seesaw, swinging from anxiety to overconfidence, and feel like you need someone to talk to, call me. Please."

"Sure thing."

∞

Wednesday, August 16, 7:00 p.m.

Hours later, Drew arrived at Dr. Khalid's Manhattan office. The elevator opened into a reception area for Empire Dental, a practice made up of four dentists. The area was deserted except for a pretty young brunette in medical scrubs busily closing shop.

Dr. Khalid appeared in an instant. Tall and dark with a full beard perfectly trimmed, his olive complexion and curly black hair suggested Afro-Arab ancestry. A well-defined physique suggested regular exercise and a healthful lifestyle. He escorted Drew down a long narrow hallway to his small office. Degrees, licenses and photos hung framed on the walls, and the desk was littered with journals and papers. He wasn't an organized man. On the desk was a family photo of a lovely wife and two small children.

Dr. Khalid cleared off a chair. "So Angel's at it again?"

"I'd like to know about your encounter and why the case was dropped."

Khalid took a deep breath. "I was hoping to have heard the last of Angel Morales, but she keeps coming back to haunt me."

Drew gave him a comradely smile. "I know what you mean. How did it start for you?"

"I met Angel about three years ago. She was dancing at a downtown club near Times Square. I'm a happily married man, but after the birth of our second child, my wife lost interest... Let's just say I started looking elsewhere. One thing led to another. I started seeing Angel regularly. She was fun, but she had a habit."

"Cocaine. And you?" Khalid hesitated. "I'm not here to judge," Drew said. "You don't have to answer that. This is completely confidential, I'm not the police. It's just any details might help."

"I'd toot the stuff during our... She liked to freebase but it inhibited my performance. And I wasn't trying to get that high."

"When did the harassment begin?"

"Her binges were getting more frequent. She supported herself by dancing, and she lived pretty well—expensive tastes, clothes, restaurants. I became a major money source for her and her habit. Then my wife and I began counseling, our marriage turned around, and I ended it with Angel. She wasn't happy. She started calling and hanging up, showing up at my office unannounced, cruising by the house and parking out front. I finally filed charges to get her to stop."

"What happened?"

"I got a visit from a friend of hers who threatened me with bodily harm but also promised to make the problem disappear if I dropped the charge and paid a certain cleanup fee, as he called it."

"Extortion."

"I'm not a lawyer."

"Then what happened?"

"I wanted the whole Angel thing to go away as fast as possible before it wrecked my marriage. So I paid, wired the money to an offshore account. End of story—until I got your phone call. At the time, it seemed like a small price to pay. Now she's back to stalking again." He smiled for a moment. "Pardon me for saying it, but I'm glad this time it's a lawyer."

"How much did you pay?"

"Fifty thousand."

"Does your wife know about Angel?"

"After a while, I couldn't hide it. Our marriage is back on track, and I haven't cheated on her since. What do you plan to do?"

"I don't know yet, but what you've told me shows a pattern. Thanks for taking the time to see me."

"No problem. Will all this come out?"

"I doubt it. As far as Angel is concerned, you're ancient history. I'm her current event. Tell me about her friend."

"Tall Latin dude, ponytail, a thuggish edge, piercing dark eyes. Scary son of a bitch, had the look of a real killer if you know what I mean. Figured he was her pimp or something worse." Dr. Khalid looked down and shook his head with regret and Drew realized he had dredged up a past the dentist was anxious to forget. A complete picture of Angel was developing.

"Thanks. You've been a great help."

Drew got the next flight back to Washington. It was time he had a talk with Angel's mysterious friend.

Chapter 14

Thursday, August 17, 10:30 p.m.

JULIO PARKED ON 16th Street near the Sacred Heart Church in front of the Lincoln Multicultural School. They walked around the corner to the address of Oscar Torres at 1460 Irving Street, unit 203. The block stretched from 14th to 16th Streets. The alley near 16th Street was busy with the evening drug traffic. The address was one of three apartment buildings grouped together next to a men's homeless shelter. At a point where the neighborhoods of Adams Morgan and Columbia Heights merged, it was a long desolate stretch to the Columbia Heights Metro station at 14th and Irving.

The area reeked of decay. Real estate speculators were gobbling up properties, and century-old homes and apartment buildings were being gutted and renovated. The intense gentrification and revitalization was sparked by the recent opening of the Irving Street Metro station. Real estate prices were soaring. Blacks and Latinos were being bulldozed out of affordable housing to accommodate the flood of urban pioneers.

Middle-aged Latinos sat on the building's stoop, catching the evening breeze. Drew and Julio got little attention as they entered the four-story walkup. The lobby smelled of urine and stale alcohol, a drunk slept on the floor in a corner. Drew followed Julio up the stairwell. On the second floor, the shouts in Spanish of an arguing couple came from one unit, a baby's crying from another and the sounds of Telemundo and Latin music from yet another. Julio knocked on a door.

"Who is it?" a muffled voice answered. Drew stepped aside out of peephole view.

"Julio."

"Que?"

"Are you Oscar Torres?"

"Who wants to know?"

"Julio. I have a check for him."

The man answered the door with a suspicious look and a little girl asleep on his shoulder. Drew stepped into view. The man reacted with fearful recognition.

"Jew. What jew want?" The man spoke through clenched teeth, whether from anger or a wired jaw, Drew wasn't sure.

"I want to talk to you, and to apologize. You understand?" The man was unresponsive. "Tell him, Julio."

Julio began to speak in Spanish but the man interrupted.

"I speak English." Oscar Torres's diction and heavy accent were labored.

"Oscar, quien es?" A young woman emerged from the bedroom. She was much younger than Oscar, who appeared to be in his mid-thirties. She was no more than a teenager with a swollen belly, and by the way she tottered toward Oscar, Drew feared she was about to go into labor. They spoke in Spanish as he handed off the child. She disappeared back into the bedroom. He closed the door behind her and returned to where Julio and Drew waited to be asked in.

"Why jew come to my house?"

"I'm sorry for the misunderstanding the other night. But you drink too much for a married man with a baby and one on the way."

He lowered his voice and glanced back at the bedroom door. "That is my business."

"I need your help and to show you I'm here in good faith, I want to give you something." Drew withdrew his checkbook and pen. "May we come in?" Oscar looked at the checkbook then stepped aside. Drew entered, followed by Julio. "I want to compensate you for your troubles. May I sit?"

He motioned Drew to the rickety table for two. Drew sat and began to write. The sparsely furnished apartment was in need of paint. A worn sofa and old coffee table sat on a bare hardwood parquet floor. In one corner the volume was low on a 26-inch color TV flickering images of a Tamale western and on the wall over the table hung a portrait of a blond, blue-eyed Christ.

Drew handed over the check. "You must have medical expenses and probably missed a few days work. I want to make things right."

Torres took the check, read the amount, and his expression of disbelief turned into a big grin. "What jew want from me?"

"I need to ask you about that night at the Palais." Again the man glanced at the closed bedroom door. Drew lowered his voice. "Besides Mendoza, you were with two other men. Who were they?"

"Tattoo and Benicio."

"Where can I find them?"

Julio took over the questioning in Spanish, translating back to Drew on the fly. Tattoo el Malo—Tattoo the Mobster—and Benicio Juarez rented rooms in the house with Oscar's cousin Adan Mendoza on Lamont Street. Benicio and Adan had done time together. Tattoo a Dominicano who, Oscar had heard, trafficked in drugs and guns. Tattoo, whom Oscar clearly didn't like, was buying the drinks that night, and Oscar and his cousin

Adan were his guests. Oscar admitted he was drunk and things got out of hand.

He turned to Drew. "I'm sorry."

"No problem. Where can we find Adan?"

He gave them an address not far away, then thanked them effusively with vigorous handshakes. Drew warned him to keep quiet about the money.

A GMC Denali was parked in front of the Lamont Street address. Drew stepped around to the passenger side and sniffed around the door and window. "This is it."

"How do you know?"

"Gunshot residue."

"What do we do?"

"Let's wait awhile, maybe he'll leave soon. We'll follow him, see where he takes us."

"What if he doesn't leave?"

"We'll jump off that bridge when we come to it."

The two returned to Julio's limo.

"Why does he want you dead?"

"Maybe I'm getting too close. Maybe he's jealous. Maybe he was just trying to scare me."

"Why are we waiting?" Julio pulled his gun from the glove compartment and checked the safety before holstering it. "I say we kick in the door and ambush him. The way he did us."

"Calm down, cowboy."

"He's a dangerous man, we can finger him for trying to shoot us, why don't we just call the Chief? Let the police take him down."

"I can't risk it."

"You're risking your life."

"He can take us to Jinx, and I need Jinx alive."

"What if he's in Atlanta?"

"I don't buy it. The only place he knows is D.C. He'll stick close to home. This is where he's most comfortable. Somebody's hiding him."

"So let the police take him down."

"Are you kidding? Lowry thinks he's J. Edgar Hoover tracking John Dillinger. He'll kill him on the spot, given half a chance. There's no glory in bringing about an outlaw's downfall peacefully. I don't want him to have any chance at all."

Twenty minutes later, Tattoo and another man appeared on the front porch. By the shadowy light, Drew couldn't get a make on the other man. They got into the SUV and drove off. Seconds later, Julio pulled out with his lights off and followed them into Rock Creek Park. He switched on his lights after they turned on Beach Drive. They exited the parkway at P Street.

"They're on their way to the Palais," Drew said.

From a safe distance, Drew and Julio watched the two men enter the Palais. Minutes later, they escorted Angel out.

"That Benicio?"

"The fourth man at the table on fight night."

"So what do we do now?" Julio asked.

"Go home."

"You said he would take us to Jinx."

"He will. Tattoo is the connection between Angel and Jinx."

"So let's get in his face."

"Not now. I have to come up with a plan."

"Don't wait too long. I don't like this dude, especially since he's already taken a shot at us."

"Somehow I have to work it through Angel."

"I don't know, dude, she's kinda unpredictable."

Chapter 15

JULIO WALKED INTO Drew's office as he was hanging up the phone. "What'd you find out?"

"A lot," Julio said. A gangbanger in his youth, Julio still kept up his street connections. "Tattoo el Malo ain't no joke. Started out as a mule for the Medellin cartel. Dude knows how to get cocaine across the border and onto the streets. Made a name for himself and then things went downhill. Word is, a big drug deal went bad and he left a trail of blood. Out of control, he got too careless and the cartel dropped him. The West Coast cops and the DEA want to talk to him. He's laying low between New York and Washington."

"What's he doing here?"

"Other than keeping company with your girl Angel, he's a freelance solo supplier to a couple of street dealers. No big threat to the crews. They let him push a stepped-on product, and worst thing, he uses most of it himself. Benicio is his strong-arm gofer, did time for manslaughter at Pelican Bay. They're bad men."

"Hardcore, huh?"

"Hardcore and loco. So what do we do?"

"I'm still trying to figure out an angle through Angel."

"Guy's dangerous, man. Let's confront the dude, cut out the bullshit, let him know we know what's up, and tell him we'll go away in exchange for Jinx."

"He's too devious. Whatever he's planning would just morph into something else."

"I say we get in his face."

"And do what?"

"Kill him if we have to. You got to get the drop on him before he gets you. He shot at you once, that's warning enough."

"He just wants money."

"And the way you're buying up information on him, trust me, that'll get back to him. Oscar probably called his cousin right away."

"I told him to keep it under his hat."

"He can't keep it under his hat, dude, you gave him a check, you think he has a bank account of his own?" Damn. "So now Tattoo knows you're looking for him. I don't like it, man. The dude will kill in a heartbeat."

"I'll take my chances."

"If you won't listen to me, call the Chief. Let him know what you're doing. I'm warning you, man. Keep your guard up."

"That's your best idea yet. I'll call the Chief. What are you doing tonight?"

"Besides maybe taking you to the hospital? Why?"

"I want to get Nina and Hernando together at my house this evening. I need to discuss my strategy for the hearing, and I want you to bring Nina."

"No problem."

"I'm also going to see if they'll agree to couples therapy. She's dead-set on a divorce. I want you there in case Hernando gets out of hand."

Julio tilted his head, his brow furrowed. "And you're set on seeing Hernando dead. I get it. We're going to whack him. Hey, I'm game."

Drew chuckled. "Shut up, Julio."

"I'll be there, and I'll bring a big roll of plastic wrap. You know like on the Sopranos. Seriously, why are you doing this?"

"I just want Nina to be happy."

"And if Hernando can't make her happy, you can. You gonna force her to make a choice."

"Gee may be locked up six months or more, that kid'll have enough to deal with in jail, I don't want him worrying about the home front. His parents need to present a united front in supporting him."

"You sound like a father now. I'm outta here." Julio stood, spun his chauffeur's cap, and flipped it onto his head with a tilt covering one eye. Drew was amused when Julio accidentally bumped into Shirley coming through the door. She could invoke a leary apprehension in Julio the same as Chevy.

"Back from lunch?" Julio asked.

"What's it to you?"

"Just asking, what's eatin' you?" Julio shot Drew a what's-with-her look and was gone.

"Angel's on line one. What should I tell her?"

"I'll take it."

Shirley shook her head and returned to her desk, leaving the door open, no doubt so she could listen. So it was Angel who upset her. He closed the door and picked up the receiver. "Hey baby. I miss you. I want to see you. When can we get together?"

She giggled. "I knew you didn't mean those things. But I got to be careful now."

"Someone else? I don't care. I need to talk to you."

"About us?"

"About Jinx."

"Oh," she said and Drew sensed that was not what she wanted to hear, he was losing her.

"And us." She didn't respond. "You still want that reward?"

"With that money, I'd go back to school, we could start over again."

"Come to my office tomorrow. Let's say around noon. Can you do that?"

"Yeah I can do that... Drew?"

"What?"

"I'm sorry for those things. Can we really start over, I mean really be together again?"

"We'll talk about it."

She sighed. "Okay."

Drew hung up and eased back in his chair. His plan was beginning to take shape, but he needed backup. He picked up the phone again and dialed.

"What's up, Chief?"

"Crime is up, so is my blood pressure."

"Better do something about that."

"I'm working on it. What can I do for you? Still dodging bullets?"

"About that, I did some investigating. My stalker Angel Morales has a drug-peddling cohort. The shooter goes by the street name Tattoo el Malo."

"You want us to pick him up?"

"That may be premature."

"What's this all about, Smith?"

"He may lead us to Jeffrey Legere. This guy's a gunrunner, drug dealer, and extortionist. I suspect I'm his next target. And I think he's hiding Legere."

"So she's your tipster? I hope you and Julio don't plan to take him down by yourself."

"That's where you come in. I'm meeting her tomorrow. She's got her eye on that reward. I think the two of us together can convince her to tell us where to find Jinx. I'll use gentle persuasion, and you apply the pressure."

"Okay, Smith, I'll be there. If your plan doesn't work, I'm running them both in. You got twenty-four hours, then I'm taking over."

"That's all I need. And leave Lowry out of this."

He had come up with a solution, but what if it didn't work? Gee's future was at stake. His son, whom he'd never really gotten to know, and now maybe never would...

Self-pity was taking hold and he caught himself sinking. Zoë's words came to him, about calling her if he needed to. There was something about her plea—tender, compassionate, caring. Not her usual careful detachment. She was right, he wasn't opening up. After all, the dreams had stopped. Despite his own efforts, she was actually helping him. He would try harder. But first he should apologize. He made another call.

"Dr. Settles?"

"Yes, Drew."

"You recognize my voice."

"I've grown attuned to it. How are you?"

"Okay. I want to apologize for the way I acted the other day. Running out the way I did."

"I understand. I'm glad you called."

"Really?"

"Yes..." she said releasing a deep sigh. "I'm terminating your treatment."

It stabbed him like a rusty knife. "What, I'm cured?"

"I've arranged for another therapist to continue your sessions."

"No, I want you. We were just beginning to click."

"I'm sorry, but I can't help any further."

"I can't accept that. We need to discuss this."

"Drew, this is the best thing for you."

"To kick me to the curb?"

"Drew, I'm your therapist, or was, not your lover."

"You're a tease, toying with my mental health."

"Drew, stop, you're upset."

"What do you expect? I'm hurt. We had a relationship—I mean we were building one. I trust you." Drew was suddenly struck by his own admission.

"This wasn't the best way to tell you, over the phone, I'm sorry."

"Help me understand, explain it to me, in person." He looked at his watch. "Can you break away this evening? I'll buy you dinner. Since you're no longer my therapist, there's no boundary to cross."

She didn't answer.

"Dr. Settles?"

"Okay, Drew, I'll have dinner with you."

"I'll pick you up at eight-thirty. Wear something nice, I haven't eaten all day, and after this news, I need a fancy meal."

He hung up before she could change her mind.

∞

Friday, August 18, 6:00 p.m.

Julio and Drew shut themselves off in the study to afford Nina and Hernando the most privacy, on the other side of the house, in the kitchen. Not even the walls and distance could keep the passion of Hernando's pain from reaching their ears. He could be heard groveling, pleading, begging at her feet, and abasing himself by every means available. Sprawled on the sectional sofa in the study watching a soccer game on ESPN, Julio and Drew tried to ignore Nina's loud accusations and charges. It was enough to make any man pop her. Every now and again, Julio would turn to Drew, shaking his head in sympathy with Hernando.

"You know what I like best when me and Chevy have a big fight?" Julio was on his fourth beer and getting chatty.

"The make-up sex."

"How'd you know?"

"We've all been there, and besides, you've told me a thousand times, after every fight. Sometime I think you pick fights just to have sex."

"I do, and I learned which fights to pick—you know what I mean. I lose, I'm sleeping on the sofa. Gotta know which fights to pick. You know, I was just thinking," Julio said. "There are three men in this house right now who at some point have been crazy about Nina. I was in high school. You were what, 26, and then came Hernando. She's still in our lives, man. Why is that?"

There was something remarkable about the woman who kept her footprint stamped on their hearts no matter how far their love had expanded, mutated, or evolved. "We're all still crazy about Nina," Drew said. "Look at us." Suddenly he laughed. "Tell you the truth, Julio, she can be a real bitch."

Julio sighed. "Either she changed or we were blind. Or both."

"I always thought I lost the best thing I ever had. But you know? I'm glad Hernando's her husband and not me." He laughed again.

The other side of the house had grown quiet. Nina came into the study alone. She looked worn and emotionally drained.

"What's the deal?" Drew asked her.

"I need time, Drew. Julio, can we go now?"

"Sure." Julio threw Drew a look and followed her out, leaving Drew with the task of cheering up Hernando. Nina would probably take Hernando back, but not before making him suffer. This would be a turning point in their marriage. If he really wanted her to stay, Hernando would have to make a number of concessions and begged for mercy at her feet. The dynamics of their marriage would change or else it was doomed.

Drew led Hernando out onto the deck. Hernando thanked him for his support, and again apologized to Drew for stealing his love that crime of long ago which neither could forget. Drew accepted the apology but didn't go so far as to thank Hernando for saving him from what might have been the same misery. Instead Drew was left to deal with the occasional stalker or bouts of loneliness the price to pay for his freedom.

On his way out, Hernando noticed some chipping around the lock on the deck's French doors. "Your door needs fixing. What happened here? You have a burglary?"

Drew kneeled to inspect the lock. It was the first time he'd noticed the damage, and the scratches were new. Someone had tried to burglarize the house and the alarm must have scared them off.

Hernando looked over the doors closely. "The hinge screws are stripped away too. They're old, it's worn. I fix for you. I hung these doors."

"I remember."

"I fix them."

"Hernando, that's not necessary."

"No problem, tomorrow morning, I come fix your doors. Please, I do this for you."

"I remember the last time you fixed things around here."

"Huh? Oh!" They shared a laugh, then Drew hurried him off. He had to get ready for his dinner date.

∞

Friday, August 18, 8:30 p.m.

Zoë's condo was in the old Hecht Company department store across from the Verizon Center. Drew remembered sitting on Santa's lap there as a small boy. She surprised him answering the door in a black mini-dress. He had forgotten how beautiful he found her the first time they met. Her stiletto heels brought them face-to-face. She had shapely legs and his eyes were drawn to the plunging neckline before he pulled them away—he was still hoping he could change her mind about dropping him as a patient.

"Don't you look nice," she said.

"You clean up nicely too." Drew wore a black linen suit, dressy Ferragamo loafers, and black silk shirt set off by a white tie. The 30s gangster look was seasonably fashionable.

"Come in. Do we have time for a drink?"

"Sure." He watched her disappear into the kitchenette. Candles imbued the room with a soft light and floral fragrance. He meandered about admiring an eclectic art collection including Southwestern landscapes and African masks. "I hope you like Asian fusion," he called after her. "I made reservations at Ten Penh."

"I do, and I love Ten Penh." She returned with two glasses of red wine. "Sit down, we can begin our talk, but first a glass of wine."

He eased down on the Egyptian cotton sofa. "Nice place." He said accepting the wine as his eyes continued to scan about. He glanced at her and was momentarily hypnotized by her dress. Shimmering, the candlelight captured speckles of glitter.

"Why are you looking at me like that?"

"I'm sorry, was I staring? Now, how come you don't like me?"

She sighed. "It's not that I don't like you."

"Then why are you terminating my treatment?"

"Drew, I'll sum it up as plainly as possible. You've become a master at keeping things from getting too close to you—including people."

"I admit, but some things aren't easy to talk about."

"My point exactly, it's not easy for you to discuss some things *with me*. Drew, we either live in love or in fear. You stay in fear. We get addicted to the feeling without knowing it. But now you're reaching out to find a way to break the loop. That's good."

"That's why I came to you. I know something's not right—"

"Let me finish. Since fear is the absence of love, you need to start opening to the possibility that you really are loved. Then you can let it show up in your life, give love a chance to help run the show."

"I'm listening."

"That's all, really. This isn't a session, and if it were, I'd be asking you questions, not lecturing. If we can't believe we're good enough to be loved, what do we have to stand on? Everything becomes quicksand, a great void, a bottomless vacuum."

He knew the feeling. "So why leave me hanging?"

"The last time we met, I sensed there was something crucial you were withholding. I can't help if you won't open up."

Drew sipped his wine, and tried to relax and compose his thoughts. "Okay, okay, I have a dirty little secret I'm not comfortable talking about."

"Drew, I'm not your therapist anymore, I'm not asking you to—"

"Don't stop me now, not if it's what's making you drop me. I've done things that I'm ashamed of." It all came out in a torrent, the fantasies he paid to make real. Ménages à trois where girls dressed up in garter belts, black fishnet stockings and heels, or leopard bustiers and feather thongs. Enjoying dominating them with money. Taking them in pairs and just watching. With those who were willing to risk it, paying more for sodomy. He summed up this confession. "That's it." He steeled himself against her reaction.

"You're hardly the first to engage in group sex or pay for it. Dressing up and acting out sexual fantasies isn't necessarily deviant behavior. But you obviously have a great deal of guilt from something. And because I'm a woman, you withheld it. That's why my associate, a man, could better help you."

"But I've opened up now, I've told you. Why can't we continue?"

"There's another reason." She avoided Drew's eyes.

"What else is wrong with me?"

"It's not you. It just won't work. It's me. And now that we've talked this out, there's not much point in having dinner together." She drained her glass and stood up.

"Hold up, hold up, what's this all about? Now you're the one who's withholding."

"I'm saying I'm too involved. I can no longer be detached, dispassionate, and rational. And that's not good." In the long silence, Drew stood and walked to the window. "I'll transition you to another therapist," she said to his back. "You seem to be beating this dream thing—"

"How come you can no longer be detached and rational?"

"You don't give up, do you?" She let out a resigned sigh. "All right. I've developed feelings for you. I find myself looking forward to our sessions, and afterwards you stay on my mind. I'm afraid I may end up just messing with you mind. I think about the women in your life, Nina and Angel, and I feel...I wonder what it must be like. Pardon my honesty, but I get just a little bit jealous. My interests have superseded yours."

"Wow," Drew whispered. "You like me after all." When she didn't say anything, he turned to face her. He'd been trying so hard to look at her as a therapist instead of as a woman, to curb the dog in him long enough to retune his psyche. "Can we at least still be friends?"

"Yes," she said. "I'd like that."

He eased down on the sofa next to her. "I can always get another therapist, but there's only one Zoë Settles."

For the first time that evening, she smiled. She seemed genuinely touched. But she remained silent, lost in a distant stare.

"What's wrong?"

"There're still two other women in your life. I don't want to get mixed up in that mess."

"I don't know how much the therapy had to do with it, but earlier tonight I realized that Nina was never meant to be. I loved and—fortunately for me—I lost. She's history."

"And Angel, what about her? What if she really is in love with you? You deceived her with your kindness and charm. What if she really meant it when she said she wanted to marry you?"

"You don't know her. She's a calculating witch. I'm the victim here. I fell under her spell. She uses sex to conquer men."

"She fell under your spell."

"My spell?"

"Yes, your spell."

"Once she's got her prey crippled, she whistles for the muscle and here comes her pimp Tattoo el Malo."

"Who?"

He stood up. "Let's not talk about Angel. Ten Penh ain't going to wait forever.."

Saturday, August 19, 1:00 a.m.

For the remainder of the evening, discussing Drew's mental health was off-limits. That would happen between him and his new therapist. Instead, he asked Zoë about herself for a while, and soon they branched out into all manner of topics—art, music, politics, a couple of mutual acquaintances, and the funny people they'd hung with when they were younger. He found her captivating—her wit, her style, her intelligence, and her humor.

After dinner, they took in some late-night jazz at Blues Alley in Georgetown. More talk and laughter cemented their intimacy. They decided to end the evening with a nightcap at his place.

He cut on the lights in the vestibule and reset the alarm while she kicked off her stilettos and gazed about the spacious living room—the dark, masculine colors, clean, crisp lines, and the deep-pile chocolate carpet, into which she dug her newly freed toes with an ecstatic sigh. She examined the painting of silhouetted chained slaves marching against the horizon, looked closer, and gasped. "This isn't what I think it is, is it?"

"Aaron Douglas."

"It must have cost you a fortune."

"Shush, not many know I have it, and most have no idea what it is. You're familiar with the Harlem Renaissance."

She continued to stare at the painting. "Not hanging-on-my-wall familiar... What a nice place you have here."

"Come on, let's have that nightcap." He stood close to her, deeply inhaling in her subtle scent. "What would you like?" He could no longer restrain himself from touching her, and put a hand on her back just above her waist.

She turned around and peered up into his face for a long moment. Then she kissed him. His hand slid down and pulled her closer.

After a wonderfully long time, their lips separated. She teetered back from his embrace. Drew grabbed her arms to steady her.

"Too much to drink?"

"No." She eased down onto the sofa. "Too much of you. I can't believe I'm here. What am I doing here?"

He laughed and sat down next to her. "All this time, we've been fighting to keep our distance, trying to find a cure for my ailment, and you were my medicine all along." He took her ear lobe between his lips then licked her neck. She cooed, and suddenly, as if things were going too slowly, she took control. She shoved him onto his back, kissing him while at the same time tugging at his pants. She found the treasure and freed it.

"Wow. I wasn't expecting all that. What are you waiting for?"

He laughed. "What happened to the staid psychotherapist? She's a super-freak."

She was coming in again for another kiss. He held her at bay, sat up, and she nearly tumbled off his lap unto the floor.

"Slow down, don't be in such a hurry."

She moved to the other end of the couch and crossed her arms. "I'm sorry, I didn't mean to... Why did you ask me here?"

"To take you to pound town baby."

"What?"

"To make love to you."

"Well...?"

"Let's get it on, huh." He laughed. "Chill baby, it's early. I want to relish every moment. I want it to last awhile. That's why you need to ease off the throttle." He stuffed away his erection with a zip. "How about some champagne?"

She sighed. "If you think I can wait."

"It'll be worth the wait."

"Promises, promises. Where's the bathroom? I need to get out of these pantyhose."

"Upstairs on the right."

In the kitchen, Drew grabbed two champagne glasses and pulled down the ice bucket and filled it around a bottle of Cristal, choosing his last 1999 over the almost as good 2000. With all the accoutrements in hand, he returned to the living room whistling, and set in motion his plan to stimulate every sense with pleasure. He set out the wine, lit a scented candle and put it in the corner where it wouldn't interfere with the champagne's bouquet, and then loaded the CD player, in its discreetly hidden cabinet, with Luther Vandross, Will Downing Jr., and Peabo Bryson. He mulled over the possibility of hors d'oeuvres and rejected it; their mouths would have plenty of other things to taste.

He heard Zoë come out of the bathroom.

"Come on down," he said, "let's get this party started."

The doorbell rang. Who could that be in the middle of the night? He went to the door.

"Who is it?" Zoë asked.

Drew looked through the window. "Damn. Angel. She was supposed to wait until tomorrow."

"Wait for what? I knew I shouldn't have come here."

Angel pounded on the door. "Please, Drew, open up. We need to talk."

"Sit down," he told Zoë. "I'll get rid of her."

"Where are my shoes? I knew I should have gone home. I'm out of here."

More pounding. "Drew, please, just for a minute."

"Hold up, don't go, I'll get rid of her."

Drew turned off the alarm and unlocked the door. It happened so quickly. Before he could even speak, Angel stepped aside and Drew was looking over the barrel of a gun into a familiar face.

"Back up, Mr. Drew Smith."

"Tattoo el Malo. I guess I don't have to ask you in."

Tattoo pushed Drew back into the vestibule. Angel followed him in, and then another familiar face. He too pointed a gun at Drew. The man's clean shaven youthful appearance and without the Bantu locks barely resembled the mug shot plastered all over the local papers.

Tattoo waved his gun at Drew. "Have a seat." Then he smiled at Zoë. "Hello gorgeous." He waved her to a chair, and as she passed, snatched the clump of pantyhose from her hand.

"What do you want, Tattoo?" Drew said.

"Some of that money you givin' away. Heard you was looking for me and writing checks. But we'll get to that later."

Drew gazed into the other, younger man's glare. "It's Jinx right?" Jinx didn't respond. "I've been looking for you, too. Expected you'd be south of the border by now. Waiting around for your mother's funeral?"

"Shut up, Smith," Tattoo said. "I'm doing the talking now."

Zoë seemed to have regained some of her composure and was studying Angel, who was leaning against the closed door, arms crossed. She looked high.

"Ah, champagne," Tattoo said. "We celebrate, no?" Unlike Angel, a New York Puerto Rican, no traces of the urban accent he spoke like an immigrant Dominicano. "But only two glasses. That's no way to treat your guests. Angel, get more glasses."

Angel pouted but didn't move.

"You hear what I said?" Tattoo cut her a sharp look.

"I want a hit."

"Don't start that again. What I tell you?"

Angel twisted her mouth and disappeared into the kitchen.

"What is this shit music?" Tattoo walked to the hidden cabinet. This wasn't his first visit, he seemed to know his way around. He switched to a satellite radio station. The Afro-Latin beat of reggaetón filled the room. Tattoo did a salsa step, holding his gun in one hand and the pantyhose in the other. Jinx looked tense as he stood watch over them.

Angel came back and set three glasses next to the ice bucket, cutting her eyes at Zoë, who met her gaze for a moment then looked away.

Tattoo stood over Drew. "Pop the cork, man."

"I'll let you do the honors." Drew wanted to get his hands on that bottle, the handiest weapon within reach, but didn't want to seem too eager, and anyway, a guy like Tattoo would insist on having his orders obeyed.

"My hands are full." He put Zoë's pantyhose to his face and inhaled deeply. "He's got her all wet. Angel, how you like that?" Again he sniffed the stockings and tossed them in Drew's face. "And do I detect a hint of Summer's Eve?"

"A cocksucker like you ought to know."

"Be nice." Tattoo suddenly brought the butt of the gun down on Drew's skull.

Chapter 16

T HE MUSIC OF Tito Puente and Celia Cruz, "Yo Soy La Voz," came from the satellite radio system. Pain pounded in Drew's skull as his eyes focused. Zoë's expression of grave concern swam into view. His head nestled against her bosom as she applied a cold towel. It all came rushing back—Angel, Tattoo, and most of all, Jinx.

"How's your head?" she whispered.

Taking her cue, he whispered back. "Hurts. You okay?" She nodded and gave him a tight smile. He turned his head to see Tattoo dozing in the armchair across the room. The gun, a Glock 17 with an eighteen-round clip, lay across his lap. Angel was nowhere in sight.

"How long was I out?"

"About an hour, he just dozed off waiting for you to come around."

"Angel?"

"Upstairs smoking crack."

"Jinx?"

"Tattoo sent him away."

With pain pounding in his head, and his arms and legs feeling miles away, was he up to taking on Tattoo mano-a-mano? But this might be his only opportunity to end the hostage situation. Whatever the risk, he had to make a move.

Son of a bitch, snoring like a pig, the empty bottle of his vintage Cristal lying raped and dead at his feet. Drew's anger gave him energy. He dizzily struggled to his feet.

She grabbed his hips and held him upright. "Where are you going? You have a concussion."

He pointed to the gun. As Zoë held her breath, he tiptoed across the room. Should he go for speed or quiet? That was easy: right now he had no speed. Fifteen feet to go. Why did he have to buy such a big house?

The candle flickered, casting Drew's jittery shadow onto the wall and making him even dizzier. Step by step—

Suddenly, footsteps on the staircase. It was now or never.

"Tattoo?" Angel called.

Tattoo's eyes jerked open just as Drew made his leap of faith for the gun. Drew's fingers grabbed the barrel at the same instant Tattoo's fingers tightened his grip on the handle. Drew crashed into him, pinning his back against the chair. With failing leverage, Drew delivered a weak punch to Tattoo's jaw. The gun fired, plaster rained from the ceiling, and the struggle halted for one shocked moment. Tattoo took advantage of the distraction and got a knee under Drew's ribcage. Drew landed on his back, his hands empty.

In an instant, Tattoo stood and his right bare foot slammed against Drew's already sore skull. His vision went black and all he could do was lie there and catch a kick to his ribs. He tried to grab Tattoo's foot but was too slow. With kicks thrown from the back of the leg, Tattoo seemed trained in Tae Kwon Do.

Tattoo jumped out of Drew's reach and in a 360-degree turn delivered another kick to the face. Zoë fell between the two men.

"Stop it! Stop!" Tattoo, his breathing ragged, backed off and pointed the gun at them. Angel stood frozen on the staircase.

"You!" Tattoo shouted at Zoë. "Get back over there!"

Zoë eased back as Drew struggled to lift himself. Tattoo, with the gun at Drew's head, collared him with an arm and jerked him to his feet. For a slim man, Tattoo was unexpectedly strong. Drew staggered to his feet only to be shoved back onto the sofa. Drained, he slumped down next to Zoë.

"Don't move, muddafucka!"

Drew glared back into his black hawk eyes. The head wound had reopened and blood dripped down his face as Zoë tried to stop the bleeding.

"No more bullshit! You hear me?"

Angel picked up her glass and walked back into the kitchen. Moments later, a key turned in the front door. Tattoo pointed the gun at the door. Jinx walked in.

Tattoo lowered the gun. "You get it?"

"Benicio said it's the last of your stash."

"Give it to Angel and give me the rope."

Jinx tossed Tattoo a coil of nylon rope and a roll of duct tape.

Angel came back in with a full glass of wine. "Tattoo—Oh Jinx, you're back. You got it?"

He pulled a plastic bag from the pocket of his baggy jeans. With both wine and crack replenished, Angel flashed a quick smile and headed directly for the steps. She paused for a moment. "You want a little hit?"

"Not now," Tattoo said. "Mr. Drew Smith wants to play games."

"Okay, but hurry up. It's not much fun without you."

"I need to get back," Jinx said. "Benicio's ready to hit the road. Says he took care of the boat."

Tattoo pulled a pocketknife from his jeans and released a hooked blade. "Cover me. If he tries anything, shoot him."

Jinx pulled the Glock from his waistband. Drew stared at him and Jinx returned a crooked smile as Tattoo tied Drew's hands together with the fireman's chair knot, which Drew remembered from his Boy Scout days. Tattoo admired his handiwork.

"Excuse me," Zoë said.

"What?" Tattoo snapped.

"I have to pee. I can't hold it any longer."

"Okay, come on, sweetheart."

"I don't need an audience."

"I promise I won't watch." He escorted her up the stairs.

Drew tried not to worry about her and instead debated whether to taunt or beguile Jinx.

"What's the plan now, Jinx?"

"What you mean?"

"There's a price on your head. Where you running to? Who can you trust? I talked to your sister."

"What you know about my sistah?"

"I know she wasn't happy to hear you killed her mother."

"She don't care. My mother never cared for us. I'm the only one who cared."

"Does Tattoo care?"

"Shut up. I ain't gotta talk to you."

"Let's talk about the cab driver. What happened?"

"I saw you in the alley with Gee's uncle. Why was you looking for me?"

"You can help Gee. You can clear him. Why don't we go to the police and tell them what happened?"

"Gee's a punk, and you his punk-ass lawyer."

"Tyrone said you shot Naomi, Josh and Rodney."

"He couldn't even shoot that fat old bitch."

Drew shook his head in pity. "No way you'll come out of this alive if you stay on the run. You know how many white cops with guns are running around looking for your ass? At least save your life. Let me take you in. Alone, you'll never be able to surrender, they'll shoot you down on sight."

"I ain't going out like that."

"You're all alone, Jinx, and will be for the rest of your life. Not even your sister will have anything to do with you. When you're locked up, no one will think of you at Christmas. Who will remember your birthdays? Who'll write? No one will visit you."

"I ain't going out like that, either."

"It's not too late to save your life. What's up with Tattoo? You think you can trust him?"

"Shut up, I said." Jinx was coming at him with his gun.

"Tattoo's a crazy snake, you know that. You're all alone."

Jinx raised his gun.

Tattoo appeared on the staircase with Zoë. "Don't let him get to you, Jinx. He's a lawyer. All talk. That's what he does. Shut up, Smith."

"How about you, Tattoo? You're a wanted man too. I heard about the mess out in L.A. DEA's looking for you, and I heard you pissed off the cartel."

"Shut up, Smith." Tattoo signaled Zoë to have a seat. She eased down next to Drew. Tattoo aimed his gun at Drew, long enough for Zoë to start whimpering softly. After a long pause, he laughed. "Smith, you talk too much. Shut up."

"Is that true?" Jinx asked.

"Both of you are being hunted," Drew said. "Tracked by bloodhounds."

Before Drew knew what was happening, Tattoo slapped him across the face. "I said shut up, Smith. Don't listen to him, Jinx. He don't know nothing."

"Now I got to pee," Drew said.

"Okay, go ahead, who's stopping you?" Drew started to stand and Tattoo pointed the gun at him again. "I didn't say you could get up. Pee there if you have to." Tattoo laughed.

Drew looked at Jinx, who in turn was still frowning uncertainly at Tattoo. Drew had maneuvered Tattoo into two choices, either of which gave Drew a chance. Tattoo could let Drew stay here with Jinx and water the seeds of doubt he'd already planted, or take Drew to the bathroom where Tattoo would have no backup.

He aimed the gun at Drew. "Okay, get up." Drew stood. Tattoo looked at Zoë then winked at Jinx. "You two get to know one another."

He followed Drew up the steps with the gun at his back and shoved him into the bathroom. "Hurry up."

When Drew tried to shut the door, Tattoo blocked it with his foot.

"You like to watch, huh?"

"I'm warning you, Smith, no funny business."

"Hey, I need some help here." Drew held out his bound hands. "Can you pull my dick out for me? I'll let you suck it."

"You find a way."

Drew fumbled with the zipper and found a way. He pretend-ed not to be able to pee. "I can't while you're watching." It would take five seconds to reach the Liquid Plumber under the sink, and one splash to blind Tattoo.

"Tough shit. Pee or we go back downstairs."

Drew released a stream, and smiled when he was done. "Like the show?"

Tattoo yanked him out by the collar and pushed him down the hall.

"Hey, I didn't wash my hands. No need to flush and rush." Tattoo shoved him against the wall. Their eyes locked. The Liquid Plumber wasn't going to happen. "What exactly is it you want, Tattoo?"

"Let's talk." Tattoo pushed Drew down the hall, into the gues-troom, and onto the bed, and closed the door. He spoke quietly.

"Let's make a deal, Mr. Drew Smith. I give you Jinx, and you give me the reward."

"I'm not offering a reward, the police are. Besides, Angel al-ready tried that."

"I know. She told me. She thought I'd be mad at her for trying to make a deal behind my back, but I thought about it and came up with a better plan. I knew she was up to something when me and Jinx saw you going into the Palais that night."

"So why try to kill me?"

"That was Jinx. You were looking for us. I wouldn't have missed. It made him feel good. Deal?"

"I'll give you the money if you let Zoë go."

"So you're worried about the woman. Good to know."

"Where do you plan to run to?"

"Atlanta, like Jinx." He laughed. "You think I'm stupid, I'm gonna tell you my plan?"

"You hand me Jinx and I'll make sure the cops give you the money. They won't even know it's you, it's anonymous, they'll give you a number—"

"I'm not waiting for the cops. I've seen your bank statements. You got that much and more. Break me off a piece. I'll give you a couple of hours to think about it. Your bank opens at nine on Saturdays."

"How do I know you won't double cross me, like Jinx?"

"You don't. But you're no good to me dead. Anyway, you'll do what's best for the woman, no?"

Drew nodded.

With hands tightly bound, Drew stumbled down the steps to the living room. Tattoo pushed him back onto the sofa next to Zoë, cut off another length of rope, and tied her hands. Then he ordered the two upstairs to the small guestroom, where he made them lie down side by side on the double bed. He must have put a lot of time into planning this takeover. He wound the rope around their chests and legs and bound them to the bed. Down the hall, Angel seemed to have set up camp in the master bedroom with the comforts of TV and stereo. Tattoo apologized to Zoë for having to tie her up, and left.

Drew turned his head toward her. "I'm sorry I got you into this."

She seemed remarkably composed under the circumstances. "It's not your fault. I heard them talking while you were unconscious."

"What did they say?"

"Once they get the money from you, somebody named Benicio is the advance man. He's leaving for the Florida Keys to charter a boat. They're going to Santo Domingo. Tattoo plans to marry Angel there, and Jinx will work for Tattoo."

"I'll figure out a way to turn this around."

"I think I can help."

"How?"

"I have a razorblade in my bra. I lifted it from your medicine cabinet."

"That's why I like you."

"Why?"

"You're smart." Her fingers strained beneath her dress to get to her bra. It wasn't easy with both hands bound at the wrist. "I wish I could help with that," he whispered. "Please don't scar that beautiful bosom." She smiled and finally sighed with relief.

"Got it."

"Cut me loose."

She took the single-edged blade and gently cupped it in her fist, then relaxed her head back onto the pillow.

He held his roped hands to her face. "What are you doing? Start sawing."

"Wait."

"For what?"

"Until they settle down and Jinx is gone."

"You're right. They'll probably come back and check on us." Drew lay back too. "For two weeks I've been looking for Jinx, I never imagined he'd show up at my door."

Jinx's and Tattoo voices could be heard downstairs. The front door closed. Moments later, Tattoo looked in on them, checked their ropes, but said nothing. His footsteps returned to the master bedroom. Through its open door, they listened to Angel's and Tattoo's laughter turn into the sounds of sex. They went at it long and hard. Drew knew Angel's stamina. It seemed they'd never end. Then it stopped.

"Cut me loose."

She delicately began slicing away at the tightly wound plastic threads. Barely audible voices drifted in from down the hall. Once his hands were free, he immediately began to untie hers, then started on the rope across their chest. Soon Angel and Tattoo were at it again, with Angel's moans and cries louder than before.

"Damn," Zoë whispered. "He must be good."

"She's a screamer. Let's go."

"They're not asleep."

"They're too busy to hear us."

"No. Wait. Soon they'll be sleeping."

"Woman, you are working my last nerve."

"Shut up and sit down."

"You sound like Tattoo." But she was probably right, and Drew did as he was told.

They waited patiently. Twenty minutes later they heard nothing but the hum of the central air conditioning and the muted street traffic.

"Now." Zoë eased her bare feet onto the carpet and was at the door when Drew pulled her back and took the lead. As they eased down the staircase, the sound of creaking boards seemed amplified. He should have had it carpeted.

At the bottom, Zoë raced to pick up her shoes at the door. Drew was behind her and quickly snapped open deadbolt. The room suddenly lit up from a table lamp.

"Hold it right there." Jinx pointed a gun at them from the sofa. Either he'd left and come back, or never left. "Where do you think you're going?" He approached them, gun held high and aimed directly at Drew's head.

Drew flung open the door—"Run, Zoë, run!"—and punched a code into the keypad. Jinx was almost on him when he dropped low and drove his head into Jinx's gut. The younger man grunted and hit the floor, and the gun slid out of reach. Zoë scrambled for her shoes but when Tattoo leapt down the steps in his underwear, she was out the door running. Drew made a grab for Tattoo but Jinx tackled him and Tattoo ran out after her. As Drew tried to kick himself away from Jinx, Zoë screamed. Her next scream sounded muffled, and a moment later Tattoo carried her kicking back into the house with a hand over her mouth. He threw her across the room then slammed the door and turned the deadbolt.

Jinx was punching wildly at Drew, who was trying to fend off fists with one hand while the other gripped Jinx's throat.

"Stop!" Tattoo shouted. He pulled Jinx off and pointed the gun at Drew. "Stop it!"

"Let me kill him now." Jinx panted and gasped, his chest heaving as Tattoo pushed him away.

"Drew Smith, you're being a bad boy." Tattoo bare foot landed up side his head.

Chapter 17

THE TWO WERE tied down again, the ropes tighter than before. Tattoo discovered the razor blade and immediately knew Zoë was responsible for the escape attempt.

"Let me have her," Jinx said.

"You go back to Angel's apartment."

"I saved your ass, man, what you talkin' about?"

"Go. And stay there till I call you. You gonna fuck things up. I have to keep you and Smith apart."

"Let me kill him now."

"That's what I'm talking about. We need him alive."

The two men left the room arguing.

Drew painfully turned his head to look at Zoë. "You all right?"

"Me? Are *you* all right?"

The doorbell rang. Drew and Zoë heard the flurry of activity. Tattoo and Jinx burst into the room and peeked through the blinds.

"Police," Tattoo said.

"It was that box, he punched in some numbers," Jinx said.

"What did you do, Smith?"

"I activated the silent alarm. You're all done now. Untie us and it'll look better for you."

"They're walking around the house." Jinx said. "What are they doing?"

"They'll be knocking on the door next," Drew said. "Let me go talk to them."

"Fuck you, Smith."

"I told you he'd fuck things up," Jinx said. "Let me kill him."

"Shut up." The doorbell rang. "Watch Smith, shoot him the first noise he makes, her too. Smith, you pay for this. Angel!" He left the room. "Angel, get up. Get up! Fuckin' crackhead." A couple of sharp slaps, some frantic whispering, then the sound of stumbling footsteps.

"What do I say? Tattoo, I'm too afraid."

"Now!"

"What do I say?"

"Think of something, tell them anything, I don't care if you shake your ass in their face, just get rid of them."

Angel dashed back to the bedroom and a few seconds later Drew caught sight of her running for the stairs in her sexy teddy. Tattoo glared at Drew with a finger to his lips and a gun to Zoë's head. He heard Angel unlock the front door. "Hi, officer, is there a problem?"

Drew had no trouble imagining the scene downstairs, the two uniformed officers staring at her, her fake attempts to hide herself behind the open door. She'd show them enough to turn on their engines and turn off their brains.

"Your silent alarm is going off, ma'am."

"Oh, I always do something wrong with it. My husband reset the password and I guess I remembered it wrong."

"Where is your husband?"

"Out of town on business."

"We'll notify the security company to reset the alarm, but I suggest you contact your husband and get that code."

"Oh, good idea."

"We don't want to have to come back here again tonight." He must have been smiling with that line, for Angel laughed.

"I'm sorry to bother you."

Tattoo watched the cops leave from the window while Angel locked the door and trudged upstairs. "That was too intense. I need a hit." Jinx tucked away his gun.

"You go now." Tattoo waved Jinx to the door with his gun. "Come back when I call you."

"You sure, man?" Jinx didn't move. "Last time—"

"Go!" Tattoo turned to Drew. "You changed the code, Mr. Drew Smith. I should known after you changed the lock. What's the new code?"

"You'd better stay, Jinx."

"I'm warning you, Smith."

"Jinx, who can you trust?"

Jinx balled a fist. "Let me beat it out of him."

"I told you, go!"

Jinx turned away from Tattoo's impatient glare.

"He's selling you out, Jinx."

Jinx spun around, pulled his gun, and pointed it at Drew's face. "Is this going down like you said, Tattoo? We're taking that boat tomorrow?"

"Shut up about that. It's just like I told you. Now get over to Angel's apartment till I call you."

"Jinx, he's already made a deal for the reward on your head. I'm your only hope of staying alive."

Jinx clenched his teeth and ground the gun barrel into Drew's cheekbone. Drew watched helplessly as Jinx's finger tightened on the trigger.

Tattoo grabbed his arm. "No, man! We need him."

Jinx stayed motionless for a moment, then suddenly stepped back. His shoulders slumped and his arms dropped slack to his sides. The gun dangled loosely in his hand. Then he turned and walked quietly down the stairs. The lock made only a faint click as he left.

Tattoo grabbed Drew by the ears and pulled his head off the bed. "What's the code?"

"Forget it." It was too soon for the security company to have reset the alarm, so Jinx hadn't set it off again when he opened the door. But the next time someone came or went, the cops would be back.

Tattoo pointed the gun at Drew. "The code."

Drew smiled. "You need me alive, remember."

Tattoo suddenly shoved the gun up under Zoë's dress and ripped it half off. "But not her." He worked his fingers between her thighs. Zoë was looking daggers at Tattoo and didn't make a sound.

"W-E-R-D," Drew said.

Tattoo tucked the gun into his waistband. "No more bullshit, Mr. Drew Smith."

⚮

Zoë lay silent while Drew wrestled with exhaustion, his mind actively running scenarios for escape and overcoming his captors. Each one ended in disaster.

At sunup, voices from down the hall let him know Angel and Tattoo were up and about. Moments later, Tattoo stood in the doorway shirtless wearing the same jeans and the same wicked grin. He swaggered to the window and yanked the blinds open, flooding the room with barbarously bright light. Zoë stirred and blinked.

Tattoo knelt bedside her. The Royall Bayrhum fragrance from Drew's toiletry bar filled the room. Thick, long black hair hung loosely over his muscled shoulders, and the freshly trimmed mustache glistened like slivers of coal against the smooth caramel complexion. "Good morning, my sweet chica." He began to untie her ropes. She turned her head toward Drew, her eyes full of fear.

Angel appeared in the doorway, arms crossed, watching Tattoo fawning over Zoë. She looked burned out from a night of sex and drugs. Even with all that had happened, Drew felt a pang for the beautiful woman killing herself slowly with thugs and drugs.

"Tattoo, what you doing with that bitch?"

Drew saw the momentary start in Tattoo's eyes, but he didn't miss a beat. "With both these bitches. What's it look like I'm doin'?"

Tattoo pulled the ropes away from both of them. Drew sat up.

"My sweet chica, would you like a shower, change into something more comfortable? It won't be much longer."

Zoë looked at Drew. No doubt the last thing she wanted was to take her clothes off with Tattoo around, but if the bathroom offered any chances for escape... "I'm not sure."

Tattoo laughed. "Course you do. Angel, get her some clean clothes."

"I don't have any clothes for her."

"I have shorts and shirts she can wear," Drew said. "The ones you wear when you sleep over."

"*Used* to sleep over."

"Do it," Tattoo snapped.

Angel turned on her heel and disappeared down the hall.

Again, Tattoo kneeled in Zoë's face. "Breakfast?"

Drew grunted. "I need to use the bathroom."

Tattoo regarded Drew for a moment. "Get up." He pulled the gun from his waistband. "Go." He followed Drew down the hall. When Drew passed the hall bathroom, Tattoo grabbed him by the back of his collar. "Hey, right here."

"Force of habit, using the master bath."

"Use this one." He shoved Drew into the bathroom and again stood at the door watching. Drew repeated the same taunts, which Tattoo ignored. Back in the bedroom, Drew plopped down next to Zoë.

Angel brought in a pair of shorts and t-shirt. Zoë accepted the clothes with "Thank you," the first words spoken between the two women. Angel didn't respond. Tattoo freed Zoë's hands.

"I get to shower too?" Drew asked.

"No."

Drew looked over to Angel. "What do you see in this man? He's only using you."

"Unlike you, huh?"

"Shut up, Smith," Tattoo said. "She ain't dumb like Jinx."

"I'm ready," Zoë said. Tattoo smiled and stood up.

Angel stepped between them. "I'll watch her." She led Zoë out of the room before Tattoo could argue. Tattoo watched them leave with a hint of annoyance in his expression, then eased down in the corner armchair with the gun across his lap. "Made up your mind, Mr. Smith?"

"I don't have a choice, the way I see it."

"Get up. Come with me."

Tattoo marched Drew downstairs to his study. His business checkbook, an emergency backup, had been removed from the drawer and lay open on his desk. The computer was up and running. Tattoo sat Drew down and produced two documents for his signature, a check drawn on his business account and printed from his computer in the amount of fifty thousand dollars, and a letter authorizing the wire transfer.

"What's this? The reward is twenty thousand dollars."

"You can take a loss."

Drew sucked in his breath and signed the documents. Tattoo compared the signature to one on a cancelled check from the desk drawer, then tied Drew securely to the chair.

"You, me, and Angel go to the bank when Jinx gets here. Jinx stays here with your girlfriend. Once we have the money, we let you go. You call the cops, get the reward."

"That's too dangerous. He'll try to use her as a hostage."

"Not my problem." He left the room.

Imprisoned in his study, Drew pulled and strained against the plastic rope, but nothing would give except his bruised skin. A thousand thoughts and fears crossed his mind. He prayed no harm would come to Zoë, and he found a little solace in the reminder that she was no weak-willed woman. She had shown bravery and nerve tempered with a practical prudence and spunk a quality that made her good at her job.

What would happen to Gee if Drew didn't survive this ordeal? To any other lawyer in town—to the entire justice system—Gee was just another black thug trying to squirm out of well-deserved jail time.

And Angel, how could he have been so stupid, exposing his personal and professional life to such a woman? But still, there was something good about her, some goodness in her—genuine love at her core, that was it. Beautiful but weak and vulnerable, exploited by the rogue Tattoo. And by a rogue like himself. All the advice offered by Julio, the Chief, and even Shirley had fallen on his deaf ears. Drew Smith needed no one's advice. He could take care of himself--right, hogtied and robbed by a whore and her pimp. Drew Smith, you asked for this.

Still, if he could appeal to the tiny spark of good still burning in Angel's heart—

A shadow moved on the deck...Hernando! Here to fix the door! He was inspecting it now. Drew tried to get his attention, but couldn't yell for fear Tattoo would hear him. Hernando pulled out his tape measure and began measuring. He was earlier than he said he'd be...damn, he must be figuring out what materials he'd need for the job, then would go away to gather them. Hernando probably thought Drew was upstairs asleep and didn't want to wake him. Drew leaned forward, tilted the chair an inch or two, and tried to inch it toward the French doors. The heavy chair hardly budged.

But the movement must have caught Hernando's eyes causing him to peer in, his hand covering the reflection from the glass, and his eyes grew wide with surprise as they met Drew's. Drew wiggled his bound hands to show that he was tied to the chair. Hernando tried the door. No! Drew shook his head. Get help! He mouthed the words. Hernando looked puzzled. "Get Julio," he said as loud as he dared. "Hoo-lee-ooh" he repeated slowly, with exaggerated lip movements. Still looking puzzled, Hernando slowly nodded and disappeared.

∞

Perched on the covered commode, legs crossed, Angel filed her nails while Zoë showered. Zoë luxuriated for the briefest moment in the freedom the shower offered, then frantically tried to come up with a plan. She'd have little chance with an improvised weapon, even if she could get her hands on one. What good would it do her to overpower Angel, which was a long shot anyway against a woman with a dancer's athleticism and probably a lot of practice defending herself from violent attacks. Her own skills were with people, getting into their heads.

Angel glanced at her with suspicion on her face; she'd lingered in the shower as long as she could get away with. Zoë turned off the water and grabbed a towel from the rack. She managed to flash a friendly smile at Angel.

"What's your name?" Angel asked.

"Zoë."

"Zoë, can I ask you something?"

"Sure." Zoe answered relieved at the thought and opportunity to establish rapport.

"How long you been sleeping with Drew?"

Easy answer, the truth. "I'm not sleeping with Drew."

"Oh, bitch, don't play me, you were here in the middle of the night."

"First date..." Don't play too innocent, and butter her up a little. "But you're right, I might have slept with him if we'd had the chance. Why are you so interested? Isn't Tattoo your man?"

Angel didn't respond.

"Do you love Tattoo?"

Angel sighed. "I don't know. He promised to take care of me. How long have you known Drew?"

Careful, she might know the answer. "About three weeks. Drew recently became my patient."

"Patient?" Angel looked concerned. "He sick?"

"I'm a psychiatrist."

"Oh." Angel pondered a moment. "He's a little bit crazy, huh?"

Zoë laughed. "Aren't we all?"

"Like Tattoo."

Tattoo was dangerously crazy. "What's he like? We heard you last night, you know…"

Angel sighed. "The sex is good, but he's no Drew. Drew's great in bed, don't you think?" Angel watched Zoë out of the corner of her eyes.

"I wouldn't know."

Angel stopped filing her nails. "You're serious, you two really haven't?"

"Nope."

"Boy, are you in for a big surprise." Angel gave her a wry smile.

Take a chance, build the intimacy. "Oh, I've seen the big surprise. I just can't get my hands on it." The two shared a giggle—bingo.

"Girl it's a lot to handle. And you've known him three weeks? He had me in his bed in three hours."

"Until last night we had a doctor-patient relationship. No fooling around. But if you hadn't showed up last night I bet I would have beat your record by two hours."

Angel smiled and her eyes softened. "Are you in love with Drew?"

"No. I don't know. Not that I couldn't be, but who knows? I think he still has a thing for you."

Angel seemed to mull that over. Zoë wrapped herself in the towel and stepped out of the tub. Draw things out but don't obviously stall. Look busy. Zoë stood at the mirror, unpinned her hair, and shook it free.

Angel offered her hairbrush. "There's a supply of toothbrushes below the sink. Drew seems to have a lot of houseguests." They shared another laugh and Zoë began to brush out her hair.

"You have pretty hair," Angel said.

"Thank you, and so do you. Are those highlights natural?"

"I wish. I did it myself."

"It looks natural. Any deodorant in here?" She opened the medicine cabinet. The razor blades were gone.

"Some roll-on."

"Your light complexion goes with any color. You have so many options. I wish I had your hair."

"You're pretty," Angel said. "You don't have to change anything. Mother nature blessed you perfectly."

"Me?" Zoë looked in the mirror. "You could have any man you wanted. If you don't mind my asking, why bother with Tattoo? You're smart. You can take care of yourself. You don't need him. He lives a dangerous life."

"I've always lived dangerously. What's the difference?"

"If something happens to him, then where will you be? He may even take you down with him. A life of crime, is that what you want?"

Angel shrugged. "I've never had what I wanted. What does it matter?"

"Angel, help us. Drew will look out for you. He can get you out of this awful life. I can help."

Angel smiled sweetly at her. "All my life men come up to me, smile, tell me how pretty and smart I am, how they can help me out. You think I don't know when I'm being played, bitch?"

"Angel!" Tattoo shouted. Someone was pounding on the door downstairs. "Angel!"

Tattoo corralled the two women into the master bedroom and handed Angel a roll of duct tape and a pair of scissors. "Tie her up and gag her. Quick!" He left and was back in moments with Drew, whom he shoved down on the bed. "Now him." They worked together and soon had them both tightly trussed.

The banging at the door increased in volume and tempo. Tattoo handed a second gun to Angel, who took it with confidence.

"I'll see who it is," he said. "Watch them."

Drew strained to hear what was going on downstairs. He recognized Hernando's raised voice. Spanish was being spoken. He was alone—where was Julio? What the hell was Hernando doing? The idiot was supposed to get help.

After a long silence, Hernando's pickup door slammed and the engine's drone faded beyond the driveway. Tattoo stomped back up the stairs and into the room. He stood over Drew and violently snatched the tape from his face. Drew cried out in pain. Angel removed Zoë's with a tad less force.

"Who is this Hernando?"

"A carpenter, was supposed to do some work for me this morning."

"I sent him away. He wasn't happy. I tell him I'm your Dominican cousin. I don't think he believed me. Why should this stranger not believe me?" He slapped Drew in the face. "Who is this Hernando?"

"I told you."

"Is he your friend? How you know him? Will he make trouble?"

Drew smiled at Tattoo, hoping to increase his fear. Damn Hernando's stupidity. Now Tattoo would only be more careful and dangerous. "Afraid he'll come back here with the police? Didn't count on that in your plan, did you?"

Tattoo slammed his fist into Drew's right eye. "Don't fuck with me, Smith."

Drew lurched sideways into Zoë. His eye quickly began to swell shut. Tattoo anxiously scuttled to the window and peeped through the shades.

"Get her dressed. I'm going downstairs to check around. I'll shoot the first thing that moves." Tattoo pointed the gun at Zoë and glared at Drew. "Or her, if you give me any more trouble."

Chapter 18

Saturday, August 19, 8:00 a.m.

A N HOUR BEFORE their scheduled trip to the bank, Tattoo was spooked. Hernando must have thrown him for a loop. He paced around the second floor, looking out all the windows, checking for an invasion force. Drew tried to engage him in negotiations, then to pick a fight, just to keep him from being so vigilant in case Hernando wasn't as dumb as he seemed.

"Where the hell is Jinx?" Tattoo muttered.

"He's not supposed to be here yet," Angel said.

"This Hernando could come back. We should go now." Tattoo dialed, then slammed down the phone. "Why don't he answer his phone?" Tattoo came back to the bedroom to check on Drew and Zoë. Angel followed. "Take Smith's car," Tattoo said, "go get Jinx. Now! Call me when you get there."

"I'm going, just be cool."

Drew caught Angel's eye for a moment. He stared at her hard, then looked at Tattoo, then at Zoë, then back at Angel with raised eyebrows. She seemed puzzled, but at least he had her attention. He repeated his pantomime. This time Angel threw a worried glance at Tattoo, then gave Drew a dismissive scowl, turned, and left the bedroom. A few seconds later, the front door slammed and a car started up and drove off.

Tattoo tied Zoë to the armchair and took Drew back down into the study and tied him to a chair. On his way out, he paused. "Now I go have some fun with your girlfriend."

"You lay one hand on her, I'll—"

"What? I go'n do to her what you did to my Angel. Fair is fair, no?" He shut the door.

The room grew darker as outside the skies clouded. A fierce morning storm was brewing. Raindrops pattered on the window. A volley of thunder rattled the windows. Drew struggled with the ropes but made no progress. Damn Hernando. How long could Zoë hold off Tattoo? He yanked on the ropes until his wrists bled.

The sudden storm passed. And then Julio and Hernando were peering through the French doors. Drew couldn't get a finger to his lips so clenched mouth shut, trying to signal Julio to keep quiet. Hernando pried open the door with a crowbar.

"Man, you look like hell," Julio whispered. "What's going on?"

"Tattoo el Malo's upstairs. He's got Zoë. We got to get her out of there."

"Figured it was him." Julio pulled a pocketknife and cut Drew's ropes.

"Where de muddafucka?" Hernando waved his crowbar. "I got something for him."

"What took you so long? Didn't the security company call you?"

"They called back and said they spoke with your wife and everything was all right. I went back to sleep."

"Julio, I don't have a wife."

"See? You need one. I figured you shacked up with Angel again."

They froze at the sound of a car pulling into the driveway. Julio peeked through the window. "Angel."

"With Jinx?"

"Alone."

Drew opened the study door so they could hear better, then they all hid behind it.

Zoë screamed . Julio grabbed Drew's arm and held him back. The front door lock snapped open and moments later, Angel's high-heeled steps quickened on the staircase.

"He's got a gun," Drew whispered.

"Me too", Julio responded.

They tiptoed across the living room to the staircase. Julio led with his gun drawn, and Hernando and his crowbar brought up the rear. Angel stood eavesdropping at the bedroom door, her back to the three men coming up behind her. Zoë cried out again, louder and more desperate. Angel burst into the room.

"Hijo de puta, cabrón, maldito. I leave you alone for five minutes and you do this."

"What are you doing here?"

"I forgot my house keys. You're no good. I can't trust you." She lifted his gun from the bureau.

"Give me the gun", Tattoo coaxed.

Angel kept him at gun point. Julio with gun raised slowly began to move in. Drew pulled him back, shook his head, and mouthed, "Zoë, Angel." Julio reluctantly nodded and lowered the gun. The three crept down the hallway.

"You stay away from me," Angel said.

"Come on, give your papi chulo the gun before you hurt yourself."

"Stay back!"

"Stupid bitch! Why you back here? Give me the gun."

"No!"

"Give me the gun, this is nothing. She means nothing to me. I'm just getting even for what Smith did to you. Now give me the gun. You know I love you. We marry as soon as we get to Santo Domingo."

"You only want to use me. Drew was right."

Drew could now see the scene through the crack between door and jamb. Angel's back was to the door, Tattoo was by the bed. Drew gave Julio a quick nod.

"Drew Smith, what does he know?"

With Drew behind Julio stepped into the room, gun pointed at Tattoo. "Hold it right there."

Tattoo dived for the gun in Angel's hand and spun her around onto the bed. She held tight and pulled back while Julio frantically tried to get a bead on Tattoo through the tangle of arms and legs. Suddenly, a loud pop. Angel trembled and Tattoo's eyes opened wide with shock. Then she went limp. "Tattoo," she whispered, in final profound disappointment.

"Angel?" Tattoo lifted her shoulders, but she was dead weight. For a moment he hovered over her, puzzled and shocked. "What have I done?"

"Stand up!" Julio shouted.

Tattoo snatched the gun from Angel's limp hand. And then Hernando's crowbar swung into the side of his head with a sickening thud.

Drew took Zoë into his arms. She was trembling violently. Tattoo had been slicing her clothes off shred by shred with the scissors, and had nearly finished. Drew covered her with a sheet. "Are you all right?"

"I will be, just give me a moment."

"Can you to go downstairs and call Chief Washington, explain what happened?"

Zoë looked about at Angel's bloody body on the bed and Tattoo unconscious on the floor. She covered her mouth, then nodded. Drew draped a robe around her shoulders. Then he took a lockbox from the closet, found the key, and removed a revolver. "Hernando, hold things down till the police get here. Look after Zoë. We'll be back shortly. Come on, Julio." He led Zoë by the hand downstairs. On the way out, he found Angel's purse, retrieved his keys, and hers as well.

"Where we're going?" Julio asked.

"I'll explain on the way."

∞

Saturday, August 18, 9:00 a.m.

The two walked down the hall toward Angel's apartment. Drew knocked on the door, waited, then knocked again, again with no response. He pulled out his cell phone and punched in Angel's number. They could hear it ringing inside. Suddenly, each reached for his gun.

"You hear that?"

"Sounded like a shot."

Drew used Angel's key and turned the knob. They entered with guns drawn.

"Hello!" Drew shouted out. No answer came from the deathly silence. Drew led the way with Julio close behind. Using couch and chairs for cover, they eased through the living room, down a narrow hall, past an empty bedroom on the left, to a bathroom on the right. Drew stepped in, then lowered his gun.

"Hello, Jinx."

Julio peered over Drew's shoulder. Jinx's head was slumped over the tub, blood oozing down the drain, tiles and shower curtain freshly splattered with flesh and blood. The place reeked of vomit. "He just killed himself?" Julio said. Drew held out his arm, blocking Julio from stepping inside for a better view. "Why he go and do that?" Julio turned to Drew. "At least Lowry didn't get to kill him."

"This is my fault. I tried to turn him against Tattoo. Instead, he must have finally realized there was no one in the whole world he could trust, and nothing left in this life for him. He said he wasn't going out like that, I should have read the signs. Now I've got no one left to exonerate Gee. Damn!"

"What's that other stuff?" Drano, bleach, and cleaning products were scattered about the floor. "Planning to clean up his own mess?"

"Probably trying to poison himself. Must have been too slow, couldn't take the pain. Decided it was quicker to blow his brains out. Anyway, it's over for him. Let's get out of here." Drew pulled out his cell phone.

"What do we do now?" Julio asked. "I mean about Gee?"

"Good question."

They waited in the hallway. It wasn't long before Lowry stepped off the elevator, followed by two uniformed officers. He frowned at Drew and Julio.

"What is it, Smith?"

"You'll find Jeffrey Legere inside."

Lowry walked into the apartment, and seconds later, reappeared in the doorway. "How did you know about this?"

"Long story. You'll find another body at my house."

∞

Saturday, August 18, 11:00 p.m.

It was early evening before the police and forensic investigators cleared out of Drew's house. Statements were taken from Zoë, Julio, Hernando and Drew. Zoë helped Drew clean up his room and Julio discarded the bloody bedclothes. Hernando did what he came to do in the first place, repair the French doors. Zoë lingered, and Drew persuaded her to let Julio drive her home. They were the last to leave. Drew wanted to be alone.

Tattoo would live, Angel had not, and Drew felt a profound sense of loss and blame. She died in his home, in his bed, the same bed they shared their sexual escapades. No matter how crazy and conniving she'd been, she didn't deserve such a death, and in truth, if he hadn't insisted on getting what he wanted from her without taking her real needs into account, and hadn't rationalized it all as simply a business proposition for her, she'd still be alive. This and all the events of the past twenty-four hours jammed and spun in his mind. All this death, and still one life remained in jeopardy. For hours he tried to focus on Gee, fearing he might lose the son he never knew. Jinx alive had been Drew's best hope, but not his last. He tried to relax and consider his young client's case. The Farragut robbery occurred in a big city full of people. Somebody had to have seen something...

The sharp ring of the phone jolted him. "Hello."

"Drew, I just called to check on you."

"I'm fine, Zoë. How about you, did you get some rest?"

"I'm still in a state. Is there anything you want to talk about?"

"I don't want to talk about it, at least not tonight."

"How are you feeling?"

"Excuse me, is this Dr. Settles, the therapist? I refuse to speak to her. She dropped me as a patient. I'll never speak to her again. However, I will talk to my good friend Zoë. Is she in? Where is she? I want to speak to Zoë. I want to speak to Zoë "

"Very funny. I don't have multiple personalities. But I'm sorry if that's how I sounded. I only asked as a friend, a friend who cares."

"I understand, and believe me, I appreciate it."

"Can I see you tomorrow?"

"I'd like that very much, but I don't think I'll have the time. Gee's hearing is coming up Monday, so I'll be working tomorrow. This is important to me."

"I understand."

"Goodnight, Zoë."

"Drew? Call me when you can."

"I promise." He ended the call. Did she feel like he was giving her the brushoff? Her standing up to danger with him had intensified his feelings for her. But he had a more pressing problem. His thoughts drifted to Hernando and Julio, enemies to allies, recalling the scene at Hernando's door.

It hit him like a bolt from the blue. He grabbed the phone and dialed.

"Julio, get up. We got work to do."

"What work?"

"Knocking on doors."

Chapter 19

T HE DOORBELL CALLED Drew away from his coffee. He greeted the courier and accepted a large manila envelope from the U.S. Attorney's Office. The reply brief's hefty weight amused him. Government lawyers seemed to believe that more paper could somehow tilt the scales of justice away from the weight of the evidence. With an interminable amount of taxpayer funds at their disposal, they could bury an adversary in paper. He once heard a horror story about a civil matter in which the sheer volume of government paper and process defeated justice and sent the litigant—bitter, bankrupt, and brokenhearted—to an early grave.

He perused the 120-page response to his 25-page arguments. It held nothing new, just the standard boilerplate citing superfluous case law. Drew tossed the document aside and picked up the phone. It was time to go to work again.

He called a couple of reporters to give them background on the hearing and ask for media coverage; while withholding details, he guaranteed a front-page story. He worked through the day and much of the night preparing for the hearing, outlining his oral argument, drafting his opening and closing statements, and devising the best strategy for deploying his new secret weapon. More time to prepare and a good night's sleep would have helped, but they were two casualties of legal warfare.

∞

Monday, August 20, 10:00 a.m.

The courtroom was filled to capacity. The invited reporters were there, front row as promised. Behind Gee sat his nervous parents, alongside Marie. In the moments before the judge took the bench, Gee had managed to turn in his chair to exchange words. The Farragut robbery was still major news, with the public still calling for blood. Lacking details, public perception saw Gee as just another violent criminal, a cold-blooded killer. To counter the spotty information spoon-fed to the public in official police press reports, Drew undertook the task not to try his case in the press, but to present a more accurate image of his client.

Ready for Dan Gaines, Drew was stunned when Quentin Rogers, the government's best prosecutor, entered the courtroom. Rogers didn't speak, but greeted his adversary with a smug nod. Gaines had been sidelined. The government had brought out its big gun.

Rogers and Drew had come up against one another many times before. They were always friendly and civil, with a mutual admiration. The brother was light-skinned, tall with a distinguished bearing, known for his intellect and quick wit, and shortlisted to become the next Attorney General. The pre-game jitters passed, and Drew prepared himself for the challenge.

Judge Upton took the bench. The case was called.

"Your honor," Rogers said, "I will argue the government's position on this motion in place of Mr. Gaines."

"Very well, Mr. Rogers, and since the government has the burden of going forward, I'll hear your opening statement."

"Thank you, your honor." Rogers stepped from behind the prosecutor's table to the dais. "It is the government's position that defendant Garcia poses a threat of flight, and therefore bail should be denied. Gustavo Garcia was an active participant in this heinous crime in which three people were murdered in cold blood. The defendant was a life-long friend of his coconspirators Tyrone Jones and Jeffrey Legere and willingly chose to drive the getaway vehicle. Granted, he has no prior arrest record. That doesn't necessarily diminish the risk of flight. Further, in light of the current climate in which criminals and guns pose an increasing danger to the citizens on the streets of the District of Columbia, it is imperative that defendants like Garcia be held in custody.

"I call the Court's attention to D.C.'s recently enacted Emergency Crime Bill, which suspends current bail restrictions. In short, your honor, Gustavo Garcia should not be released, set free on the street, and given the opportunity to flee this jurisdiction to continue his criminal activities.

Rogers took his seat. Drew stepped forward.

"Your honor, the Bail Reform Act requires the court to engage in a two-step inquiry before ordering the defendant released or detained pending trial. The court must first make findings as to whether defendant presents a risk of flight if not detained, and then determine what conditions or combination of conditions would reasonably assure defendant's presence at trial. The burden is on the government to show absence of such conditions by a preponderance of evidence.

"I will attempt to prove that defendant Garcia does not pose a threat to the community, and that in accordance with the statute, he should be granted bail pending trial. Indeed, the defendant is so confident in his innocence that he has no reason to flee the jurisdiction. And further, in support of the motion, I'd like to call the defendant, Gustavo Garcia, to the stand."

The gallery reacted in an undercurrent of whispered exchanges.

Rogers stood up. "Objection, your honor. May I approach?"

"Very well." The two men approached the bench.

"Your honor, we've had no opportunity to conduct discovery with regard to this witness. This is a trial by ambush. I object. We're here to argue a motion, not proffer evidence."

"Your honor, this is a hearing, not a trial, and defense has every right to offer testimony. Counsel will be free to conduct discovery at pretrial."

"Mr. Rogers," Judge Upton said, "one would expect the prosecutor to relish an opportunity to examine the defendant. Overruled. Step back, counselors." She signaled the clerk to call the witness.

After taking the oath, Gee settled back. He appeared self-conscious. Drew met his eyes with a smile, hoping to relax him. Quentin Rogers was applying the old law-school teaching: object and argue anything and everything however ineffective. This boosted Drew's confidence.

"Please state your name, age, and occupation for the record."

"Gustavo Agusto Orlando Garcia, I'm 20 years old. I'll be 21 in November, and I'm a student at George Mason University. I'll graduate in May with a BS in computer sciences."

"Very good. Now, Mr. Garcia, have you ever been arrested?

"No sir, never."

"Ever been in any kind of the trouble with the law?"

"No, sir."

"How long have you known Tyrone Jones and Jeffrey Legere?"

"Most of my life. We grew up and went to school together. That is, until we got to high school. They dropped out. Well, Tyrone dropped out. Jinx was expelled."

Drew had successfully laid a foundation presenting Gee as a fairly clean-cut well-behaved college student, but that wasn't enough. Many a college man for various reasons had been convicted of armed robbery, rape, and other violent crimes.

"Tell us what happened on Sunday morning, August sixth."

"Actually, it started the day before when Jinx asked me to drop by, said he needed a favor."

"Okay, did he say what kind of favor?"

"No, he was very mysterious. I didn't give it much thought. At first I figured he wanted to borrow some money, and I'd already made up my mind to tell him no."

"Why?"

"Jinx didn't like to pay you back." This got some smiles from the spectators. "When you asked him for your money, he'd pick a fight."

"What was this favor?"

"I dropped by his house around noon. I was in a hurry 'cause I was planning to go to the movies with my girlfriend. Tyrone was there with him—"

"That's Tyrone Jones, the codefendant."

"Yes sir."

Now go back and tell us everything that happened that Saturday morning when you arrived at Jinx's."

∞

Saturday, August 5, 11:00 a.m.

"What's up?" Gee, fresh and cool in his white tee-shirt and jeans shorts, pulled off his sunshades and took a seat in the armchair.

"You," the two answered in sync.

"What you doing today?" Jinx asked.

"Got a date, going to a matinee."

"What's a matinee?" Tyrone said.

Gee laughed and looked to Jinx, who seemed equally baffled. Was their world so small? But they seldom ventured out of the neighborhood, much less the city.

Jinx sneered. "You picked up some fancy new words from that college."

"Matinee isn't a fancy word." Why did he have to defend himself for not remaining ignorant? "It's an afternoon show—a movie."

"Why don't you just say a movie?"

"Matinee says more than just a movie, it tells the time, so you say two things in one word—"

"Whatever, who's the female? Anybody we know?" Jinx shifted his weight, keeping an eye on Gee.

"As a matter of fact you do. Marie Davis."

"Marie Davis?" Tyrone said. "Fine-ass Marie Davis? You got a date with her? Cheerleader at Coolidge?"

"I remember the stuck-up bitch," Jinx said. "Gee always had a thing for her but she wouldn't give him the time of day. Ain't that right, Gee?"

"I got to go get ready. What's this favor? If it's money, I can't help you."

"It ain't money. I need a ride."

"Not now, I got plans."

"Tomorrow. I got a job. But it's early."

"Catch the bus."

"Buses ain't running that early. It's the first day, after that I can hook up a ride."

"Where's this job?"

"Out in Maryland."

"What time?"

"Early, six in the morning."

"Oh, hell no."

"Come on, help a brother out. You made it out the hood. Don't forget where you come from."

"Okay, okay, but I ain't picking you up. Be out front of my house at six."

"Solid, brother. I'll be there."

"And I never left the hood. I'm still here." Gee got up and walked out the door.

∞

Gee's testimony was going well. He came across as intelligent and articulate, holding the judge and courtroom rapt.

"Now tell us what happened that Sunday morning."

∞

Sunday, August 6th, 5:55 a.m.

After closing the Farragut, Gee only had four hours sleep. He got up five minutes before six, dressed, washed his face and brushed his teeth, all the while wondering about Jinx's mysterious new job. Jinx had been a little too vague. What kind of job started you out on a Sunday morning? Must be delivering papers or something. And how did he suddenly get a job? Jinx was never one to punch a clock. He'd quickly made a mess of things after Gee got him the job at the Farragut last summer. It was definitely time to cut Jinx and Tyrone back. Jinx was bad news, always had been. Gee grabbed his keys and was suddenly seized with an inexplicable fear, and when walked outside and saw the two sitting on the hood of his car, the eerie foreboding intensified.

"What's up?" he said. "Tyrone, you got a job too?" Tyrone looked puzzled and didn't respond. Tyrone was never one to suffer a loss of words.

Backpack in his lap, Jinx slid down off the hood of the car. "Let's go."

Gee halted. "Hold up. Something ain't right."

Jinx spun around and pointed a gun at Gee. "Get in and drive."

"What the fu—"

"Get in the car, I said."

"You tripping or what?" Gee looked toward Tyrone for an explanation. Tyrone shrugged. "What are you up to, Jinx?"

Jinx gritted his teeth with a crazed stare and fierce determination in his eyes.

"Fuck you, Jinx. Shoot me." Gee headed back into the house.

Jinx came up behind him, spun him around, and pressed the gun against his forehead. "Right now I got the nerve to kill you, maybe go into your house and kill your mama and daddy in their sleep. And then go fuck that pretty little sister of yours before I put her to death. And you won't be around to stop it. So either you drive me to where I want to go or I go into your house and have some fun."

Gee's shoulders drooped. He had never seen Jinx like this before, but he knew he was serious. Always bitter and angry, something had exploded inside him. Gee got in behind the wheel. Tyrone was ordered to take shotgun and obeyed like a puppet on a string, avoiding Gee's stare.

"Where to?" Gee hit the ignition.

"The Farragut, and you're going to help us rob it, Mr. College Man with his cheerleader girlfriend, Mr. Goodlife."

"What?"

"You heard me."

"That your problem, Jinx? It bothers you that I work a real job, finished school, went to college? That it?"

"Shut up and drive."

Jinx had always tried to make him feel bad for having two parents with jobs and for going to school. He accused him of not having what it takes to be real, a gangsta thug, a street soldier, of being too soft.

There was silence in the car as he drove up Michigan Avenue to the Farragut. Gee wondered what next, how Jinx planned to pull it off. Theo and the opening crew would be there. They all knew Jinx. The young chef, Josh, had frequently butted heads with Jinx and finally had him fired. Naomi would be making her famous brunch biscuits, and Rodney would be setting up and helping Josh with the food prep. Gee, like Jinx, had worked a couple of brunches before and knew the setup. And then it struck him—Theo had both hired and fired Jinx. Jinx had a grudge. Was this his revenge? Gee had often witnessed the quick, ugly temper, but only now saw how dangerous Jinx could be.

"What's my role in this, besides driver?"

"That's it, just enough to make you an accessory so you keep your mouth shut. You don't think I'd give you a gun, do you? You don't have the balls. And don't even think about snitching. I'll hunt you down and kill your family. Understand?" Jinx tapped the back of his head with the barrel of the gun.

Gee glanced at a visibly shaken Tyrone.

"Don't look at Tyrone. He'll finger you too."

"You'll never pull this off. You'll go to jail for a long time. Trust me, you don't have a chance."

"See, that's what I mean, you ain't got the balls. Drive to the corner of Monroe and park. Wait there until we come back. And don't think about leaving us. Afterwards you'll drive us back to my house and you can go on your way, this is our little secret. Understand?"

Gee didn't respond quick enough for Jinx. More forcefully, he again tapped Gee's head with the gun barrel. "You hear me?"

"I hear."

"Trust me, I'll hunt you down."

The car pulled to the corner. The two hopped out and Gee watched them walk around the corner to the Farragut. There was nothing to stop him from running to get help.

∞

Gee had scored a lot of points, but how would he hold up under cross-examination?

"No more questions, your honor." Drew returned to his seat.

"Mr. Rogers, your witness."

The prosecutor stood slowly, buttoning his jacket. "Mr. Garcia, do you have a bank account?"

"Yes, a checking account and a savings account."

"How much is currently deposited in each account?"

"I have about two hundred dollars in my checking account and twelve hundred dollars in my savings. That's for my tuition."

"Do you have a passport?"

"Yes."

"When was the last time you used it?"

"Two years ago, I went to visit my grandparents in San Salvador."

"Mr. Garcia, how long would you say Legere and Jones were inside the Farragut?"

"About five minutes."

"And for five minutes you sat outside waiting?"

"Not the whole five minutes."

"That's right, you drove around the block when you saw the manager, Theo running away, is that correct?"

"Right."

"You didn't tell us about that. Why not?"

"I couldn't remember everything. It wasn't important."

"Theo was your boss?"

"Yes."

"How did you get along with your boss?"

"Fine."

"So let me get the facts straight. You drove your two best buddies to the Farragut, you knew they were going to rob the place, and yet you sat and waited. Even when you saw your boss run out, you didn't stop him or go get help, but drove away so he wouldn't recognize you."

"Objection, counsel's leading the witness."

"Sustained."

"Mr. Garcia," Rogers continued, "if you had a good relationship with your boss, weren't you afraid for him? You could have just picked him up and the two of you could have gotten help, but instead you now expect us to believe you were so scared."

"Objection, argumentative and leading."

"Sustained."

"I'll rephrase the question. Mr. Garcia, why didn't you help Theo Jackson when you had the opportunity?"

"I didn't think of it. I didn't want Theo to think I was part of it."

"But you *were* a part of it. The three of you planned it together. The truth is you didn't want to be recognized by Theo."

"No, that's not it at all."

"No more questions, your honor." Rogers returned to his seat.

The government had not misjudged the case, as Drew had hoped. Pairing Rogers was a brilliant strategic move. Their golden boy Gaines was less competent, but Rogers had the years of experience and an intuitive judgment that Gaines lacked, knowing where the witness's vulnerabilities lay and how to attack. And he was immune to the race card. The process required a focus and concentration that Gaines had yet to acquire, and Rogers did his damage, first by establishing that Gee had the means to flee the country, and second by attacking his credibility.

"Redirect?" The judge looked to Drew.

"Yes, your honor." Rogers had posed the most perplexing question. Gee had plenty of time to run and get help. Why stick around and make the getaway with them? It didn't make sense, but none of this made any sense. Drew had the task of rehabilitating his witness, and to make sense of Gee's action, he had to find a logical explanation. He stood up. "Mr. Garcia, why didn't you drive off?"

"I was afraid."

"Afraid Jinx would hurt you?"

"I fought Jinx a lot coming up. We were evenly matched. Even though he had a gun, I wasn't afraid of him."

"Then what were you afraid of?"

"Of what he would do to my family."

"So you weren't thinking about your own welfare or the people inside, not even Theo's welfare, but the safety of your family."

"That's right."

"Did you receive any money from the robbery?"

"No sir."

"Did you ever meet and discuss how the money was to be divvied up?"

"No sir."

"No more questions, your honor."

"Mr. Rogers?"

"No questions, but I reserve the right to recall the witness at a later time, your honor."

"Granted. Mr. Garcia, you may step down. Mr. Smith, do you have another witness?

"Yes, your honor, I would like to call Mrs. Glenda Fitzpatrick."

Rogers jumped to his feet. "Objection, your honor, who is this witness?"

"Mr. Rogers, we'll all soon find out who this witness is. Again, I remind you this isn't a trial but a de novo hearing. Objection overruled. The clerk will call the witness."

Drew's secret weapon walked slowly into the courtroom on Julio's arm. The grandmotherly African-American had a light-brown complexion and a graceful, dignified deportment. Prim and proper, powdered and perfumed, outfitted for church, she wore a summery blue floral suit and a hat adorned with large silk roses. She seemed slightly nervous, but for her age, moved with a spry step.

As she settled into the witness stand, Drew offered a friendly smile, hoping to ease the witness into her testimony. "How are you today, Mrs. Fitzpatrick? I understand you have an asthma condition."

"I'm fine, Mr. Smith. My asthma is under control, and thank you for asking. I'm a little nervous, I've never testified in court before." The retired secondary-school teacher spoke with perfect diction.

"There's nothing to be nervous about. If at any time you feel uncomfortable, don't hesitate to say so. Before we get into the gist of my examination, let's establish the facts with regard to your residency. Please state for the record your address."

"I live at 1324 Ingraham Street, Northwest."

"And how long have you lived there?"

"For thirty years. My late husband, Mr. William Fitzpatrick, and I bought the house thirty years ago. He's been dead for seven years now."

"Sorry to hear that. Now, do you know the defendant, Gustavo Garcia, seated at the defendant's table?"

"Oh yes, he lives across the street. We call him Gee. I've watched him grow into a fine young man. And I know he could never have done those terrible Farragut killings. I don't care what they say—"

Rogers was on his feet. "Objection, your honor."

"Sustained." Judge Upton leaned into the witness and spoke softly. "Mrs. Fitzpatrick, please answer the question as to the facts and try not to offer your opinion."

"Oh, I'm sorry, Judge. I thought that's what I was doing."

Judge Upton nodded for Drew to continue. He had to keep his witness on a short chain. His intent was to present the image of a lovable granny with no hidden agenda. It wouldn't be easy. From their prior conversation, he knew she had some very strong opinions and didn't hesitate to voice them.

"So, Mrs. Fitzpatrick, how well do you know the defendant?"

"He's been cutting my grass since he was big enough to push a lawnmower. Whenever I had chores or needed handy work around the house, he or his father, Hernando, were always there to help, all I had to do was ask."

"Your honor." Rogers stood. "Do we have to listen to this over-the-fence, apple-pie testimony? It's immaterial and irrelevant."

"If the court will indulge me," Drew said, "the witness's testimony will bear out the events leading up to the Farragut robbery."

"Overruled. Sit down, Mr. Rogers. Continue, Mr. Smith, but get to it quickly."

Rogers threw up his arms, cut the judge a look, then collapsed into his chair.

Drew couldn't contain his smile. "Now, would you please tell us what you saw on that Sunday morning?"

"Well, it was around six a.m. I remember because the sun was rising. I woke up earlier and couldn't sleep. My breathing was labored and I was afraid I was about to have another attack. So I took my medication and decided to sit in my rocker at the open window. It faces the street, and I was about to pray my rosary when I saw these two fellows sitting on Gee's car. It wasn't long before Gee came out. The fellows had some words, and they didn't appear too friendly to me. Gee turned to go back into the house when one fellow jumped off the car and ran up and grabbed him from behind. He had a gun pointed at Gee. I don't exactly know what was said. But Gee wasn't going along willingly. They forced him. He got in behind the wheel while the fellow kept the gun aimed at him, and they drove off."

"Did you get a good look at the other young men?"

"Oh yes, I recognized them. They were his friends. I'd seen them often on the block visiting Gee. Although I must say I never cared for them, baggy pants and all, heads all plaited up. Hip-hop gangstas and hoochies, that's what they call themselves. They're on BET in those disgusting videos, girls running around shaking their hindpots. They put anything on TV nowadays."

"Objection, your honor."

"Sustained. Mrs. Fitzpatrick I don't want to have to remind you again. Just respond to the questions, tell us only the facts as to what you saw."

"Yes, your honor. I'm sorry."

"Continue, Mrs. Fitzpatrick," Drew said.

"As I was saying, if Gee had been my son, I would have kept him far from that element."

The gallery snickered and Judge Upton grimaced. The boy was in fact Drew's son, and like Mrs. Fitzpatrick, he too had been powerless against the influences on Gee's life. He nodded toward Rogers. "Your witness."

Rogers began his cross-examination with a smile and a friendly tone. "Mrs. Fitzpatrick, in general, how is your health?"

"It's been better. But I feel fine."

"I'm glad to hear that. Are you under a doctor's care?"

"I am, for my asthma."

"What medications are you on?"

Drew rose to his feet. "Your honor, I object. How is this relevant to the witnesses' testimony?"

"Your honor, I'm simply trying to show that the defendant is of a mature age and may have been under the influence of some condition or medication that affected her vision or judgment that morning, or her memory now."

"I'll allow it."

"Your honor, I object. This line of inquiry is irrelevant and immaterial. Counsel is on a fishing expedition attempting to undermine the competency of my witness."

"I've made my ruling, Mr. Smith. Mrs. Fitzpatrick, do you have your medications with you."

"I do, your honor. Mr. Smith instructed me to make up the list."

Impressed, the Judge shot Drew an amused look. Defense counsel vigilant in pressing his objections had nevertheless been prepared for this line of questioning.

Mrs. Fitzpatrick fumbled through her purse and retrieved a list identifying each medicine, the warnings on the label, and possible side effects. Rogers examined the list and handed it up to the judge, requesting that it be proffered into evidence. Drew didn't object. None of the prescriptions affected her mental alertness. Rogers moved on with his cross-examination.

"Mrs. Fitzpatrick, you say you've known the defendant Garcia most of his life."

"Yes."

"You also said the defendant and his father performed chores around you house."

"I did."

"So, are you close to the Garcias?"

"I wouldn't say close. We're good neighbors."

"When you saw the fellow pulled a gun on Gee, why didn't you call the police?"

"I thought of it. But I recognized the boys as Gee's friends. I thought they might have been playing around, though the gun did cause some concern. But nothing happened, Gee got in the car and they drove off. When later I saw him come home all right, I just dismissed it, and didn't think much of it until I read that Gee was involved in the robbery. Then I knew something wasn't right."

"When did you and Mr. Smith first concoct your testimony?"

"Objection! Question is argumentative, and irrelevant."

"Sustained."

"I'll restate."

"Please." Judge Upton watched Rogers with narrow eyes.

"At any time did you and Mr. Smith go over your testimony?"

"We talked yesterday."

"Did he tell you what to say?" No doubt expecting an objection, Rogers turned to Drew, but none came.

"He told me to tell the truth, the whole truth, and nothing but the truth. And so help me God, that's what I've done."

The gallery laughed and the judge smiled.

"Thank you." Rogers ended his cross-examination and returned to his chair.

"Mr. Smith?" Drew declined to redirect. "I'll hear your closing argument, Mr. Rogers."

Once again Rogers stood and approached then bench.

"Your honor, clearly this matter of bail is a moot point of law since the City Council recently enacted the Emergency Crime Bill, which excuses the court from considering usual bail standards. And even assuming there were no such statute, Garcia fails to meet the standards necessary for bail as set out in the Reform Act. The defendant Garcia met with his coconspirators the day before the robbery. They planned it. His job was to drive the getaway car. Now, to save his own skin, he's concocted this self-serving testimony with a questionable witness and expects us to believe he was forced into the scheme at gunpoint. His story is farfetched and beyond belief." Rogers paused a moment and then raised his voice as though to underscore his final point. "To secure the safety of the community, I urge the court to deny the defendant bail pending trial. Further, in light of the city's enactment of the Emergency Crime Bill, standard bail requirements are suspended to which the court must take judicial notice. It is the will of the people that Garcia be held until trial. I have no further arguments."

"Mr. Smith."

Drew stood and approached the bench. He looked up into the judge's eyes, making his appeal to no one but her. "Your honor, the defense has shown by clear and convincing evidence defendant was neither an accessory nor coconspirator, but as much a victim as those whose lives ended that morning. Only, Gustavo Garcia lives. Although it may be argued that he was an accomplice, that he aided and abetted Tyrone Jones and Jeffrey Legere, nothing could be further from the truth. This was never his intent. My esteemed associate claims that Garcia doesn't meet the standards necessary for bail. However, he fails to enumerate or explain which standard. The Bail Reform Act is very clear on the standards to be applied.

"Gustavo Garcia acted as a reasonable man complying with the orders of a cold-blooded killer, a man so crazed and vicious he killed his own mother. Garcia went along in fear of his own life, as well as his mother's, sister's, and father's, and did what any reasonable man might do. Jeffrey Legere was capable of unspeakable acts, to which the body count bears witness. Gustavo Garcia knew this because he had known Jeffrey Legere most of his life. Your honor, in conclusion, based on the testimony of both the defendant and Mrs. Fitzpatrick, who told the truth, and nothing but the truth, the court must free this young man on bail.

"The government's argument that the city's Emergency Crime Bill overrides federal law is without merit. Judges in all D.C. courts were given the right to deny bail and detain adults and juveniles charged with violent crimes. It is a right to be considered, not an absolute fiat. While the court may give full faith and credit to the legislation, it falls short of trumping existing federal law. It is the will of the people that justice be served.

"The court can only make one finding today, that Gustavo Garcia does not pose a threat to the community, and grant the defendant bail pending trial. Such a ruling would best serve the legislative intent of the 1984 Bail Reform Act. The defense rests."

"Thank you, Mr. Smith and Mr. Rogers. The court will recess for one hour, at which time I'll deliver my decision." Judge Upton banged her gavel and rose. The clerk announced the recess. Drew was already considering his next move, a writ of habeas corpus to the Court of Appeals.

As the courtroom emptied, Julio offered to take Mrs. Fitzpatrick home, but she insisted on staying for the decision. Drew took Gee's support group to lunch in the courthouse cafeteria. With little appetite, over coffee and cokes, they waited out the hour. Nina appeared frustrated and impatient, expressing her displeasure with the recess. Hernando too showed signs of frayed nerves.

Normally such rulings were handed down immediately, but Judge Upton would know what was at stake. Her decision was subject to an immediate appeal, she wanted to avoid any misinterpretation or flawed reasoning, and so would provide a well-written opinion.

∞

Monday, August 20, 11:30 a.m.

Judge Upton reconvened and began by delivering her lengthy decision with a history of the Bail Reform Act with clarity and precision, leaving no doubt as to her reasoning, and anticipating an appeal. Drew couldn't tell where she was going—not a good sign. Fighting back his anxiety, he strained to listen.

"In 1984, Congress enacted the Bail Reform Act in response to the inadequacy of its predecessor, the 1966 Bail Reform Act. The 1966 Act's primary goal was to guarantee a defendant's presence at trial. The impetus for the 1984 revision was the inability of the 1966 Act to protect society from the crimes committed by accused criminals while out on bail, and so the purpose of the 1984 Bail Reform Act was to prevent defendants from committing crimes while released on probation."

The judge continued for what seemed an endless time, citing examples that would raise a rebuttable presumption favorable to the detention of the defendant. Holding everyone on the edge of their seat, the cadence and timbre of her words slowed as she approached her conclusion. She had covered all her bases.

"In determining whether the defendant should be granted bail, the court must determine whether the accused, Gustavo Garcia, poses a danger to any victim, witness or other person. The burden of proof remains with the prosecution, and in accordance with the facts presented in this case, that burden has not been met.

"In setting conditions for bail, the defendant is hereby ordered not to leave a fifty-mile radius of this court, and to turn over his passport. The court will in addition freeze both his checking and savings accounts."

Drew breathed a huge sigh of relief. But the judge wasn't finished.

"It appears to this court that there is some question as to whether probable cause exists to bind this defendant over for trial. But in accordance with the statute, I hereby order the defendant released with a bail set at twenty thousand dollars."

The probable-cause dicta came as a bonus surprise for Drew and a warning to the prosecution that it might be traversing shaky ground. The task of securing an acquittal for Gee no longer seemed impossible, but Drew knew the road was rocky and the mountain was high.

"Am I free?" Gee asked.

Drew beamed at the young man then turned to face Nina and Hernando. "Not yet. Not until your father—Hernando—gets two thousand dollars to the bail bondsman. It'll take a couple of hours."

Hernando sprang from out his seat "I'm on my way to the bank. Get the papers," he told Nina. He ran for the exit, then ran came back to give her a quick hug and a happy kiss on the cheek.

Gee hugged his mother, whose eyes were brimming as the marshal led him back to the detention cell. Gee threw Marie a kiss just before disappearing through the door. Drew thanked Mrs. Fitzpatrick again though worried. Drew worried all the excitement might trigger one of her asthma attacks, but she assured him all was well before Julio escorted her home.

Drew packed up his briefcase and laptop and was suddenly surrounded by a group of reporters anxious with questions. He assured them he'd issue a statement from his office before their deadline.

Outside the courtroom, he found Nina waiting for him. "Drew, how can I thank you?"

"For what?"

"Taking care of this. I hope you'll continue to represent him at trial."

"He's my son, Nina. And although he may not know it, I don't intend to let you forget it."

"Please let me handle this my way and in my time."

"Have I ever interfered?" Drew stepped around her. "Don't worry, no one will know your secret."

She caught his arm. "I've given your offer some thought."

"Which offer?"

"Leaving Hernando and moving in with you."

"It's no longer on the table. I couldn't do that to Hernando. He loves you too much." Drew turned and walked away, resisting the urge to look back. What had she been going to say about that offer?

Drew spent the afternoon in his office fielding questions from the media. All were eager to profile Gee in a positive light and tell his story. Requests for personal interviews were referred to

Nina. The biggest surprise came when Rogers called with an offer to drop the charges against Gee if he would testify against Tyrone. Drew accepted the offer without hesitation or his client's permission.

Chapter 20

ON A BALMY MAY afternoon nine months after the Farragut robbery, Drew and Zoë lounged on the deck. She was immersed in a psych journal while Drew was opening mail brought home from the office. Shirley had the week off, and he was trying to catch up before her return. The smell of honeysuckle filled the air. Spring had slowly restored the wooded park to its lush dark greenery and the dogwoods were in bloom. Drew opened an envelope, read the first few lines, and began to chuckle.

Zoë looked up. "What is it?"

"Remember I told you Lt. Lowry filed a complaint against me for slugging him during the Farragut investigation? The Grievance Committee dismissed the complaint and found no evidence of professional misconduct."

"That's good news."

"Better than that, it's the final word on the Farragut robbery."

"That seems so long ago now. I wonder how Gee's doing."

The doorbell interrupted their conversation.

He stood up. "I'll get it. Probably a Jehovah's Witness."

"Be nice," she shouted to his back.

Moments later, Drew returned to the deck followed by a younger man.

"Zoë," Drew said with a big grin. "You talked him up. I'd like you to meet Gee."

"Oh, Gee," she said. "I've heard so much about you, I feel as if I know you."

"Really?"

"Drew is quite fond of you. She rose to offer a handshake. "Have a seat. I'll go get us something cool to drink."

"Make it champagne," Drew said. "We'll celebrate the graduate."

"Congratulations. I'll be right back."

Still with a broad grin Drew couldn't hide if he tried, he motioned Gee toward a wicker armchair. The young man's eyes darted about, taking in the rich setting of the big house nestled on the edge of the woods.

"Is that your girlfriend?"

"I guess you could say that. She's a psychiatrist."

"I like her. She's nice."

"I'll tell her you said that. What brings you here?"

"I came by to thank you for that generous graduation gift."

"You're welcome. What are your plans?"

"I have a job in Atlanta. I'll be leaving in a couple of weeks."

"And Marie?"

Gee smiled. "Yeah, she's there, still in school. I also want to thank you for getting those newspaper stories published. You know, I could never understand why you did so much for me."

"It's no big deal. I just couldn't stand to watch yet another young man—"

"It is a big deal. My name should be Smith. I always thought I was a brutha."

Drew's jaw dropped.

"Mom told me."

"I'm sorry, Gee. I didn't know until—"

"I know you didn't. I don't blame you. It's a shock, and at first I didn't know how to deal with it. But I realized it's not such a bad thing. Like I said, I always thought I was a brutha. I like rap, hip-hop, R&B, and jazz and meringue and salsa and all things Latin."

"Yeah I guess you got that Africanism from me."

"Mr. Smith—I mean Drew...maybe I should call you Dad."

"Whatever makes you comfortable. Not sure Hernando would like that."

"He's Papi. You know I've always admired you. Now I'd like to get to know you."

"It makes me happy to hear that." Swept up on an emotional tide, Drew's chest tightened. He fought back tears until Zoë rescued him from what could have been an embarrassing moment.

"Here we are." She held three glasses by the stems in one hand and a bottle of champagne in the other.

Drew relieved her of the bottle and busied himself into composure. He popped the cork without overflow, filled their glasses, and made a simple toast.

"To our future."

Their glasses kissed.

Minus One

At the start of a legal career Drew Smith is drawn into a criminal practice while searching for a relationship, along with best friends Julio and Medhat. Taking on crime and the system, they were all for one, an inseparable trio, until one woman destroyed it all.